Confessions of a Slightly Neurotic Hitwoman

Confessions of a Slightly Neurotic Hitwoman

JB LYNN

AVONIMPULSE

This book is a work of fiction. The characters, incidents, and dialogue are drawn from the author's imagination and are not to be construed as real. Any resemblance to actual events or persons, living or dead, is entirely coincidental.

EPub Edition February 2011 ISBN: 9780062134662

Print Edition ISBN: 9780062134639

10 9 8 7 6 5 4 3 2

Acknowledgements

This book would not have been possible without the support of the following people:

My amazing critique partner Cyndi Valero who bugged me to write with "that voice" for a couple of years, before I wised up and took her advice.

Victoria Marini, my agent, who enthusiastically embraced "that voice" and this story.

My editor, Lucia Macro, who pledged to help me maintain that voice, and to the entire team at Avon for their great work.

Those who read the manuscript early on (I'd tell you who they were, but then I'd have to kill you) and let me know the voice was working.

Doug . . . who has the misfortune of living with "that voice" in real life.

And last, but certainly not least, Mr. Coffee . . . who fuels that voice.

Confessions of a Slightly Neurotic Hitwoman

Prologue

You just know it's going to be a bad day when you're stuck at a red light and Death pulls up behind you in a station wagon.

I'd been using the rearview mirror to touch up my lip gloss when I spotted him. Okay, maybe he wasn't really Death, but dressed in a black raincoat with the hood pulled up covering his face, he sure looked like he could pluck a scythe out of thin air.

It was one of those days when I kept catching the specter of Death everywhere. I'd catch a glimpse of him in the condensation on the bathroom mirror as I stepped out of the shower, or burnt into my morning toast, or in the pile of dog shit I narrowly missed stepping in . . . or didn't.

Death was idling behind me, and I was kinda freaked out. Which was why, completely forgetting about the damn April showers that had been falling for three days straight, I floored my crappy, beat-up, not-gently-used Honda the second that light turned green.

Hydroplaning, the car spun out into the intersection,

with me pumping the brakes while wondering if I should have been steering into the skid or out of it, and berating myself for not having paid more attention during my high school Driver's Ed course.

I knew I was gonna die. I could already hear the angels singing.

Three months before, I'd had the same feeling as another car slid out of control. I hadn't been driving then; my sister's idiot husband had been behind the wheel. I'd been in the backseat, singing "Itsy Bitsy Spider" to my three-year-old niece Katie, trying to distract her from the argument her parents were having in the front seat. Suddenly the car swerved and squealed, and as we rolled over onto the driver's side, I distinctly remember thinking, *Dear God, please don't let us die.*

I didn't think that three months later. In this moment I was resigned to my fate.

But then, miraculously, my little Honda gained traction, and I achieved a semblance of control over the vehicle. I wasn't in the clear, though. Squinting at the rearview mirror, I could see that Death had followed me through the rain-soaked intersection.

And I could still hear the singing of the angels, but it wasn't a heavenly sound.

It was loud. It was annoying.

From the floor of the passenger seat, I snatched up the bag of crickets that I'd bought for Godzilla. They were making an unholy racket. I shook it hard. That shut the little fuckers up.

When I first became responsible for Godzilla's care,

I tried giving him freeze-dried crickets. But that damn lizard, he's got a discerning palate and insists on the live version, which is a pain in the ass because I hate bugs. Really hate 'em. Just looking at them gives me that awful creepy-crawly feeling, but I'd pledged to Katie that I'd take good care of the only pet she'd ever been allowed.

There was no way of knowing whether she even knew I'd made her that promise. She'd been in a coma, a "persistent vegetative state," as the doctors liked to call it, ever since the car accident. Her parents had died on impact, according to police. I'd walked away unharmed . . . except for the fact that I can now talk to a lizard.

"Call me God," he'd insisted the first time I'd thought to feed him.

He'd never spoken to me before. I mean animals, or reptiles or amphibians, or whatever the hell he is, don't talk. I know that. I haven't gone totally around the bend.

But the thing is, ever since the car accident, we can converse. And we do. A lot.

Maybe I've got brain damage, or maybe it's the emotional trauma of having my sister die and almost losing Katie, but I swear that I've turned into Doctor-freakin-Dolittle.

Of course, I haven't told anyone about my newfound ability. They'd lock me up in a funny farm like my mom. Or run a bunch of tests. Or run a bunch of tests and then lock me up. And if they did that, I wouldn't be able to visit Katie. And she'd be left all alone there, lying in a hospital bed, with only the witches to look after her.

My three aunts aren't really witches. I'm not so delusional as to think they've got magical powers. They're just extraordinarily evil in their own "helpfully" meddlesome way.

So I keep the secret conversations with God to myself. To the rest of the world, it probably appears that I'm coping pretty well. I wash my clothes, bring the newspaper in, and have even gone back to work in hell (also known as an insurance company call center).

My piddly paycheck isn't going to make much of a dent in the pile of hospital bills that are piling up faster than a Colorado snowfall, but it's a decent cover. It's not like I can go around putting HITWOMAN on my tax return.

Death, or at least the driver in the station wagon, coasted past as I turned my blinker on to signal my turn into Apple Blossom Estates. There's no such thing as apple blossoms. Three months before, God, licking his lizard lips after chowing down on a cricket, had pointed out that even he knew that. But it sounds fancy right? Or at least like the over-promising prose of a condo developer's advertising. It's not. It's just a fancy name for a brain injury rehab, or as they like to call it, a "premium care facility."

Parking in the visitors' lot, I left the bag o' bugs to their chirping (which sounded suspiciously like Madonna's "Like a Prayer") and headed inside. It was time to tell my boss that I was ready to kill a man.

But you're probably wondering how a nice girl like me got a job like this. . . .

Chapter One

Sometimes I think my first memory is the sound of the three witches cackling. Sometimes I think it's tumbling—no, wait, tumbling might insinuate that I had some sort of grace or plan. I wouldn't want to give you the wrong impression of me. I am—have been for my whole life and always will be—without an iota of grace. And planning has never been my strong suit. Okay, so sometimes I think my first memory is falling/crashing/plummeting down an entire flight of stairs and breaking my left arm when I was two.

Both those memories rushed back at me. I'm guessing it was because my entire body hurt, and I could hear the three witches. I am, if you choose to believe the traitorous date imprinted on my driver's license, thirty-two. Lying there with my body aching and my head throbbing, all I wanted was to have a good cry and take a nap. But the witches wouldn't shut up.

I cracked open one eye and squinted at the three women in their fifties gathered at the foot of the bed, huddled around what looked like some sort of clipboard. I didn't recognize the bed, or the room, or the clipboard, but I did know the three women. I groaned.

"She's awake!" Aunt Leslie, the most emotional of my three aunts, hit a note that sliced through my skull with the precision of a Ginsu knife dicing butter. Racing around the bed, she stuck her face in my face like an inquisitive cocker spaniel. "Can you hear me, Margaret?"

Recoiling, I tried to get away from the noxious fumes of her sickeningly sweet perfume. At least I told myself it was perfume. It could have been the residual odor of her daily joint (medical marijuana, she claimed, though she didn't have a prescription and hadn't seen a doctor in over a decade). Unfortunately I couldn't figure out a way to answer her without inhaling. "I hear you."

For some reason those three words made Aunt Leslie burst into tears.

"It's a miracle!" Aunt Loretta cried, as though she was praising Jesus. "It's a miracle! I have got to go find that doctor and share this happy news!"

But first she had to give herself a quick once-over in her compact mirror to make sure that her lipstick wasn't smudged and her nose wasn't shiny. Reassured that she looked her best, she shimmied out of the room in her too-tight dress and too-high heels. Even closing in on sixty Aunt Loretta was convinced that she was giving Sophia Loren and Raquel Welch a run for their money as she rocked a sex-kitten wardrobe.

"What's wrong? What happened?" I asked her twin

sister, Aunt Leslie, who had worked herself into full-blown sobs in record time.

Wiping her eyes with the corner of the bed sheet, she just cried harder.

A vise of panic tightened around my solar plexus, choking off my air supply, as I tried to figure out what was going on. Everything was so fuzzy.

"Margaret," Aunt Susan, the third and oldest sister, got my attention from where she waited at the foot of the bed. If Aunt Leslie is the family pothead, and Aunt Loretta is the resident nympho, Aunt Susan is the straight arrow. She might be a pain in the ass, but I know from experience that she can be counted on to make sense in the midst of chaos. "There was a car accident."

And it all came back. The car. The rain. The fighting in the front seat. The "Itsy Bitsy Spider." The skid. The roll. The screeching and squealing of metal. The impact. The pain. Screaming.

Katie.

"Katie!" I sat straight up, and the room spun. I was weak and dizzy and nauseated. I broke into a cold sweat. The sensation reminded me of the last time I'd gone with Darlene on the tilt-a-whirl. I didn't want to think about that. I couldn't.

"Katie's alive," Susan said.

The assurance acted like a super-concentrated dose of Dramamine. The room stopped spinning. The desire to puke my guts up abated. Collapsing back down onto the pillow, I closed my eyes.

"Theresa didn't make it," Aunt Susan said softly.

That made Aunt Leslie cry harder.

I kept my eyes squeezed tightly shut as I tried to convince myself this was all a dream. After my baby sister Darlene died fifteen years ago, I'd been plagued with terrible nightmares. In them, all my family members died, one by one. Maybe this was just another bad dream. Maybe my big sister Theresa was still here.

Aunt Susan couldn't leave me well-enough-alone with my happy delusion. "Dirk died too."

Aunt Leslie didn't shed a tear for him. That's how I knew it was all real.

I thought about the submarine movie. It was a foreign film, without subtitles. I don't even recall the title. All I remember was the scene when the ship is in danger of sinking. The captain makes the decision to seal off a room, or compartment, or whatever it's called on a submarine, forfeiting the lives of the sailors trapped inside in order to keep the ship afloat.

Even though I couldn't understand a single word of dialogue, it was a horrifying, heart-wrenching scene. The idea of sacrificing part in order for the whole to be saved didn't make any sense to me.

Until my sister Darlene died. Then I understood it perfectly. In order to keep functioning, to keep my head above water, I had to shut off my emotions.

Unwilling to deal with the loss of Theresa, I slammed the door shut on the tidal wave of pain and emotion that threatened to drown me. It was the only way to survive.

I opened my eyes as Aunt Loretta came click-clacking

back into the room on the heels of a white-coated doctor. I could see why she'd been so eager to find him. He sorta reminded me of Tom Selleck in his *Magnum, P.I.* heyday.

"How are you feeling?" he asked as he pulled out one of those annoying lights doctors like to shine in your eyes.

"Like shit."

"Language, Margaret!" Aunt Susan admonished.

Did I mention that straight arrow of hers is stuck up her ass?

"Well that's understandable, considering . . ." He leaned in close to make his examination. His touch was cool and gentle as he tilted my chin.

"She's in shock," Aunt Leslie supplied helpfully, even though no one had asked for an opinion. "Often with a concussion a patient—"

Dr. Magnum P.I. rolled his eyes. No doubt Aunt Leslie had quoted every fact she'd ever read about a head injury to the poor man. I pitied him. Aunt Loretta rested a hand on his arm, pretending to get a better look at me, while groping his bicep muscle.

"Let the man do his job," I muttered.

The doctor smiled, apparently relieved that at least someone in the family wasn't going to hassle him. "I'm going to have to ask you ladies to step out while I examine my patient."

"I saw online—" Aunt Leslie said.

"But we're family," Aunt Susan protested

"Is there something wrong with her?" Aunt Loretta asked, almost hopefully. I half-expected her to press the back of her hand to her forehead and pass out.

A nurse bustled in and hustled the witches out.

The doctor poked and prodded me. "You're one fortunate woman. Most adults don't wear their seatbelts when riding in the back of a car. Yours saved your life."

"I normally don't wear it."

"Lucky you did."

"I was just trying to set a good example for my niece." I swallowed hard. A ball of misery had lodged itself in my throat. "Can I see her? Can I see my niece?"

"As soon as we're finished here."

Once he'd finished a physical examination and I'd answered a couple dozen questions for him, he told me that with the exception of some bruised ribs, and the bump on my head, I had miraculously escaped unharmed. True to his word, he instructed the nurse who had joined us to take me to see Katie. She helped me into a wheelchair and rolled me through a series of hallways, explaining that Katie was in the pediatric intensive care unit. She also told me how lucky we were that Katie had been brought to this hospital and not to another. I found it supremely irritating that everyone kept telling me how lucky I was.

She wheeled me to Katie's bedside and left.

My eyes burned, but no tears fell, as I looked at her small, frail body, lost in the big bed. The top of her head was encapsulated in some kind of cast. Bruises and scratches marred her face. She was attached to a myriad of blinking and beeping medical monitors. She looked more like a horrible science experiment than my beautiful niece.

Always pale, her skin took on an almost translucent quality beneath the harsh hospital lights. I traced the blue vein that snaked down her cheek, imagining I could infuse my life force into her with a mere touch. It was a foolish fantasy, but one I couldn't give up.

"I'm here, Katie," I whispered. "Aunt Maggie's here."

Before the accident, it scared me how much I loved this little girl. Her smile made me happy, her laughter, giddy. My heart squeezed every time she slipped her hand into mine, and contentment flooded through me when she climbed into my lap.

I stuck my index finger into her palm, hoping that she'd reflexively grab onto me like she used to when she was a baby, but her fingers remained limp.

"You're going to be okay, Baby Girl. Aunt Maggie will take care of you. I promise."

I'm not big on promises. I don't like making them. Maybe it's because I'm commitment-phobic, or maybe I'm just lazy.

Worse than making promises, though, is believing in them.

I know this from experience. I'd made the mistake of telling my sister Marlene that her twin, Darlene, was going to be okay a long time ago. I'd paid the price, or, more accurately, she'd paid the price, ever since.

That's because a broken promise, no matter how well-intentioned it may be, is like a pebble in a shoe. At first it's uncomfortable. Then it's irritating. Finally it becomes downright painful. And if you don't figure out a way to purge it from your shoe, or, in this case, your psyche, you can end up with a giant, raw blister than can easily infect your soul.

At least that was the theory I came up with after I broke my promise to Marlene. I had nothing else to do all those sleepless nights when she'd drifted away. Nothing else to do but blame myself for what had happened. All because of my broken promise.

I didn't get to dwell on my failures as a sister for long before Aunt Susan came into the room.

"We were looking all over for you, Margaret." There was more rebuke than concern in her voice. There always was.

I ignored her admonishment, too tired to come up with an excuse, too far past caring to offer an apology. "I don't understand. I've barely got a scratch on me, and Katie . . . she. . . . Why didn't the car seat protect her?"

"There are some papers you need to sign."

It was my turn to roll my eyes. That was Aunt Susan, all business, all the time. "Papers?"

"Authorizing me to make decisions regarding Katherine's care. With Theresa . . . with both parents out of the picture, the hospital needs a guardian to sign releases, that kind of thing."

"I can sign them." Theresa had made me sign off on a million legal papers to make sure that I'd have the right to do just that. At the time, I'd thought it was a giant headache over nothing, but now I saw the wisdom of her choice.

I heard Susan's sharp intake of breath even over the

noise of Katie's monitors. She was displeased. I didn't give a damn.

"We should talk about this in the hallway, Margaret."

Grudgingly, I attempted to wheel away from Katie's bed. But no matter how hard I pushed, the damn wheelchair wouldn't budge, a none-too-pleasant reminder that I hadn't been using my gym membership.

"There's a brake," Susan muttered.

Fumbling around, I finally disengaged it, and the wheels started to turn. I tried to make a graceful exit, but instead I ended up slamming into the pole holding Katie's IV and then some other beeping machine. I made enough noise to wake the dead, but Katie didn't stir.

"Oh for goodness' sake," Susan muttered, grabbing the wheelchair from behind and steering me out of the room.

"I've never driven one of these things before. There's a learning curve."

We barreled down the hallway, causing nurses and orderlies to leap out of our path for fear of losing their toes. "Your whole life has been a learning curve, Margaret, and you're failing at it."

I winced. I couldn't come up with a clever rebuttal, because I knew she was right. I also knew I wasn't going to give her the satisfaction of knowing her barb had hit home. "I'm Katie's legal guardian. Theresa wanted me to make the decisions regarding her care."

"You can't make a decision about what socks to wear!" Aunt Susan slammed the chair to a stop, almost dumping me onto the floor.

"Hey! There are no seatbelts with these things!"

Rounding my chariot, Aunt Susan took a deep breath, preparing to hex me, or curse at me, or, worst of all, tell me how "lucky" I was to have her around to pick up the pieces.

Lucky my ass.

I wasn't going to take it sitting down. I struggled unsteadily to my feet. My blood pressure surged, and I swayed woozily, but like a boxer facing a knock-out punch, I stayed on my feet.

And the damndest thing happened. Something, some expression I had never before witnessed on my eldest aunt's face, something that looked a lot like respect, gleamed in her eyes. Pursing her lips, she considered me carefully.

I braced myself for the harangue, the lecture, the litany of my shortcomings, but she stayed silent. We stood there, locked in silent battle for the longest time. I refused to back down. I didn't look away. I knew enough to not open my mouth and stay something stupid.

Finally she cleared her throat. I lifted my chin defiantly.

"The doctor wants to keep you overnight, but one of us, probably Loretta, since she's enamored with all the wealthy, handsome doctors, will be back in the morning to drive you home."

I shook my head. "No need. My apartment is only a couple of blocks from here."

I thought for a moment I'd pushed my rebellion a bit too far, as her hands planted themselves on her hips.

"When I said we'd bring you home, I meant to the house." The three aunts still lived in the house they'd grown up in, although now it had been turned into a prosperous bed-and-breakfast catering mostly to pharmaceutical executives tired of staying in stark hotel rooms.

The B&B is located two blocks from the middle of town and is only a fifteen or twenty minute drive to three pharmaceutical complexes, but it's tucked into a quiet residential neighborhood. My aunts' neighbors are normal Jersey folks, not the kind who show up on ridiculous reality shows, but the type who, during the summer, have sprinklers that are synchronized better than any Olympic swimming team, and during the winter indulge in a penchant for oversized inflatable holiday directions that stay up from October through March.

My apartment complex, on the other hand, is on the "seedy" side of town. It's not the best of neighborhoods, but it's not as bad as my family makes it out to be. Although there is the occasional drug bust or domestic disturbance to keep things interesting, it's mostly harmless blue-collar folks who think going "down the shore" is a dream vacation. It's the best I can afford and worth every nickel to be out from beneath my aunts' stifling roof. "No, I want to go back to my apartment," I told my aunt firmly.

Aunt Susan wrinkled her nose as though she'd smelled a skunk, but all she said was, "As you wish."

Like wishes ever come true.

Chapter Two

IT TOOK ME two days to remember the lizard.

Two days of conferring with doctors about Katie's condition and care.

Two days of making the arrangements for the funeral. It shouldn't take two days to make those kinds of plans. All you have to do is talk to a black-suited funeral home employee, someone to officiate, and a girl making minimum wage in the obit department of the newspaper. You let the people who do this every day do the heavy lifting.

But the decisions regarding this funeral were more complicated than the Middle East peace process because everything had to be agreed upon by both our family and Dirk's, since he and Theresa were to be buried together.

Everything was a "discussion" down to what color the lining of their coffins should be (dusky rose, if you're interested). Personally I couldn't understand what the hell the big deal was. It wasn't like anyone was going to even see the inside of the boxes, since we'd been gently told that their bodies were too mangled to have open caskets.

By the end of the negotiations, I was ready to murder someone. My first choice was the drunk driver who'd run a red light and killed Theresa and left Katie unconscious and parentless, but that selfish, irresponsible bitch had died on impact. Which meant that the person I wanted to kill was Dirk's idiot sister Raelene, who kept prattling on about how "lucky" it was that neither Theresa nor Dirk had lost the other. That it was a blessing they'd gone together. She kept saying how "lucky" they were to get to spend eternity side-by-side.

It got so bad that every time she opened her mouth, I imagined my hands around her throat, squeezing the life out of her.

On the afternoon of the second day, once we'd agreed on what the dearly departed would wear for eternity, I drove to the state prison to tell my father that a second of his daughters had died.

I hadn't been to East Jersey State Prison for years, but I drove as though on automatic pilot, trying to figure out what I'd say when I saw him. I'd considered just calling and asking a prison chaplain to pass along the sad news, but I knew Theresa wouldn't want him to find out that way. Even after everything, she'd been devoted to Dad, driving out to visit him every two weeks, giving him regular updates on everyone, like a cuckoo clock chiming the hour.

She was a more forgiving person than I'll ever be. She was a better person.

Which was why, after handing over my driver's license and enduring a pat down that made me feel like I was as much a criminal as the person I was visiting, I sat in the prison visiting room, at window three, my stomach in knots, waiting to talk to a murderer. Some kids have teachers, steel workers, or doctors for dads. I had a killer.

"Must be my lucky day!" my father boomed the moment he walked into the room and saw me.

I was grateful that this was midweek, and therefore a "window visit." "Contact" visits are only allowed on weekends. The plexiglass partition prevented him from hugging me. "What makes you think that?" I asked.

"It's not every day I get to see my Maggie May."

He settled into the seat opposite me. He didn't look like a criminal who belonged behind bars. Twinkling blue eyes, white beard, and a belly like a bowlful of jelly—if you gave him a red suit and hat, he could be the freakin' Santa Claus in the Thanksgiving Day parade.

"Theresa's dead." I didn't prepare him. I didn't make an effort to sugar-coat the news or ease him into it. I just spit out the cold hard fact like a bullet.

It found its target.

The smile dropped from his face, and his jaw went slack. His shock and pain were plain to see.

And I was glad. Glad that for once I was able to hurt him.

But that moment of petty satisfaction only lasted a moment. I wasn't in the habit of intentionally hurting people. I immediately felt guilty. Small. "I'm sorry. I shouldn't have—"

"How?"

"A drunk driver. Dirk was killed too."

"And Katie?" His question was just a whisper, as though he was afraid fate might overhear him.

"Katie . . ." My eyes ached. I ground my palms against them, trying to rub away the pain. "Katie's in a coma."

"A coma?"

"Uh huh." I waited for him to spout some useless platitude about how *at least she isn't suffering*, but he surprised me.

"Does she have that stuffed dinosaur she loves so much?"

I shrugged.

"She should have it. She loves that thing." Two fat droplets slowly slid down his plump cheeks.

It bothered me that he was able to cry, while I hadn't shed a single tear. I'd built up such an impenetrable emotional dam over the years that I was no longer capable of a simple thing like crying. Dry-eyed, I envied his release. I looked away, unable to face my shame.

"What do the doctors say?"

I shrugged. "That only time will tell. That she needs round-the-clock care. That all we can do is wait."

"And what about the witches? What are they up to?"

"Don't call them that!" It was okay for me to call them that—I'd put up with them for all these years—but he wasn't allowed.

"Theresa didn't mind."

"Well Theresa isn't here! You forfeited the right to badmouth them when they got stuck with raising us because you got yourself locked up in here."

Any trace of benevolent Santa disappeared. Leaning

forward, he snarled through the glass, "I wouldn't be in here if it wasn't for those bitches!"

"Witches," I corrected. It startled me how much I sounded like my mother in that moment. How many times had I heard her make that very correction?

"You sound just like your mother."

I frowned at him, at myself, unhappy he'd confirmed my observation. I sure as hell didn't want to be compared to her. Not ever.

Sitting back in his chair he smiled kindly. "The hospital bills must be astronomical."

"It's only been a couple of days."

He roared. "You waited a couple of days to tell me?"

I flinched at his shout. "I've been busy."

He raised his hands in surrender. "I'm sorry. This has all been a shock is all."

"To me too."

"About the bills . . . what are you going to do about them?"

"There's life insurance . . . car insurance . . ."

"It's not going to be enough."

I knew he was right, but that was a problem I couldn't deal with at the moment. I had more important things to focus on. Namely getting Katie to open her eyes.

"Whatever you do, Maggie, don't do anything stupid. No matter how desperate you get, no matter how much you want to cure her, don't do what I did."

"I wasn't planning on robbing a bank."

"You're a lot like me, Maggie May." There was no pride in his voice, only sad resignation. "You're prone to tilting at windmills. The inability to do anything, the frustration will eat away at you, making you capable of doing things . . . the kinds of things you can't even imagine."

"I'm not like you."

"No? Then why are you here? Certainly not because you've forgiven me or because you didn't want me to hear from a stranger that Theresa's . . . gone."

I inclined my head slightly to signal my agreement with his assessment.

"You're here because you're fiercely—bordering on perversely—loyal to those you love. You knew damn well that Theresa would have wanted you to tell me in person, so you subjugated your own desires and drove here."

"You must be doing a lot of reading."

He blinked. I'd caught him off guard. "Huh?"

"You're using terms like 'tilting at windmills' and 'subjugated' during this father-daughter bonding session."

"Changing the subject doesn't change the outcome, Maggie May."

"Meaning you think I'm going to become a bank robber or a murderer?"

He winced. I knew what he was thinking. He'd said it often enough during his trial. How many times had he tried to explain that the bank teller's death hadn't been his fault? Someone had believed him because his state-appointed idiot defense lawyer had managed to plead the charges down from first-degree murder to second-.

"What I think, daughter of mine, is that you're capable of doing whatever it takes for someone you love. Whatever it takes."

Chapter Three

LIKE I SAID, it took me two days to remember the lizard, and that was just because Katie's grandfather reminded me of her favorite toy.

I let myself into Theresa's house with the key she kept by the solar-powered garden gnome in one of those fake rock/key-hider things.

Their house was in one of those cookie-cutter neighborhoods that dot the landscape of New Jersey, tucked between industrial parks, protected Green Spaces, and spots where George Washington had stopped to take a leak during the Revolutionary War. The streets in the development all had bird names.

Theresa and Dirk had bought on Cardinal Court, not because it was the best house in the area, but because cardinals were our mom's favorite bird. Theresa had said it was a sign. Personally, I don't believe in signs, premonitions, vibes, or luck, but I hadn't said a word, because I'd figured a dead-end street was probably a safer place to raise a kid.

It was dark as I fumbled for the light switch.

"It's about time." The man's voice, English and dripping with disdain, scared the shit out of me. Who the hell was in the house? Pressing my back to the wall, holding my breath, I tried to figure out where he was. All I could hear was the chirping of crickets.

"What are you waiting for?" His voice, coming from Katie's room, was familiar. Haughty. Full of contempt. "I said, 'What are you waiting for?'"

I exhaled in relief. Alan Rickman. It was Alan Rickman's voice. Theresa must have left a Harry Potter DVD running. I'd once suggested that I thought Professor Snape was too scary for a three-year-old. Big mistake. I got the whole, "parents know what's best for their kids" speech, as though having a child somehow improved the judgment of an adult.

Switching on the light, I made my way to Katie's room to turn off the movie and find the dinosaur.

Flipping the switch just inside her door, I illuminated her pink and frilly bedroom. The TV was dark. That was weird. A quick glance at the bed told me Dino wasn't there, so I dropped to my knees to look underneath.

"Hello? I'm over here."

Goosebumps sprang to life all over my body. Why did it sound as though Professor Snape was talking to me? I shook my head. I was being ridiculous. I lifted the bed skirt and peered beneath.

"I'm not under the bed you imbecile. I'm over here."

Rocking back on my heels I dropped the bed skirt. It really did sound as though he was talking to me, but that couldn't be. I closed my eyes and forced myself to take a slow, deep breath. No need to panic. I was just tired. And stressed, definitely stressed.

"Here, you moronic biped. By the mirror."

I opened one eye and slowly swiveled my head in the direction of the dresser. No one stood in front of it.

"Up here! Up here! ON the dresser!"

Slowly, I raised my gaze. Not believing what I was seeing, I blinked. I still saw it. Squeezing my eyes shut, I counted to ten. I looked again.

Yup, the lizard was still standing up and waving at me.

I gulped. Holy crap, I'd lost my mind.

I crawled over to get a better look at Katie's pet lizard in its glass terrarium. About six inches long (most of it tail) it was muddy brown with a dark stripe down its back. It wasn't what I'd call a cute and cuddly pet. And it didn't look anything like Alan Rickman.

"I'm starving. You'd better be here to feed me. And I need to be misted. All this dry air has just wreaked havoc with my complexion."

"Would it kill you to say 'please'?" I asked.

The little guy fell over backward, his tail twitching. He scrambled back up and stared at me with those shiny eyes of his. "You can hear me?"

I nodded. Heaven help me, I thought a lizard was talking to me. Apparently my father had been right to compare me to my mother. Like her, I seemed to be delusional too.

"I don't believe it." His tail twitched.

"Me neither."

He rubbed his chin with one of his front feet as though he was trying to make sense of this odd development. I waited for him to speak again, hoping he could make sense of all this. Pathetic, I know.

"You are here to feed me, aren't you? I haven't eaten for days."

"What do you eat?"

"Crickets."

"What else?"

"Just that. Crickets. I could eat other things, but I prefer crickets."

I swallowed hard. The idea of eating a cricket disgusted me. "What other kinds of things?"

"Fruit flies, meal worms, maggots."

I gagged. They were even grosser than crickets! "Okay, okay, where do they keep your food?"

"In a bag in the closet."

Opening the closet door, I found a plastic bag containing a couple of live crickets. It vibrated in my hand as the bugs jumped around. It took all my self-control not to drop it on the floor and stomp it. I hate bugs the way Indiana Jones hates snakes. "They're alive."

"Mmmm . . . fresh meat!"

I swear I saw him lick his lips. "What are you waiting for? Feed me!"

"Please."

"Please what?"

"When you say *please*, I'll feed you."

"You have got to be kidding me."

I dangled the bag above the terrarium. Not only did I think I was conversing with a lizard, but now I was trying to teach him manners. That probably made it official that I'd lost my mind.

"*Please*, feed me the fucking crickets!" he bellowed.

"No need to be snippy about it." I hastily untied the plastic sack, making sure the insects couldn't jump out and touch me. Pushing aside the glass lid of the enclosure, I dropped the entire bag of bugs inside.

"Food! Glorious food!"

Totally grossed out, I turned away as the gecko feasted, resuming my search for Dino. I rummaged through Katie's toy chest. I didn't find the dinosaur, but I did find six Dora the Explorers.

"Wha' are you doin'?"

I made the mistake of turning back to look at him. He was chewing on a cricket's leg like it was a toothpick. "You shouldn't talk with your mouth full."

Ignoring the reprimand, he said haughtily, "Whatever it is you're searching for, I can help you find it."

"Katie's dinosaur."

"I'd guess it's in the washing machine or dryer. She vomited on it a couple of days ago. I haven't seen the shabby thing since. Which reminds me, where is the child?"

"In the hospital. There was a car accident. Theresa's dead. Dirk's dead. Katie's hurt."

"That's terrible!"

I didn't dare look at him for fear that he, too, would shed a tear for Katie. I lay down on my niece's pink big-girl bed and rested my cheek on her princess pillow. I was so tired. I closed my eyes for a minute.

"Is she going to be all right?" There was no trace of arrogance in the lizard's tone, only concern.

"I don't know."

"So you're going to be responsible for my care?"

Hearing doubt in his snotty voice, I threw the pillow at him. It bounced off the glass harmlessly and slid to the floor.

"No need to get violent, Maggie."

I squinted at him. "How do you know my name?"

He shook his head as though he couldn't believe how slow I was. "Katie calls you Aunt Maggie." In a falsetto that sounded surprisingly like my niece, he parroted, " 'Aunt Maggie coming to tea pahty!' 'Aunt Maggie reads *Where the Wild Things* to Dino!' "

"All right. So what's your name, smart ass?" I couldn't believe I was asking a lizard what his name was and actually expecting an answer.

Standing on his back legs, using his tail for balance, he drew himself up to his full height (all two-and-a-half inches of it) and declared pompously, "I am Godzilla!"

I swallowed a chuckle. It wasn't really his fault he had such a ridiculous name, and you know how little guys get when they think they're being laughed at. "Nice to meet you, Godzilla."

"But you may call me God."

"God?"

"Of course. Godzilla sounds pretentious."

"And God doesn't?"

"You prefer Maggie over Margaret, don't you?"

I nodded.

"Well I prefer God over Godzilla."

"God it is then."

"Are you going to live here?"

Startled, I shook my head. "The thought hadn't occurred to me."

"Then you must take me to your home."

"I must?"

"Well you can't leave me here all alone. Katie would expect you to provide me with fresh food and water and companionship."

I frowned, knowing that he was right. I was really getting tired of doing what I imagined others would expect of me.

"Do you live alone?"

I nodded.

"By alone, I mean do you have any pets? Any predator that might try to eat me, like a dog, or a cat, or a bird?"

I shook my head.

"Good. It's decided then."

"It is?"

"It is."

"Can I ask you something?"

"You may."

"Do you talk to people, humans I mean, on a regular basis?"

"You're my first. Not for a lack of trying though. What about you? Do you talk to many non-human species?"

"Nope. Then again, I'm not really talking to you."

"You're not?" He flicked his tail.

"No, this is just some sort of side effect from the accident. It's my mind trying to make sense of a terrible situation. You're not real."

"I beg your pardon, but I most certainly am real."

"No, no, no. I know that you, the pet gecko, are real. I just mean this whole, us-having-a-conversation thing, is a figment of my imagination."

"I am NOT a gecko!" he shouted, snapping his tail like a bullwhip.

"You're not?"

"Do I look like a gecko?"

I squinted at him.

"Oh sure, one lizard gets on TV, and you automatically assume we're all just like him."

"You do look alike."

He bobbed his head, and his beard turned from tan to black. "You did NOT just say that."

Raising my hands defensively, I stepped back.

"You ignorant—"

"I didn't mean to offend you."

"I am an anole. A brown anole." He puffed out the little orange goatee-like thing beneath his chin to make his point. "I am NOT a gecko!"

"Okay, okay! Whatever you are, I'm going to bring you home with me. Katie would never forgive me if I let anything happen to you."

Chapter Four

I WENT TO visit Katie straight from the funeral. The idea of going back to the B&B with my aunts and all the well-meaning (but ultimately draining) friends and neighbors who had come to pay their respects was just too much for me to handle. That and the fact that I was still itching to strangle Dirk's ditzy sister, Raelene. I guess it was lucky none of his other family members had bothered to attend, or else I might have snapped.

Instead of riding in the family limousine with the witches and Raelene, I drove my crappy Honda in the procession to the cemetery. That meant that the moment the graveside service was over, I was outta there.

I was overdressed for a hospital visit in my best black dress and heels, but I was pretty sure no one would notice.

My maternal grandmother, the witches' mother, and the woman I think was responsible for creating the basket case that is my mother, used to shake her head sadly every time she saw me and say, "You are the most remarkably unremarkable girl I have ever known, Margaret."

She was an utterly lovely woman . . . not.

Other kids had grandmothers who baked cookies and sang lullabies. Mine delivered insults every chance she got . . . may the poor dear rest in peace.

Given the opportunity or an audience, she was always more than happy to elaborate on my shortcomings. "She's not particularly tall, and her body isn't especially attractive. She's not all that smart, or pretty, or funny, or kind."

In short, I was an average-looking girl, of middling intelligence, with an unexceptional personality. The same could be said of me at thirty-two, except now you could add, ". . . who lives a boring life."

That was why I could be fairly certain that no one would miss me at the wake.

I was so engrossed in my thoughts about how remarkably unremarkable I am, I almost missed the creepy guy lurking at the end of the hallway. I'm not sure I even saw him, but I definitely felt him.

Out of nowhere, a chill skittered down my spine, and my legs turned rubbery.

He was a small guy, my height, maybe a little shorter, not the slightest bit physically imposing. I examined his pinched face and receding hairline, trying to place where I might know him from. I drew a blank.

But I knew I didn't like him.

My breath caught in my throat as his gaze met mine. I'd seen convicted murderers with teardrop tattoos dripping down their faces—symbols of multiple kills—when I'd visited my father in prison, but none of them seemed as scary as the man in the hallway. At least in the prison there were plexiglass and guards between the evil and me. Here there were no protective barriers.

I swallowed hard.

Realizing how frightened I was, his eyes narrowed and a slow, sly sneer stretched his lips, making him look like a deadly predator. He winked at me.

My heart skipped a beat, and bile rose in my throat.

And then he was gone, disappearing down another hall.

Feeling shaky after the encounter, I leaned against the wall. After a moment, I got a little pissed at myself. Sure I'd had a rough few days, but was I really going to let myself turn into a spineless, quivering mess when I had Katie depending on me to keep it together?

So I took a deep breath, squared my shoulders, pushed off the wall, and marched (well, okay, tottered because of those damn heels) toward my niece's room.

I was so busy beating myself up for my momentary cowardice that I walked right into a man hurrying to enter the room beside Katie's.

"Uhhh!" I cried out eloquently as our bodies collided. I teetered precariously on my high heels. Unaccustomed to wearing anything other than sneakers, I thought for a moment I was going to topple over and end up splayed on my ass in the middle of the hallway.

"Watch where you're going," he growled.

"Sorry." Regaining my balance, I looked up at him. Tall, dark hair, olive skin, a cleft chin, he was definitely handsome. Of course he was. I'd just done something klutzy and embarrassing. It made sense I'd do it in front of an attractive man.

He glared at me. Something fluttered uneasily at the base of my spine, causing me to stand up a little straighter. "Sorry 'bout that."

"You should be."

I blinked. How rude! "It was an accident."

"Get out of my way!"

He shoved me, literally shoved me, backward into the wall. Pushing past, he rushed into the room.

Startled by the physicality of his attack, I stood there for a long second, trying to catch my breath.

I couldn't, though, because I was so incredibly pissed off. All the injustices of the past few days welled up within me. It wasn't fair that Theresa was gone. It wasn't right that poor Katie was hurt. I loathed the drunk driver who had done this. I despised the doctors who spouted statistics and best-case scenarios. I hated the world. I hated life itself.

In that moment I realized there was only one person I could take this overwhelming anger out on: the Jerk who couldn't accept a simple apology and had the nerve to assault me.

I, remarkably unremarkable Margaret May Lee, had had enough. I charged into the room, ready to give it to the stranger with both barrels.

Looking back, I had to admit that it was probably a good thing I'd seen a brown anole lizard standing up and waving to me the night before. If I hadn't, I'm not sure my mind could have made sense out of what I was seeing.

The Jerk was pressing a pillow down over someone's face, smothering them. A little someone, probably not much older than Katie, I guessed from the outline of the tiny body tucked beneath the hospital blanket.

I am not a violent person. Okay, maybe I'm a tad bit overzealous when it comes to swatting flies or grinding creepy-crawlies under my heel, and sure Theresa and I used to whale on each other when we were kids, but I hadn't struck another person in decades.

Something snapped in me, maybe the tether of my internal monster, when I saw the Jerk suffocating that kid.

I'm not much of a planner, but I somehow had the foresight to arm myself. Grabbing the plastic and metal visitor's chair by the side of the bed, I launched my attack . . . as well as someone can do that in high heels.

"Aaaaah!" I screamed the kind of full-throttle, gone native, sound that leaves your throat bleeding and triggers that primordial fight-or-flight instinct of anyone within earshot.

He half-turned at the sound of my battle cry. Raising the chair overhead I smashed it, as hard as I could, into his face.

Stumbling backward, sending medical equipment crashing in all directions, he tried to escape, but I chased after him, fueled by all the anger and grief I'd kept bottled up for days.

The chair glanced off his shoulder as I connected with a second blow.

"Aaaaah!" I shrieked again. There were no words to

express my rage, even the primitive yell didn't do it justice. Hoisting the chair again, I swung at him.

Ready this time, he deflected the blow. Ripping the chair from my grasp, he stared at me with an animalistic rage. "You are going to pay for that, you stupid bitch!"

He lifted the chair, and I just knew he was going to split my skull open. I didn't know karate, or jujitsu, or kung fu. I'd never even taken a basic self-defense class. I'd never had any specialized training of any sort. Except once. A very, very long time ago.

With nothing to lose, I tried the long-ago learned evasion technique.

I stopped.

I dropped.

I rolled.

Stop. Drop. And roll. Fire safety 101. A lesson I'd learned in kindergarten.

And I'll be damned, but it works when a psycho-killer jerk is after you too.

Especially when hospital security enters the room. It's helpful to be on the floor so that they can leap over you and tackle said psycho-killer jerk.

The little boy in the bed survived the attack, security hustled psycho-killer jerk away, and I was called a hero by the doctors, nurses, and the boy's family for saving his life.

It was that praise that led me to become a contract killer.

Chapter Five

I WAS SITTING at Katie's bedside singing "Itsy Bitsy Spider," manipulating her lifeless fingers so that she'd mimic the pantomime of the song, when the man who would become my boss strolled in. I knew who he was instantly. Anyone who reads the newspaper or watches the local news would.

Tony Delveccio.

Or maybe he was Anthony.

According to rumor, Ms. Delveccio, an Atlantic City showgirl, hadn't been the brightest bulb on the marquee. She'd named her twin boys Tony and Anthony, never realizing that Tony is of course the shortened version of Anthony.

Anyway, the Delveccio brothers, identical twins, allegedly ran the local crime syndicate. I stress *allegedly* because they've never actually been convicted of so much as a parking ticket despite the effort of cops, local D.A.s and federal prosecutors. A case based on eye witness testimony falls apart quickly when there's always an identical twin with an airtight alibi waiting in the wings.

Delveccio stood just inside the room with his leather loafers, a shirt unbuttoned halfway down his sternum (so not an attractive look for a guy pushing sixty) and a pinky ring with a diamond the size of an eyeball, staring at me.

Like I wasn't having a bad enough week.

"You the broad who took a chair to Alfonso's head?"

I considered lying. After all, I certainly didn't want a mobster after me, but then I realized the nurses had probably already told him I was in here. There was no point in lying about it. At least if I was going to get thwacked . . . or is it whacked? . . . I'd do so honestly.

I tried to answer him, but my throat was closed tighter than the doors at Walmart before they open for shopping on Black Friday, so I just nodded.

"I thought you'd be more . . ."

"Remarkable?" I croaked.

"Huh?"

"You thought I'd be remarkable?"

Shrugging, he switched his attention to Katie's still face. "Poor kid. She's your niece, right?"

I panicked for a moment, wondering how the hell he knew that. Then I realized the flock of gossiping magpies at the nurse's station had probably told him that, too. What worried me more was why the crime boss cared.

I jumped to my feet, putting myself between Delveccio and Katie. "It wasn't her fault I hit your goon."

The corners of his mouth twitched. Turning his back

on me, he moved toward the hall. A surge of hope rocketed through me. He was going to leave us alone.

That fizzled the moment he closed the door of the room, isolating us. My stomach roiled nervously and acid rose in my throat, scorching flesh still tender from my earlier screaming. Wrapping my fingers around Katie's IV pole, I prepared to use it to knock a gun from his grip.

But when he turned back around, his hands were empty. I didn't let go of the pole.

"Alfonso ain't my goon."

I breathed a little easier.

"That little guy," he jerked his thumb in the direction of the boy's room where I'd scuffled with the psycho-killer jerk, "he's my grandson. Dominic."

"I'm sorry." I loosened my grip on my weapon. I knew how much it sucked to have a relative in this awful place.

"Everyone says you saved him. Brave thing."

"I really didn't think it through."

"And yet you live to tell the tale without a scratch on ya. You're either very good or very lucky."

I bit the inside of my cheek to keep from rolling my eyes at the mention of the unfortunate "lucky" term. No need to piss off the nice mobster. "Glad I could help."

"That goon you tangled with? Alfonso? He's my son-in-law."

"Oh."

"My daughter inherited my mother's lack of sense."

"Uh huh." I really didn't know what he wanted me to say.

"He's Dominic's father, the one who put him in that bed. Threw him down a flight of stairs."

"Bastard!"

Delveccio smiled approvingly at that. "Family: You can't live with 'em, ya can't get away with killing them yourself."

Thinking of Dirk the Jerk and his idiot sister Raelene, I muttered with feeling, "I know exactly what you mean."

"Which is what brings me here, Miss Lee."

I gulped. "How do you know my name?"

He twirled his pinky ring. The rock was huge. "I know your name, where you live, where you work, and that you're the legal guardian of that little girl. I also know how much your annual salary is, that you have no criminal record, and what's in your bank account. Most importantly, I know how much this "premium care" costs. People say I'm a crook, but the medical establishment has got nothing on me. They just know how to bleed you dry legally. And *that* is why I think you might find yourself amenable to the offer I'm going to make you."

"You've lost me."

"Think of this as a lucrative job opportunity. A chance to make some extra cash to care for little Katie."

Delveccio stepped closer.

I tilted the pole toward him, a clear signal that I wouldn't go down without a fight.

The move seemed to please him. "I like you. You're a feisty one. That's why I'm offering you $100,000 to take out Alfonso."

My mouth went dry as I stared at him. I asked, "You mean like take him out to the ballgame? Or take him out to dinner?"

He tilted his head and raised his eyebrows knowing damn well that I'd understood his offer and was just playing cute and/or stupid with those questions. The man had just offered me a boatload of bucks to kill his son-in-law.

He watched me intently, studying my reaction.

"I can't."

"Why not? You took a chair to the man's head earlier."

"But that was the heat of the moment. I'm not . . . I couldn't . . ."

"Sure you can. It's in your blood. You are Archie Lee's kid."

I flinched at the mention of my father. I guess I shouldn't have been surprised. The mobster seemed to know everything there was to know about me, but I was still startled that he'd brought up my dad.

"I know I've given you a lot to consider. You don't have to decide right now. Think about it. Sleep on it. I've got obligations the next couple of days. I'll be back here on Friday. You can give me your answer then."

"I don't think—"

He held up his hand to silence me. The diamond sparkled like the freakin' North Star.

"If you decide to accept my offer, I'll set you with one of my guys. We'll get you some on-the-job training so that you get the job done and get away clean. I'll be in touch, Miss Lee."

I didn't respond in kind. I just stood there, staring at him slack-jawed.

He opened the door and strolled out with the same studied ease as when he'd come in.

I ran into the bathroom, leaned over the sink, and gagged. Nothing came up beside dry heaves. Splashing water on my face, I studied my reflection.

I didn't look like a killer.

Chapter Six

THE PROBLEM WITH someone offering to pay you to kill someone is that you can't talk to anyone about it. Not anyone. Usually when you've got some sort of monumental, life-changing decision to make, you run it past your family, your friends, your confidants, strangers on the street. But I couldn't breathe a word of it to anybody. Not that there was a decision to make. I'd made up my mind I wasn't going to become a hired killer. But I've got to admit that it was all I thought about. Not the actual act of killing, but what it meant that Tony (or was it Anthony?) Delveccio thought I was capable of such a thing. Could he see something in me that I'd never admitted to myself?

I went back to work the next day, because I figured that I didn't need to lose my job on top of everything else. But my heart wasn't in it. Not that it ever was. I hated my job taking insurance claims for automobile accidents. You can never fully grasp the true stupidity of your fellow man until you've worked at a service call center. Between calls I thought about Delveccio's offer. A lot. By the time my lunch hour, or more accurately my lunch *half* hour, rolled around, my head was spinning.

My best friend at Insuring the Future hobbled toward me across the break room. Armani Vasquez consistently earned the lowest scores on our customer service call audits, but she's never in danger of losing her job. *"I'm a female, Latina, gimp," she declares proudly. "I got the Americans with Disabilities Act covering my ass. Ain't no one gonna fire someone missing three fingers with only one good leg."*

She is, of course, right. No one dares to discipline her for fear of a discrimination lawsuit. As a result, she takes ridiculously long breaks and mouths off to managers on a consistent basis. She can be a royal pain in the ass, but I like her. Maybe it's because she says what she thinks, or maybe it's because more than once I've caught her taking the blame for mistakes other employees have made. Something she does with some regularity and with no expectation of reciprocation. She's not nearly as self-centered as she pretends to be . . . but she is damn good at the pretending.

"I got a reading tonight." Breathlessly she flopped into the chair opposite me.

She's got one of those cool scooter things, but she refuses to use it most of the time, preferring instead to drag her bad leg behind her, lurching like a drunken sailor. She's fiercely independent that way. It's another reason to like her. "I got a reading," she repeated.

"Good for you."

Besides being the poster child for the Americans with

Disabilities Act here at Future, Armani Vazquez was starting a side business . . . as a psychic. While I don't believe in signs, premonitions, vibes, or luck, Armani does.

"Referral from a former customer."

"Uh huh." I considered asking her why she hadn't foreseen the car accident that had just demolished my life or the runaway Zamboni that had ruined her leg and chewed up her missing fingers.

"I tried googling the girl, but I didn't come up with much."

"Not even Facebook?"

Armani shook her head, her face appearing and disappearing behind her thick curtain of dark hair like a magician's trick. Her hair was part of her mystique and she played it for all it was worth. "Girl's pretty cagey about revealing personal information online."

I raised my eyebrows. "How inconvenient for you."

Armani liked to scout out details about her clients before they met her. She claimed it helped her get a better idea of the big picture of their lives. She may have almost fooled herself into believing her own bullshit, but I wasn't buying. Fortune-telling was just a con, designed to take money from some poor, desperate sap who was looking for a couple blanket reassurances—you're not going to die alone; you'll find love—that kind of crap.

"She's a four," Armani announced with disdain.

"Excuse me?"

"A four. Lisa. L-I-S-A. Four."

"Which means . . . ?" Like all good con artists, Armani had put her own spin on things. Some so-called-psychics read palms, other cards, and still others tea leaves, but Armani Vasquez read Scrabble tiles.

Yes, Scrabble tiles. She'd ask a mark to pull a handful out of a cloth bag and lay them on the table. Then she'd spell out words or make up anagrams and "read" the future. She practiced here in the break room on unsuspecting co-workers all the time, perfecting her act, reading their tells.

She'd never offered to look into my future. Maybe she sensed that I'd seen enough in my past. Maybe she figured I wasn't quite as dumb as the rest of these idiots we called our peers.

"You know how I feel about fours." Armani judged everyone based on the numerical value (as determined by Scrabble letters) of their name. Armani equaled eight. Vasquez was like hitting the jackpot in her book. It equaled twenty-eight.

My last name Lee is only worth three, but I'm saved by the fact that my first name is a ten, if I go by Maggie, or twelve if I use Margaret. Otherwise I don't think we'd be friends because she doesn't trust anyone five or below.

I didn't respond to her comment about fours. I had more important things on my mind. Like why Delveccio thought I was capable of murder.

"What's wrong with you? " Armani asked sharply, jolting me out of my morose musings.

I couldn't tell her the truth, that my future might hold a murder. "I dunno. My sister's dead. My niece is in a coma. Excuse me if I'm not going to win Little Miss Sunshine today."

"Today, my amiga, you are not even in the running."

"So go sit somewhere else if you don't like my company."

She ignored that as she started rummaging in her purse. "What you need is to channel your inner Chiquita."

"You want me to channel my inner banana?" I knew what she meant, but I liked teasing her. For as long as I've known Armani, she's been trying to get me to set my "true self" free. I was too bottled up for her taste. I didn't tell her that my reserve was something I'd carefully constructed over the years. The ability to control my emotions, to lock them up and refuse to express them, was a conscious choice. It was what separated me from my crazy mother. I wasn't about to let loose any time soon . . . or ever, if I could help it.

Still, Armani kept trying to get me to let go by calling it different things: "Let the world see the real you" and "Be your bitch self" were just two of the previous campaigns she'd waged. She'd dropped it right after the accident, but apparently she'd decided I'd been my mopier-than-usual self for long enough.

"Let that cute, smart, passionate girl that's inside you out, Chiquita. You have a big heart stuck in that petite persona you show to the world." She pulled a bottle out of her purse and spritzed my arm with some Glow by J Lo perfume. "You've gotta get your glow on."

"You just put your Glow on me, which, by the way, is not cool. I don't care if you are a cripple, you try that shit again, and I will lay your ass out."

She beamed. "Yes, that's it! Send some energy out into the universe, and let it come back at you ten-fold!"

"You have lost your fucking mind!" I jumped out of my chair before she could spray me again.

"And you have lost your way, Grasshopper. But I believe that you will find your path."

Right then I was worried that the path she was referring to might lead me straight to the death penalty, but of course I couldn't tell her that. Instead, I went back to work, knowing that as soon as my shift was over I was going home to talk to the other living . . . being I could talk to.

Chapter Seven

I SHOULD HAVE known that my plan to go home and spend a nice quiet evening talking with a lizard, who calls himself God, about whether or not I look like a stone cold killer, was doomed from the start.

Aunt Leslie waited for me in denim overalls and a Grateful Dead t-shirt, her white hair waving in the wind like a flag of surrender. She was hammering something above my front door, a difficult task for most women, but at six-four, she rarely needed a ladder.

"What are you doing?"

She swung around in my direction, almost causing me thousands of dollars worth of dental reconstruction. I jumped back, narrowly escaping a hammer to the mouth. Oblivious that she'd almost taken my head off with her hammer, she threw her arms around me, enveloping me in that disgusting scent she wore. She squeezed my rib-cage like she was trying to get the last drop of toothpaste out of a used-up tube.

"We missed you at the wake."

Extricating myself from her grip, I backed away a few feet to where the air was fresh and clean (or at least where I could breathe in the familiar smog that passes for fresh air in New Jersey). "What are you hanging?"

Aunt Leslie beamed, obviously proud of her find. "A horseshoe."

"A what?"

"A horseshoe. It's supposed to ward off bad luck."

Kinda late for that, I thought. "You know I don't believe in that kind of stuff, right?"

Her smile turned upside down into a pathetic, pouting, frown. Her lower lip trembled ominously.

"But hey, it can't hurt!" I wanted to avoid one of Aunt Leslie's emotional outbreaks like a lingerie model wants to avoid cellulite. "I'll take all the help I can get. Thanks, Aunt Leslie!"

She smiled and I breathed a sigh of relief (albeit a shallow one, since I was still trying to avoid the noxious fumes emanating from her person). A mini-meltdown had been avoided.

"So was that all you wanted? To hang the horseshoe?"

"That, and to check on you. You've been so strong through all of this. I just wanted to see how you're holding up."

I briefly considered revealing how I'd snapped and attacked a man with a chair.

"And . . . ," she said, a little too brightly. "I wanted to see if you'd like to visit your mother."

"No." I didn't have to think about it. The answer was automatic.

"But . . ." Her voice cracked, a sure signal the tears would start any moment. "But I know she'd like to see you."

"And you know I wouldn't like to see her."

"Susan said you'd refuse, but I thought if I could just talk to you . . ." The waterworks started on cue, just like those sprinklers that go off in the produce section of the supermarket just when you're reaching for a head of lettuce.

I held my breath, waiting to exhale a sigh of exasperation. But there was no need to upset her more. She was just trying to be a good aunt and sister. I couldn't fault her for that.

Closing the distance between us, I wrapped my arms around her waist. "I appreciate you coming to check on me, Aunt Leslie. And I appreciate the horseshoe. I even appreciate the invite to visit Mom, but I'm sorry, with everything else that's happened, I can't. I just can't take any more. Can you understand that? Can you forgive me?"

Hugging me back, she pressed a kiss to the top of my head. "There's nothing to forgive, Maggie. When you're ready, I'll be here to go with you. Until then you take care of yourself."

She walked away, taking her cloud of stinky perfume with her. I watched her go, feeling guilty for upsetting her. I knew she meant well. I knew she loved me. I knew she didn't mean to meddle.

"Oh," she yelled as she reached her car. "I forgot to tell you that Susan says that when you decide that Katie is too much responsibility for you, just let her know."

My good will toward her evaporated instantly. Meddling fools!

I was muttering as I unlocked the door and walked inside my apartment. "She makes it sound like this was all my idea. I mean it's not like I ever had any desire to have a kid. I'm a realist. I know I'd suck at it."

"Suck at what?" God asked in that self-important tone of his.

I was so upset about Aunt Leslie's visit that I'd totally forgotten I'd left him and his terrarium in the middle of my kitchen table.

His voice was so unexpected that I jumped back, knocking a framed family portrait photograph off the wall. It crashed to the floor, the glass shattering.

"Dammit! Look what you made me do."

"What do you suck at?"

"Raising a kid. I know I'd end up screwing up a kid just the way my . . . just the way I was screwed up. Why would I want to do that? Why would I want another living soul to inherit that kind of legacy? The world really doesn't need one more fuck-up."

Picking up the frame, taking care not to look at the photograph, I leaned it up against the wall.

"That's why I balked when Theresa asked me to be godmother to her unborn child. Katie hadn't been born yet, and Theresa was already asking me to make a commitment to be responsible for the kid if something should happen to her and Dirk. I turned Theresa down the first two times she asked me. I caved the third time, when she pulled out the big guilt guns, *If you don't agree to take her, she'll end up with the coven.*"

"That's an excellent impression of her." The lizard sounded impressed in a bored kind of way. "Spot on."

"And of course nothing could get me to quit shirking my responsibilities quicker than the impending threat of the coven, also known as the three witches, also known as my three aunts. Not that Susan, Leslie, and Loretta are bad witches, or women, or aunts. I actually think they mean well most of the time, but sometimes their meddling feels downright evil."

"And what horribly, evil thing have they done to you, that you've labeled them witches?" God managed to make every single syllable drip with disparagement.

"*I* didn't label them. My father called them the three bitches. My mother changed bitch to witch every time. As a kid Theresa thought that meant they were the three witches. The name stuck."

"And you never outgrew the childish name-calling."

Ignoring his chastisement I rummaged in the kitchen pantry for my dust pan and brush to clean up the broken glass in the foyer. "If I'm totally honest, I've gotta say that there have been plenty of times I've wondered whether the nuthouse locked up the right Ginty sister. I mean, sure my mother is delusional, but I don't think she's any crazier than her loony sisters."

"You do realize you're telling all this to a lizard, don't you?"

I sighed. "I was trying not to dwell on that particular fact."

"You're not very sensitive."

"About what?"

"Mental illness. You toss around *nuthouse* and *loony* like they're beads at Mardi Gras."

"Are you trying to tell me that you've been to Mardi Gras?"

"I'm trying to tell you that the stigma of mental illness runs rampant, and you shouldn't be so callous as to perpetuate the stereotypes."

"I'm being lectured by an amphibian."

"Reptile."

"Whatever."

"And I'm not telling you anything you don't already know. You should be ashamed of yourself."

I glared at God. It's really difficult to stare down a lizard. They don't have eyelids, so you know they're not going to blink first.

He just stared at me with that infuriating implacability of his. "You're angry, Maggie?"

"It's a double standard."

"What is?"

"Understanding. I'm supposed to understand. Be patient. Excuse and forgive."

God licked his eyeball, his equivalent of blinking. It's disgusting to watch. "You're not making a lot of sense."

"Maybe that means I've gone 'round the bend. Over the bridge to grandmother's house I've gone."

"You're going to your grandmother's house?"

"Over the river and through the woods to grandmother's house . . . Oh never mind. It's just a song Mom used to sing when I was little—before she went 'round the bend and over the edge. I have a headache. I don't want to talk about this any more."

"You speak of her with such . . . disdain."

"I love my mother."

"All the time?"

Busted. I hung my head. He was right. There were times when I didn't love her or even like her. It was my secret shame.

"Tell me why."

I shook my head. It was bad enough that I was confiding in a lizard. I sure as hell didn't need to confess to him, too. I couldn't even look at him.

"Why, M&M?

The old nickname caught me like a sucker punch to the gut. The air whooshed right out of me on a pained gasp. How did he even know to call me that?

Only one person had ever called me M&M (Margaret May): my youngest sister, Darlene. I did my best not to think about her. It just hurt too much. It had been over ten years since she'd been kidnapped from the traveling carnival passing through town. Almost nine years since her body had been discovered and identified.

God summoning her memory was a low blow.

Before I could even process the renewed sense of grief, he delivered the knockout punch.

"Why do you hate your mother?"

"Because it's all her fault!" The accusation came from somewhere deep in my core. Like lava it bubbled up and out, obliterating everything in its path. There was no reason or logic left, just the searing pain.

I fell to my knees in the foyer, shards of glass tearing at my flesh. My eyes burned. I wanted to cry, to let it out, but no tears came.

"I should have been keeping an eye on the girls, but I was so busy watching her, making sure she didn't do anything crazy, that they wandered off." Speaking softly didn't dampen the ugliness of the admission. I hated my mother because of my own failure to protect my little sisters.

"You are going to feed me soon, I hope."

Disbelievingly, I turned to give the scaly little guy the evil eye. Here I was, pouring out my heart, and he was worried about his stomach?

"Typical male," I muttered.

God flicked his tail, a sure sign he was displeased. "What's that supposed to mean?"

"It means that the minute I start talking about my feelings, you go and change the subject. Typical. A guy *says* he wants to know you, but that's a lie. All he cares about is food, sex, the latest app on his phone, or the score of the game."

"There's a game involved? I like games!"

I began sweeping up the broken glass with short, choppy strokes. "Never mind."

"No. I want to understand about this game."

"There is no game! I just meant guys are always checking on a baseball, football, or basketball game."

"I enjoy more intellectual pursuits. I am not into sports."

"I didn't say you were."

"You did say I was a typical male."

I considered throwing the swept up shards at him, but he was too well protected by his cage. I'd just have to sweep them up again.

"Just to be certain I've assessed this situation correctly: you hate your mother, you hate your aunts, and you hate all males. Is that correct?"

I shook my head. Geez, when he put it like that, it made me sound like the most bitter, lonely woman on the planet. No wonder I'd been reduced to talking to a lizard. "I don't hate my aunts. It's just that they drive me insane." I winced at my unfortunate choice of words. "And I don't hate men."

"Then what's with the unprovoked male bashing?"

"It wasn't unprovoked! You—"

"All I said was that I'm hungry."

I took a deep breath. If men are from Mars, and women are from Venus, that must mean lizards are from Zargon. We were never going to understand one another. "Fine. I'll feed you."

I hauled myself to my feet. A million splinters of pain set my knees on fire. Looking down I saw glittering chips of picture frame stuck through my pants. "I just need to get this glass out of me first."

Carrying the dust pan, which tinkled with every step, I limped into the kitchen. I dumped the contents into the trash can before hobbling into the bathroom where I grabbed my first-aid kit.

I glanced at the light fixture above the sink. A light bulb had blown out in the morning, but being late for work, I hadn't had time to replace it. As a result, it was too dark to perform minor surgery.

Walking lamely back into the kitchen, I turned on all the lights and slumped into a chair. This practically put me at eye-level with the lizard.

"You're going to need tweezers."

"They're in the kit."

"And antiseptic."

"It's in there."

"And bandages."

"Thank you, Doogie Howser. I think I can treat my own wounds."

His tail flicked, but he stayed mercifully quiet.

Gritting my teeth against the pain, I used my fingertips to pull the biggest shards of glass out of my knees. It hurt like hell. I tried to remember whether I had any Percocet left over from the root canal I'd had three years earlier.

"Can we watch *Wheel of Fortune*?" the lizard asked.

"You like *Wheel of Fortune*?"

He nodded. "I'd like to buy a vowel."

The little guy was full of surprises. I glanced at the microwave clock. *Wheel* didn't start for another forty minutes. "Can I ask you a question?"

"You're wondering how a creature with a brain the

size of mine can spell? I told you, I enjoy intellectual challenges."

"Uh huh. That's cool and everything, but I had a question about me."

He stood up, balancing on his tail, and crossed his arms over his . . . chest. "Go ahead."

"Do you think I look like a killer?" Grabbing the tweezers I attacked the smaller particles imbedded in my knees while he mulled over his answer. When an uncomfortable pause stretched on, I glanced over at him.

Head cocked, he was stroking his chin with one of his . . . hands, obviously deep in thought. Finally he spoke. "That's an odd question, Mags. Even for you."

"Never mind. Forget I asked." Something told me I didn't want to hear his answer.

"I'm curious as to what spurred this line of inquiry."

I sighed. I'd really hoped to avoid getting into this whole thing. "Someone offered me money to kill someone. I was thinking maybe he could see something in me . . . see that I was capable of that."

"Thomas Alva Edison once said, *If we did all the things we were capable of doing, we would literally astound ourselves.*"

"Yeah, but he was inventing light bulbs, not playing the part of the Angel of Death."

"Do *you* think you look like a killer?"

I shrugged, plucking the last piece of glass from my flesh. I watched a small, red rivulet of blood spread over the torn-up skin. "Everyone says I look like my father. He's a killer. So maybe I do."

"Did you accept the offer?"

"Of course not!" I pulled the pack of alcohol-soaked pads from the first-aid kit. I ripped it open with my teeth. "How could you even think I would?"

"Sometimes questions reveal more than answers," he replied mysteriously.

"I couldn't kill someone."

"Then why ask the question?"

"Because it's been bugging me. I was wondering if I give off some crazy-eyed Charles-Manson-wannabe vibe or something."

"I wouldn't say so. No."

"Then why'd he ask me?'

"He didn't give you a reason?"

"He said . . . Well, here's the thing. I sort of attacked, physically attacked, the guy he wants dead."

"You did?"

"But the psycho-killer jerk totally deserved it. He threw his son down the stairs, and then he tried to smother the kid with a pillow. I had to stop him from doing that."

"So perhaps he deserves to die."

"I'd considered that possibility." Actually I'd come to that conclusion, but I wasn't about to voice the thought. I swiped the alcohol pads over my knees. It felt like I was being stung by dozens of hornets. If I could have cried, tears would have come to my eyes. I should have found and taken the Percocet. "Fuck! Fuck, fuck, fuck that hurts!"

The lizard waited for my pained outburst to subside before he asked, "So you saved the boy's life?"

"That's what they said."

"Interesting."

"What is?"

"The whole dichotomy of taking a life versus saving one."

I rolled my eyes. "Fascinating. Does this mean you think I'm capable of killing someone?"

"Do you think you are?"

Chapter Eight

"HEY THERE, CHIQUITA!"

"Hey." I really wasn't in the mood to chat with Armani.

I'd spent the night before plunked in front of the television with the talking lizard. Who, in case you're interested, really sucks at *Wheel of Fortune*. He just doesn't get the clues. At all.

I actually was feeling pretty damn superior when Pat and Vanna waved good-bye. I'd done a much better job at solving the puzzles than God. My victory was short-lived.

The lizard is some sort of *Jeopardy*-savant. You know the annoying kind who knows the most obscure trivia, does the *New York Times* crossword puzzle in pen every day of the week, and actually understands what the hell Pi is.

So I'd gotten my ass whipped watching a game show while I chowed down on a gourmet feast of microwaved Lean Cuisine, half a bottle of wine, and a bag of chips (not the single-serving size mind you, but a real, honest-to-goodness, bag).

I'd fallen asleep on the couch and woken up coated in the grease and crumbs of the chips. And here I'd been thinking I'd inhaled them all.

I had to take a shower to get the smell of rancid vegetable oil out of my hair. The water felt like it was slicing and dicing my knees all over again.

Finally I'd managed to drag my hungover self in to work.

Of course, once I was there I took a string of automobile accident claims. That's my job. Unfortunately all of my callers were vying for the Stupidest-Driver-Ever-Allowed-Behind-the-Wheel award.

I got a woman who didn't know how to spell the names of the passengers who were in her vehicle (they were her children), a guy who didn't know what car he'd been driving, and someone using one of those creepy voice distortion machines who didn't want to give his/her name or policy number and then threatened to report me to a supervisor for not helping them.

By the time my lunch break rolled around, I had a throbbing headache and an upset stomach, not to mention the fact that I was seriously considering taking a chair to Harry's head, despite the fact he's my boss.

Smelling like week-old pepperoni, he kept leaning over my shoulder under the guise of looking at my computer monitor when what he was really doing was checking out my cleavage.

So I really was in no mood to chat with Armani.

That is, until she suggested, "Let's eat outside."

Outside. Away from phones, computers, and Harry. "Sounds good."

I logged off the system and got to my feet. My knees were killing me.

Shuffling like an old lady, I followed Armani outside, shielding my eyes from the abnormally bright sun.

"Jesus," she said, looking back at me, "You move worse than me. What's wrong?"

"I fell. Cut up my knees on some broken glass."

"You should be more careful."

"Ya think?"

We settled at a picnic table under a tree. A brook babbled nearby. It would have been a nice, peaceful place to nurse my hangover headache . . . if Armani had just shut up.

"Remember that reading I told you about?"

I nodded. Bad idea. My stomach roiled mutinously at the movement. I lay down along the length of the bench and closed my eyes. That was a little better.

"Ends up she didn't want a reading."

"I thought you said she was a referral."

"I did. She was. For sex."

"You, the great and powerful psychic, couldn't predict that?"

"Bitch!" She fell silent for a long time.

I wondered if I'd hurt her feelings. I couldn't afford to lose someone else right now. "I'm sorry. Don't mind me. I'm hung over."

"A three-way."

I sighed. Armani Vasquez is not only the Latina poster girl for Americans with Disabilities at Insuring the Future, she's also been voted "Most Likely to Spill her Sexual Exploits." Whether or not you have any interest in hearing them.

I considered covering my ears and belting out "God Bless America," but I didn't think she'd take the hint. Instead, I remained motionless and silent, hoping she'd think I'd fallen asleep.

"They were both DPWs."

I didn't make a peep. This stuff was too much for me on a good day, forget about it when I'm hung over. Apparently there's some whole sexual fetish thing concerning people who are disabled or disfigured. I don't get it, and quite frankly, since it's not my thing, I don't particularly want to get it. I feel the same way about math, fashion, and white bread.

But it is Armani's thing. She's always hooking up with these people.

"Wait!" she said suddenly. "Did you just say you're hung over?"

"Uh huh."

"So you took my advice? You embraced your inner Chiquita?"

"I still don't understand how my WASPy Caucasian self could possibly be a Chiquita."

'And I told you. It's a state of mind. A Chiquita is a cute, smart, passionate girl. I know she's inside you."

I wasn't so sure.

"Did you get your freak on?"

Yes, she actually uses that phrase in conversation.

"Did you party 'til dawn?"

"Oh yeah. Me, Pat, and Alex had a wild night."

Armani squealed with delight and slapped her thigh (her version of clapping). "I want to hear all about it!"

"Be real. I haven't had a date in a year, let alone sex, and you think your spraying me with Glow and telling me to set my inner Chiquita free turned me into some—"

"Miss Lee?"

That was not Armani's voice. It was too deep. It was too male. It was too damn amused.

Oh crap, how much of my outburst had he heard?

Opening my eyes, I bolted upright.

I had to clap a hand over my mouth to keep from puking the previous night's feast on the picnic table.

"I'm Detective Mulligan. I'd like to ask you a few questions about your . . . altercation with Alfonso Cifelli."

I looked up at him. I knew we'd never met, but his face seemed oddly familiar. Both his forehead and his chin seemed a bit long, which gave his face an almost oblong appearance. Aviator sunglasses hid his eyes. A stack of red hair, almost copper in the sunlight, was being ruffled by the breeze. I barely glanced at the badge he held out for my inspection.

"I know who you are!" Armani cried excitedly.

I winced as her shriek drilled into my brain.

"You're the Courageous Cop!"

It was his turn to wince. I wondered why. I also wondered how I hadn't recognized him myself. Footage of a dramatic rescue he'd made had played on the news. His picture had been on the front page of the paper. His face was plastered on billboards all over the state.

"Wow, an honest-to-God hero." Armani sighed reverentially, like she was seeing the Holy Mother or something.

Personally I thought it was a bit much.

"Just doing my job, ma'am."

Armani frowned. She hated the ma'am label.

"Which is actually why I'm here. As I said, I need to ask Miss Lee some questions."

"Is she in trouble?"

I shot her a dirty look to let her know that I'd heard that hopeful note in her voice. She gave me a big, all-teeth smile in response.

Secretly I was glad she'd asked the very question I'd been wondering myself. Maybe someone had overheard my conversation with Delveccio. Or worse, what if someone had been listening in on my discussion with Godzilla?

"No, ma'am. She's not in trouble, but I would like to speak to her in private if you don't mind."

I was shocked when Armani stood without an argument. Usually she wanted to be smack dab in the middle of everything. "See you later, Chiquita." She winked at me, an overly exaggerated wink signaling . . . what? She thought I should try my Chiquita charms on the nice police detective who'd heard me talking about hooking up with strangers I met on the street?

I waved her off. Still smiling, she limped away.

Detective Mulligan slid into the seat opposite me. "This won't take long."

"I already told the officer at the hospital everything."

"This is just standard follow-up. Nothing to worry about." He was more soft-spoken than I'd expect in a man of action, willing to put his life on the line.

"Your sister is a patient at the hospital?"

"My niece. Katie. My sister's daughter."

He nodded. "Can you just explain how you came to . . . interrupt Mr. Cifelli?"

"I collided with him in the hall."

The detective seemed to go still. I wished I could see his eyes, but the sunglasses hid them.

"And I tried to apologize, but he was a jerk. I'd just come from my sister's funeral and I was distracted. I—"

"I'm sorry for your loss," he murmured gently.

I wondered how often he had to utter that phrase in his line of work. I was surprised that he managed to make his condolence sound sincere. "Thank you. I was distracted. I didn't mean to run into him, and I did apologize right away."

He nodded, offering silent encouragement to continue with my story.

"And then he shoved me into the wall." My hands curled into fists at the memory. "I just got so mad. I followed him into the room to tell him off."

The detective pulled a roll of wintergreen Lifesavers from his shirt pocket and offered me one.

I could smell the minty-fresh flavor from across the table. In my hungover state it made me want to retch. "No, thank you."

"So . . . you went in the room to tell him off, and . . ."

"He had a pillow over Dominic's face."

"You knew the boy's name?" He popped the mint into his mouth and chewed, slowly and deliberately.

"Not then." Apparently he didn't understand that the point of the candy was to allow it to dissolve on one's tongue. The relentless crunching grated on my nerves.

"But you found out later?"

"Yes."

"How?"

I hesitated for a second. It probably wasn't a good idea to mention Tony/Anthony Delveccio. That was a can of worms better left unopened. "Someone told me."

"Who?"

"I really don't remember. There were so many doctors, nurses, and other hospital staff milling around."

"Family?"

I considered playing dumb, but decided that was too far-fetched, and I'd end up getting caught in the lie. "Yes, of course! I probably heard some family members use Dominic's name."

"Probably. So you see the pillow and then what?"

"I hit him with a chair. Twice. But then he got it away from me and . . ." My voice cracked as I remembered my terror in that moment.

"Take your time."

"He swung it at me."

"And he missed?"

I nodded emphatically. He'd most definitely missed.

"That's the part I don't get. Alfonso Cifelli is a bad guy. He's got multiple assault-and-battery arrests on his record, but you, who, as far as I can tell, have no special hand-to-hand combat training, managed to beat him." His soft voice was now laced with tempered steel.

"No, no! I didn't *beat* him. I avoided him."

"How?"

I looked away. I couldn't believe that I was about to admit my stealthy ninja move to this man. I blurted out my confession as one long word. "Istoppeddroppedandrolled."

"You what?

I sighed. "I stopped. I dropped. And I rolled. He was swinging that chair at me. It was the only thing I could think to do. Fire avoidance 101."

The corners of his mouth quirked, but he had the good grace not to actually laugh at me. "Like they teach to kindergartners?" The edge in his voice was gone. Now he just sounded amused.

"Exactly!"

"I never understood why they drill that into five-year-olds who will probably never get near an open flame, but they don't even mention it to adolescents when they give them Bunsen burners in junior-high chemistry classes."

I grinned. "I never thought of it that way."

"Maybe they're afraid that having boys and girls rolling around on the floor together would necessitate additional sex-ed classes."

For a split second I thought there was a spark of sexual tension hovering in the air. Yeah, I was so lonely that the mere mention of the word *sex* in conversation had me misreading signals.

He grinned and continued, "Or maybe they've just figured out that people don't retain much after the age of ten."

The guy was certainly *not* hitting on me.

Embarrassed by my desperateness, I managed a weak smirk. "Or in my case, five."

"That was a very brave thing you did, Miss Lee. Dumb, but brave. Thank you for your time."

He got up and left me sitting alone at the picnic bench. He was right about one thing.

I was dumb.

Chapter Nine

YOU KNOW IT isn't good news when a social worker shows up at your door looking depressed yet determined. I have, due to a lifetime of experience dealing with social workers, determined that only those freshly out of school and in their first placement wear an *I'm ready to change the world* expression. The rest—underpaid, overworked, and drowning in red tape—look like the woman who stood in the doorway of Katie's hospital room.

I appreciated that she allowed me to finish reading *Where the Wild Things Are* before she cleared her throat. Content in the knowledge that Max had made it home to sleep in his own bed, I joined the woman in the hallway.

She clutched the clipboard she held as though it were a shield that wielded magical bureaucratical protection. "I'm sorry to interrupt your visit with your niece, Miss Lee. I'm Stacy Kiernan, the hospital's patient liaison."

She stuck out her hand.

I wondered whether she'd remembered we'd met before. Twice over the past couple of days in fact.

I shook her hand. Just like the other two times, it was warm and firm. She made sure to make eye contact. I'm guessing that's Social Worker 101—make a connection, create a rapport.

"We've met before, Ms. Kiernan."

"Oh good, you remember that."

"Yup." I'd lost my mind, not my memory.

"Some people don't. For some, all this," she waved her arms as though encompassing the entire building, "is too much."

"Uh huh."

"Perhaps we could sit down?" Without waiting for a response, she hurried toward a "guest" area at the end of the hall. The whole place was littered with impromptu waiting spots, clusters of two or three chairs tossed into every available corner. Since patients were only allowed two visitors at a time, family members spent shifts rotating from bedside to "guest" areas in a macabre game of musical chairs.

When we were both settled in chairs facing one another, Stacy Kiernan slid the glasses on top of her head down onto her nose. She looked down at her clipboard, making a show of reading the papers attached to it.

She didn't fool me for a second. I knew that she was stalling for time, putting off the inevitable. She was the bearer of bad news.

I didn't know exactly what the bad news was, but I was ready for it. I had been since the moment I'd seen her standing in Katie's doorway.

I wanted to tell her that it was okay. I wished I could tell her to just spit it out. I wasn't going to collapse, or cry, or freak out. I've heard it all before: *Your father's been arrested for murder. Your mother needs help. Darlene's body has been found. Marlene's left a note, she's run away. There's been an accident. Katie's in a coma.* I'm as accustomed to receiving bad news as some ridiculously lucky people are to yell "BINGO!" on a weekly basis.

I couldn't tell her all that, though. I would have sounded crazy. So instead I just waited, watching as she adjusted her glasses. She and Katie were currently in a dead heat when it came to scintillating conversation.

Finally, unable to bear the uncomfortable silence for another second longer, I blurted, "You're kicking her to the curb, aren't you?"

Stacy Kiernan reared back as though the very idea was offensive, as though she'd never considered doing such a thing, like that wasn't the exact reason we were sitting there.

"I . . . I. . . ." she stuttered.

I literally had to sit on my hands to keep from saluting her and saying, "Aye, aye, Captain!" Instead I fixed an expectant stare on her.

She couldn't meet my eyes. "Well, I would . . . I wouldn't have . . . I'm sorry, but the insurance . . ."

She seemed incapable of stringing a complete sentence together.

I took pity on the unfortunate woman. It must really suck to have to tell people their loved ones are getting booted from the best care facility because of astronomical medical bills. "It's okay. Can I get you a cup of water or something?"

Her gaze skittered in my direction. Poor thing was still waiting for me to blow up at her.

"It's not your fault. You're just doing your job."

The clipboard slipped from her fingers, crashing to the floor. She made no move to pick it up, because she was sobbing.

She wasn't teary, or sniffling, or crying. No, she was sobbing. Body-shaking, gut-wrenching, soul-cleansing sobs.

For a brief moment I envied her liberal expression of pain.

People up and down the hallway cast furtive glances in our direction. I fought the urge to shout that I was the one who should be crying. I was the wronged party here. I deserved their pity and sympathy, dammit!

I was embarrassed for Stacy Kiernan. After all, this was her place of employment. At the same time it angered me. More than was called for. More than I liked. Her unrestrained crying jag reminded me too much of my mother's emotional outbursts.

I yearned to slap some sense into her like they used to do to hysterical women in black-and-white movies, but that was socially unacceptable. Instead, I put a hand on her shoulder and murmured, "It's okay. Everything is going to be okay."

It never fails to amaze me the way that simple little lie delivers so much comfort. It did its job. Her sobs quickly petered out into occasional hiccups as she confided that she'd had a terrible week.

I somehow managed not to tell her that she had no idea what a terrible week was until she'd lived my life. I listened to her complain that her coworkers were mean, her mother demanding, and her ex-boyfriend needy. Then she told me that I was the nicest, most understanding person she'd talked to all week.

I ended up listening to her litany of woes for more than an hour. When she was finally done, I'd made a new friend.

A friend who told me that if I couldn't come up with a lot of money pretty quickly, Katie would be transferred out of this premiere treatment center to a state-run hospital.

"How much will that hurt her chances of recovery?" I asked my new friend.

Stacy, her face still blotchy from crying, shook her head. "I'm not a medical doctor."

"Ballpark it for me."

She glanced around to make sure no one else was within earshot. "They earn the big bucks here for a reason. These guys are the best. They may be obnoxious. They may have God complexes. But they work miracles. I've seen it. If I were you I'd do whatever it takes to keep her here. If there was a way to sell your soul to the devil for cash, I'd take the deal."

At that moment Tony/Anthony Delveccio strolled past. The devil himself didn't even look in our direction.

I knew with a certainty that chilled me to my bones that I had to take him up on his job offer.

I WAS JUST ABOUT to stroll into Dominic's room to tell Tony/Anthony Delveccio that I was willing to kill his son-in-law when someone tapped me on the shoulder.

Fervently hoping it wasn't poor Stacy Kiernan coming back to unload more of her angst, I slowly turned around. I was shocked to see a familiar, statuesque blonde, who could pass for Heidi Klum's sister, staring at me with tears in her eyes.

I wondered for a moment if this was another delusion, like believing I could talk to a lizard. Was I just imagining that my oldest and best friend, the only person who'd never let me down, all through my mom's craziness, my dad's incarceration, Darlene's death, and Marlene's running away, was actually standing in front of me?

"You look like hell, Maggie."

Throwing my arms around her, I said (and actually meant), "Alice! It's so good to see you!"

With her genuinely sweet disposition and easy laugh, Alice is one of those people who brightens every room she steps into. I'd desperately missed her light during these dark days. Not to mention how much I missed her unwavering support.

"Oh, Maggie. I'm so sorry. So sorry about Theresa and Katie. I'm sorry I wasn't here for you. How's your dad holding up?"

I tensed, mid-hug. Alice and I were best friends, but there are two things we always argue about: her abysmal taste in men and the fact that she adores my father. Ever since he'd stopped her own dad from molesting her by beating the crap out of him and running him out of town, she'd worshipped him.

"He does know, doesn't he?" she asked.

"I told him."

"Good. That was the right thing to do. I'm proud of you, Maggie."

I took a step back so that I could see her properly. Besides being ridiculously good-looking, my dear friend Alice was an amazing humanitarian who traveled to exotic spots all over the world to teach English . . . or is it irrigation? Either way, she enriches lives, while I, on the other hand, ask people if the police had given them a ticket when they crashed their vehicle. "What *are* you doing here? You're supposed to be gone for another three months."

She patted her stomach.

"You're sick? You picked up one of those exotic nasty bugs or worms, like they're always trying to diagnose on *House*, didn't you?"

She shook her head.

"Then what? Your iron stomach finally surrendered and you couldn't take the local diet?"

Out of the corner of my eye, I saw Delveccio amble out of his grandson's room. Dammit! I needed to talk to him, but I couldn't very well do that while chatting with Alice.

She shook her head again. An angelic smile spread across her face, making her eyes sparkle and her skin glow.

I was still too slow to get it. In my defense, I did have an awful lot on my mind.

"I'm pregnant, Maggie."

I blinked. I looked down at her stomach. She didn't appear to have one. I looked up into her face again. Maybe this was another of my delusions. "I don't understand . . . how?"

"The same way men and women have for centuries."

"What man? Who's the father?" The last I'd heard she'd sworn off men. A prudent decision, considering her last boyfriend, who I'd told her repeatedly was bad news, had beaten her to within an inch of her life. That scumbag was rotting in prison.

Speaking of prison, my favorite mob boss had disappeared from sight.

Alice pointed to a dark-skinned man, taller than a refrigerator and almost as wide, perched uncomfortably in one of the too-small waiting chairs. He waved. I swear his hand was bigger than my head. He smiled, teeth shiny, gleamy white against chocolate pudding skin. The fact that I was mentally comparing him to chocolate pudding told me I'd eaten too many of my meals in the hospital cafeteria.

I waved weakly in reply.

"C'mon. I'm dying for you to meet him." Alice grabbed my shoulder and propelled me in his direction like she did when we were seven.

"Where is he from?" I figured it was more polite to ask that than to come right out and ask if he spoke English.

"Chicago."

Whew! I speak Windy City. Sorta.

"Lamont, this is Maggie," Alice chirped. "Maggie, Lamont."

"Nice to meet you." I extended my hand only to have it swallowed whole by his.

"I'm sorry we have to meet under these circumstances. My condolences on your loss."

"Thank you. Welcome to New Jersey. How do you like it so far?"

"We-l-l," he said carefully. "It's not exactly what I was expecting."

"If you drive an hour or two in any direction, you can find whatever you want, mountains, ocean, New York city, farms . . . we've got it all. Plus, we have all four seasons." I knew I sounded like some Board of Tourism hack, but I couldn't stop myself. "Movies and TV haven't been terribly kind in their portrayal of our fine little state, but I promise there's plenty here to like."

Unable to take any more of my sales spiel he said quickly, "I already found what I like." He pulled Alice toward him. For once she didn't tower over the guy she was dating.

"How'd you know I was here?" I asked my oldest friend.

"All my stuff's in storage, and I'd given up my apartment before I left, so I called the bed and breakfast to see if they had a room available. Your aunts filled me in."

"Which of them?"

"All three." Alice, who usually had the patience of a saint, rolled her eyes.

I winced. “Sorry ’bout that.”

She shrugged. “Wasn’t your fault. Susan said you’d probably be here, so we borrowed Leslie’s car, which, by the way, reeks of pot. She really shouldn’t be driving while smoking that stuff. We really wanted to get away from Templeton, your Aunt Loretta’s boyfriend. Have you met him?”

I shook my head. He’d exhibited the good taste to skip the funeral, and since I’d ducked out of the wake I hadn’t made the acquaintance of Loretta’s latest love of her life. “I haven’t had the pleasure.”

“You’re going to hate him,” Alice said. Besides being my best friend for decades, she had grown up next door to the B&B, so she was well acquainted with Aunt Loretta’s loves. “Anyway, we rushed over here to check on you.”

Eager to get rid of them so that I could talk to Delveccio, I spun in a circle doing the hokey-pokey. “As you can see, I’m fine.” I glanced at the big guy. “How ’bout you? Meeting all three of my aunts at once must have been . . .”

“A bit overwhelming,” Alice supplied helpfully.

I shook my head. “You’re too kind.”

“I survived,” Lamont said with an easy smile.

Shaking my finger at him, I warned, “Whatever you do, don’t eat the love muffins!”

“Pardon me?”

“At breakfast. Don’t eat the love muffins. They’re terrible. Aunt Loretta, the sex-addict-slash-baker keeps putting weird aphrodisiac ingredients to them.”

“She’s not a sex addict,” Alice said.

“Why? Because it’s only PC to say a man’s a sex addict? The woman has had more lovers than Cassanova!”

Delveccio strolled back in. He glanced in my direction. I thought I saw a tad of annoyance in that look. I really had to find a way to get rid of my Amazonian friend and her even bigger boyfriend. Soon. Preferably before I changed my mind about taking the job, or the offer was rescinded.

"Anyway," Alice soothed, blissfully unaware of my dilemma, "I just wanted to come check on you."

"And I thank you for that, but you must be tired from your trip. Why don't you go back to the B&B to rest, and I'll call you tomorrow to catch up?"

Tony/Anthony was talking to one of the nurses. I hoped that didn't mean he was leaving already.

"But I haven't seen Katie yet. Leslie says it's terrible, wires and machines everywhere."

"It is. Maybe now isn't the time? Maybe come back when you're feeling stronger?" After all, Alice had been the kid who fainted at the sight of her own blood when she'd fallen off her bike and skinned her knee.

"Is it okay if Lamont comes with me?"

"Of course." It meant I'd be rid of both of them. "Only two visitors allowed in the room at a time. Third door on your left there."

"Okay. We won't be long."

Hand-in-hand, the two giants moved toward Katie's room. I looked over to Delveccio. He was still engrossed in his conversation with the nurses. I tried to catch his eye, but he didn't look up.

Now what the hell was I supposed to do?

I sank into one of the waiting-area chairs and nodded

encouragingly at Alice and Lamont. They were hovering in Katie's doorway, much the same as the social worker Stacy Kiernan had. I wondered why people did that. Was it a lack of commitment on their part to step over the line? Did crossing the threshold irrevocably change things?

They disappeared from sight. Leaning forward, I dropped my head into my hands as I tried to figure out exactly what I should say to Delveccio. A pair of leather loafers that probably cost more than I made in a week stepped into my line of vision.

"Mind if I sit here?" Tony/Anthony asked, motioning at the chair beside mine.

"Of course not."

He sank into the seat, his shoulder rubbing up against mine. I flinched. The scent of his expensive cologne managed to overpower the antiseptic smells of the hospital. "I didn't recognize you at first. Good disguise."

"Disguise?"

"Yeah. The dressed-down look, not attracting attention, smart move."

I hadn't dressed to camouflage my existence. I was wearing my usual work uniform, khakis, long sleeves, and flats.

"Personally," the mobster continued, "I preferred the femme-fatale look you were working the other day, but I appreciate your business decision."

Deciding that my wisest course of action was probably to just keep my mouth shut, I didn't tell him that my *femme-fatale look* was a result of my not having anything else to wear to my sister's funeral.

"Who's the big dude?" Delveccio asked.

"My friend's boyfriend."

"He a linebacker?"

"Don't know."

"A bodyguard?"

"I don't know."

"A bouncer maybe."

"I don't know. I didn't even know he existed until about five minutes ago. I've never met him before. I have no idea what he does."

Tony/Anthony raised his hands in mock surrender. His diamond pinky came within inches of my face. "No need to be touchy about it."

"I'm not being touchy. I just don't want to talk about him. We have more important things to talk about."

"We do?"

"Yes."

"Like what?"

"Like that . . . job you offered me?" I kept an eye on Katie's door, half-expecting to see nurses flying in to revive Alice.

"You wired?"

"No. I haven't had any coffee since this morning."

"Are you for real?" Tony/Anthony turned to look right at me. I studied his face, wondering if this was even the twin who'd offered me a hundred grand to kill his son-in-law. If he wasn't, I could be getting myself in a whole lot of trouble by opening my mouth, so I kept it closed.

He spoke with exaggerated slowness, so that I could keep up with his line of questioning. "Are you wearing a wire? A listening device? A bug? Are you going to try to rat me out to the cops?"

I shook my head and whispered, "Are you?" Cuz that was all I needed, to be sent to the big house by a career criminal.

He chuckled. "What did you want to talk about?"

"The job."

"What about it?"

"I'll take it."

"You're sure?"

I nodded.

He leaned back in his seat and fixed his gaze on Dominic's door.

"You try to screw me with this and I'll kill your whole family. Every, single last one of them."

Cold fingers of fear clawed at my chest, making it difficult to breathe. "I . . . I believe you."

He templed his fingers beneath his chin. To any would-be witness it probably looked as though he was praying. "I'm not convinced this is the best idea."

Truth be told, neither was I, but I was too scared to voice my concern. I needed this job. Katie needed it.

He slid a sidelong glance in my direction. I probably looked like a puppy desperate to be thrown a bone.

"Okay. We'll give it a shot. Meet my guy at the Galaxy Diner, nine tomorrow morning. He'll teach you what you need to know."

"I have to be at work at nine."

"Call in sick. Or, if you don't show up, I'll assume

you're walking away from our deal and this was all one big communication error."

As Alice and Lamont, fingers still entwined, emerged from Katie's room, Delveccio got to his feet.

"Wait!"

He looked down at me.

"How will I know your guy?"

"He'll know you."

"He will?"

"But if it makes you feel better, he'll be stacking condiments."

"What?"

He walked away without explaining.

I switched my attention to my best friend, who was even paler than usual. "You okay?"

"She looks so . . ."

"Small? Weak? Lost?"

Alice nodded.

"I noticed."

"How are you getting through this?"

I glanced at Delveccio's back as he turned the corner and disappeared from sight. "I'm doing whatever it takes."

Whatever it takes. Exactly what my dad had predicted. The thought made me frown.

Alice must have thought I was going to cry because she thrust a tissue at me.

For a second I considered confessing that I hadn't been able to cry through this whole ordeal, but I didn't want to burden my friend with that knowledge. I knew

Alice. She's a worrier. Worse than that, she's a fixer. Tell her about a problem, and she'll move mountains to make it better. It's one of her most endearing traits, but it can also get annoying because she's never willing to admit that there are some problems that just can't be solved. Smiling weakly, I took the tissue from her. "Thanks for coming by."

"We're going to be at the B&B for a while, so if you need anything, anything at all, you know the number." Alice hugged me hard, like there was some correlation between how tight she squeezed and her concern.

"It was nice meeting you, Lamont." I wheezed.

That got Alice to ease up. She didn't let go, but at least her embrace was no longer painful.

"I've heard a lot about you." The big man smiled. "Don't worry," he joked, "most of it's good."

"I bet you have." Alice and I have been best friends since second grade. "There's a lot to tell." I'd endured her entire line-up of loser boyfriends. I had to admit that so far Lamont didn't have me urging her to get a restraining order.

"Oh crap!" I cried, smacking my palm to my forehead like in those V8 commercials.

Lamont took a step back, as though afraid I was going to hit him next.

"I totally forgot your good news. Congratulations! Both of you. Congratulations! Fuck! I am such a screw-up of a friend! I am so sorry! I'm happy for you! So frea-kin' happy for you!"

Alice giggled and shook her head. "Give yourself a break, Maggie. You've got a lot on your mind."

"But still I should have . . . right away, I should have congratulated you. It's huge."

"I'm going to be huge soon," Alice sighed, putting her hand on her non-existent belly. "You're going to be the kid's godmother, right?"

I glanced at my other godchild's room. I hoped I wouldn't have to kill for this unborn child. "Of course."

Chapter Ten

I ALMOST CHICKENED out the next morning. Big surprise there, right? I got dressed for work and everything, but the thought of poor Katie being stuck in a state institution had me calling in sick.

I pulled into the parking lot of the Galaxy Diner, a place bordering the seedy side of town, and took some long, slow, deep breaths. They didn't help. My heart was still racing and my stomach was churning. I watched my car clock turn to 9:00 A.M., then 9:01, then 9:02, and 9:03. I made a deal with myself to get out of the car before 9:05.

I knew that once I did, my life would change forever. The simple act would transform my existence in ways I couldn't even imagine. I guess this is how people who are selected for those makeover shows on TV feel. I was about to throw myself at the mercy of a stranger for cash and prizes. Okay, just cash (with the prize being Katie opening her eyes).

The clock changed to 9:04. I opened my door. "Katie

needs you, Maggie," I muttered to myself. "You can do this. Whatever it takes. Whatever it takes."

Taking a deep breath, I spun my lower body out of the car.

I almost snapped my damn neck.

The fucking seatbelt cut into my throat. I gagged. I choked. If I could have cried, my eyes would have watered. "Idiot! Fucking idiot!"

I unclasped the seat belt. Disentangling myself from it, I stumbled from the car. I didn't dare look at the clock, afraid I'd missed the 9:05 deadline with my fumbling.

Pissed at myself, I stalked into the diner in search of a man stacking condiments. Since when was playing with your food some sort of covert signal?

"I'm meeting someone," I growled at the hostess before she could ask me how many were in my party. Pushing past her, I scanned the place.

Typical diner: booths, chairs, a counter, the smell of bacon grease and burnt toast.

A familiar face, or at least a recognizable shock of red hair sat at the far end of the counter. Sure enough he'd made a tower of syrup containers on top of a bottle of catsup.

He didn't look like a killer.

Then again, according to God, neither did I, but maybe that was because I hadn't actually done the deed yet. Maybe once I did, took a life, maybe then my sin would be written clearly on my face for all to see.

At the end of the counter Detective Mulligan cocked his head as if he was trying to see me at a different angle, in a different light. Maybe he was trying to spot the wannabe killer lurking in the shadows of my soul.

Maybe I was being melodramatic.

Maybe he had something in his eye.

Sliding off the stool he'd been on, he slid into a booth where he began to start another tower of condiments. That was the sign that I should join him. If you asked me, I would have said it was a stupid-ass signal, but no one asked.

Feet numb and face hot, I shuffled toward him. The only sound I could hear was the frenetic beating of my own heart.

Without his sunglasses, I could tell he had blue-green eyes. He was older than I'd originally guessed, probably in his mid to late 40's. He didn't look like a killer.

And I sure as hell didn't feel like one.

"Have a seat, Miss Lee." Just like our earlier encounter, his voice was disconcertingly soft.

During that first conversation it had seemed gentle. Now it sounded menacing.

Swallowing hard, I slid into the booth opposite him.

"Coffee?"

I blinked.

"The waitress is going to be here in a second," he prompted. "She'll ask you if you want coffee. You have to answer her."

I nodded my understanding.

"Coffee?" the waitress asked, as if on cue.

"Please," Detective Mulligan said.

"Cream, okay?"

"Of course."

She looked at me. "Coffee?"

Jerking my head in her direction, sort of like the Tin Man did when he needed oil, I nodded.

"Cream?"

My mouth was too dry to speak. I nodded again.

Turning on her heel, she strode away.

I jerked my head back to look at Detective Mulligan.

"You can still walk away, Miss Lee. I'll tell our mutual acquaintance you never showed."

I considered that for a long second. I really wasn't cut out for this. I couldn't speak, let alone kill. I slid along the bench and stood up.

Mulligan's stayed very still, only his eyes followed me. He really didn't look like a killer.

I stood there at the end of the table, frozen with indecision. Part of me, the logical, law-abiding part of me, wanted to bolt. To forget this had ever happened. But my feet didn't move.

"Restroom's round the corner," the waitress offered, reaching in front of me to put a cup of coffee down.

Stiffly, I moved toward the rest room, feeling like I didn't have a brain, or courage, or a heart. Thankfully there was no one else in the bathroom. I stared at my reflection in the grimy mirror. No, I didn't look like a killer.

But I did look like Katie's aunt.

"Fake it 'til you make it," I muttered at my distorted mirror image.

I marched back into the dining area and planted my butt in the seat opposite Detective Mulligan.

He arched his eyebrows but didn't say anything. Instead, he raised his coffee cup to his lips and sipped, considering me carefully over its chipped rim.

I cleared my throat, hoping that when I made the attempt this time, words would come out. "I need the job."

"Why?"

"Why? Is there some sort of job interview that goes with this? Am I supposed to tell you what my greatest weaknesses and strengths are?"

"Do you want something to eat? They make great waffles." He waved the waitress over with two fingers.

"Can I get two poached eggs over waffles instead of toast? And a side of sausage? Oh, and a large orange juice."

"Sure." The waitress scribbled on her pad. Without looking at me, she asked, "What can I get you?"

I stared at the man across the table from me. Was I really about to break bread, or in this case waffles, with a killer? I mentally shrugged, as I realized it really wasn't all that different than sitting across the breakfast table from Dad. "Just waffles for me. No eggs. No sausage. No juice."

As she walked away, he picked up his coffee cup again. He gave me that inscrutable stare again. It made the back of my neck itch.

"Why don't you tell me why *you* do it," I challenged.

The corners of his mouth twitched. "Family."

"Are you kidding me?" Obviously he knew about Katie, guessing that she was my motivation for agreeing to take part in this insane scheme.

Putting his cup down, he shook his head. "I've got kids in college. It's expensive."

I stared at that sphinx-like expression of his. I couldn't tell whether or not he was fucking with me. "You need the money so badly, how come you're not . . ."

His eyes narrowed, transmitting a warning to choose my words carefully.

" . . . helping our mutual friend?"

"I'm here, aren't I?"

"But you're not going to do the actual . . ." I searched for a euphemism for committing murder.

"Chore," he supplied helpfully.

"You're not going to do the actual chore."

He shook his head.

"Why not? Why farm it out to me, to an amateur, to someone who's never—"

"Done that kind of work before?" he interrupted.

"Yeah. Why me?"

"Because," he said, matter-of-factly, "as your . . . friend pointed out yesterday, I'm the Courageous Cop. Probably the most recognizable law enforcement officer in the state. It's cramping my style."

"So you play hero, and it screws up this other thing?"

"I wasn't *playing* hero. It wasn't my fault the news crew caught the whole thing on tape. They were there to film a piece about peacocks who'd escaped from the zoo, not me!"

"And now your style's cramped?"

He nodded. "Now you tell me, why do you need this job?"

"You know."

"Assumptions are dangerous things. I'd like to hear it from you."

"Family." I parroted his own reply back at him.

He tilted his head to the side. I could almost hear him thinking, *Touché!*

"I need the cash in order to make sure that my niece continues to get the best possible care. I'm her godmother. I'm responsible for her."

He nodded, but said nothing.

I waited for him to say something, anything, but he stared down at his coffee cup.

"I need this job."

He didn't look up. He didn't respond.

My stomach flipped nervously. Katie's life hung in the balance. If he turned me down . . .

"Please," I said, reaching across the table to grab his wrist. "I need this job."

"I know you do." He looked at where our hands met. He used his other hand to cover mine, trapping me there. "I'm just not sure you're up to it, and if you're not . . ."

The unspoken threat hung in the air. If I wasn't up to killing Alfonso, Delveccio would have someone kill me . . . probably the very guy who was using his thumb to explore the hills and valleys of my knuckles.

He released me as the waitress arrived with our food. I clasped my hands together in my lap, an almost prissy, lady-like gesture. My aunts would have been proud, prouder still if I crossed my ankles while I was at it.

Detective Mulligan broke his egg yolks so that they

seeped into the waffle. It was one of the most unappetizing breakfast combinations I'd ever seen. Spearing a sausage, he stuck the whole thing in his mouth. He considered me carefully as he chewed.

Unwilling to meet his searching gaze, I busied myself with slathering butter into every crevice of my waffle. "You'd think it would be more cost effective to put more product into bigger packaging," I muttered, struggling to open my third pack. "No one ever uses just one or two."

"Maybe," he said, prying the plastic from my fingers. "They figure people will give up because they can't get them open. So therefore they use less."

He peeled back the lid with no problem and handed it back to me.

"That might work for the diner owners, but how does that benefit the butter producers?"

"Damn, she forgot my juice."

"Maybe," I suggested, "they charge per hundred packets or something like that."

"I need my coffee refilled too." He held up his cup so that the waitress could see, the universal sign to top it off. "Can I get my juice, when you get a chance?" he asked as soon as she was within earshot.

"You said no juice," the waitress said, petulantly snapping the wad of chewing gum that made one side of her face look like she was a chipmunk undergoing dental work.

If she'd spoken that way to me, I would have cracked wise at her, but Mulligan just sort of smiled and said quietly, "Actually I asked for a large orange juice. She," he inclined his head in my general direction, "said no juice."

"Fine. Large orange juice." Refilling his coffee, she got almost as much in his saucer as she poured in the cup. Without asking me if I wanted mine warmed, she flounced off.

"I said the waffles were good, not the service," my tablemate said before I could even open my mouth to make a crack about the service with a smile. He pulled a handful of napkins from the dispenser and layered them between his cup and saucer. They quickly turned brown as they soaked up the liquid.

The charming waitress smacked a large tumbler of orange juice in front of him as though she was using the glass to tenderize the table.

"Thank you," he murmured politely.

I wondered if maybe he thought killing someone with kindness was actually possible.

"You got any experience?" He crammed a mouthful of egg and waffle into his mouth.

"Experience?"

"With the chore. Have you done it before?"

"Do I look like I've done it before?" I squeaked a little. Did he too think I look like a killer?

"I thought maybe your father. . . . never mind. Do you have any special skill sets?"

"How do you know about my father?"

"The whole force knows about Archie Lee."

The bank teller my father had "accidentally" killed was the wife of a cop. Yet another reason he would spend the rest of his life rotting in a cell.

Detective Mulligan put his fork down and sat up straight, as though an idea had just occurred to him. "Why don't you just ask him where his stash is? He got away with what? A million? That would go a long way toward paying hospital bills."

I'd already thought of that. He hadn't offered when I'd gone to visit him in prison. I sure as hell wasn't going to ask him for it, but I wasn't about to get into that with the redhead sitting across from me. "According to the prosecutor it was just under ten million. He didn't get that much cash. Most of it was in the form of jewels."

"I never got that. Why knock over a bank in the middle of the day for gems? Why not just hit a jewelry store at night? Less chance of getting caught."

"Less chance of an innocent bystander getting killed."

He let that go. "There was probably some fraudulent insurance claims filed for so-called stolen jewelry, so split the difference. He's probably got five mil or so hidden somewhere. He's never gonna use it. Why not ask him to help his granddaughter?"

Not wanting to make eye contact with him for fear he'd spot the depth of my anger, I carved up my waffle savagely. "He wouldn't give it up. I'm sure he's got some crazy-ass plan to break out of prison. He's done it before."

"To visit your mother."

I looked up at him. Those blue eyes trapped my gaze. I swallowed convulsively. "You've done your homework, Detective."

"It's kind of romantic."

I stared at him. "What?"

"The guy breaks out of prison. Twice. And both times he goes to see his wife. He must really love her."

I shook my head.

"He doesn't love her?"

"He's addicted to her drama. Her mental state is like a game to him. Shake her up and see where the dice fall. Delusion? Twenty points. Mania? Ten points. Catatonia? One hundred big ones. Archie Lee is not a romantic, Detective."

"Patrick. If we're going to be working together you should call me, Patrick."

It took me a second to change gears and catch up with him. "Does that mean you think we'll be working together?" I tried to sound matter-of-fact, but I knew a hopeful note or two got through.

"We should get started right away. When can you start?"

It felt like I'd just passed a job interview and was being asked when I was available to begin my new career. "I called in sick today."

Patrick smiled. "Okay, Life Lesson Number One. Don't—"

"Life lesson?" I interrupted, suddenly feeling ill. What if this whole conversation had been a massive miscommunication? What if he was just a guy who liked to play with his food? What if he wasn't the one I'd been sent to meet? Life lessons didn't sound like Contract Killing 101 to me.

He bent forward across the table, beckoning for me to lean in. He whispered, so that only I could hear, "Life lessons: how to take one and how not to end up with a life sentence."

He leaned back.

I let out the breath I hadn't even been aware I was holding.

"Life Lesson Number One: Don't get caught."

Chapter Eleven

ONCE HE WAS done consuming his massive breakfast and had gotten three blueberry muffins for the road, Patrick Mulligan paid the diner check and led the way out to the parking lot. Right after we'd inhaled a lungful of second-hand smoke from the patrons huddling outside, sucking down their fix of nicotine, that he suggested we go for a ride in the country.

I eyed him suspiciously. "Is that some sort of euphemism?"

"I buy you breakfast, and now you think I want a roll in the hay in return?"

That hadn't been what I was thinking, but to be honest the idea wasn't revolting. There was something about this soft-spoken redhead, maybe it was the way he seemed to be focused on me one hundred percent of the time, something I hadn't known a man was even capable of, that was sort of sexy.

I must have spent too long considering his question,

because he shook his head, waved for me to follow him, and walked away.

Like a fool I hurried after him. "I meant, is *going for a ride in the country* hired-gun speak for *I'm going to kill you now.*"

Taking out his keys, he used the remote to unlock a nearby SUV. "I wasn't planning on it, but if you insist on being such a pain in the ass . . ."

His delivery was so dry, I wasn't sure whether the threat was genuine or a joke.

"We'll leave your car at the mall. I'll meet you over by the food court." He climbed into his vehicle, shut the door, and started the engine.

I hurried over to my car, still not convinced this wasn't part of his elaborate plan to execute me. Not for the first time, I wondered what the hell I'd gotten myself into. But, remembering that I was doing this all for Katie, I obediently drove over to the mall. I kept looking in my rearview mirror, but I never spotted Patrick's truck. I guess spotting a tail isn't part of my skill set.

As per his instructions, I drove to the parking lot outside the entrance to the mall's food court. Mulligan was nowhere in sight. I had no idea what to do next.

I pulled out my cell phone to see if he'd called to give me more cryptic instructions. He hadn't. According to the call log, I'd missed calls from Aunt Susan, Alice, and Armani. I didn't bother to listen to the messages they'd left. I had more important things to worry about, like where my cop/killer had gotten to.

A horn tooted behind me. Glancing in the rearview

mirror, I realized my assassination advisor had arrived. I jumped out of the car and into the passenger seat of his SUV.

"Rule Number One: Don't get caught." He pulled out of the parking lot heading west. "That means you don't talk to anybody. Not your family. Not your friends. Not your boyfriend."

"I don't have a boyfriend."

"Good, one less person to worry about. You can't talk about this to anyone."

I wondered if the lizard fell under the purview of this rule. "So you're breaking your own rule by talking to me?"

"Are your smart-ass tendencies the reason you haven't stayed at the same job for more than two years at a time?"

"I get bored."

"Part of not getting caught is leading a boring life. You've got to stay in your same apartment, keep the same friends, and work the same crappy job."

"I hate my job. I'd been planning to look for a new one when the accident happened."

He shook his head. "Bad idea. Stay at the insurance company. Nothing more dull than that."

"Tell me about it," I muttered.

He turned onto Route 80, the interstate that runs across the country. I wondered if he was planning to cross state lines and then kill me. I'd watched enough cop shows to know that crossing state lines always hampered investigations.

"What's bothering you?" he asked.

"Nothing."

"You pinch your bottom lip between your thumb and forefinger when something's bothering you."

Realizing he was right, I yanked my hand away from my mouth.

"So what's on your mind?"

"Nothing."

"You can't back out now. One of our mutual friend's employees saw us together at the diner. That seals the deal."

"I wasn't backing out."

"Then what?"

"I was wondering whether you're taking me to Pennsylvania to kill me."

"Why would I need to take you to P.A. to do that?"

"So you don't get caught?"

He threw back his head and laughed. His amusement echoed in the cabin of the vehicle. "So I don't get caught. That's rich. You are a unique one, Ms. Lee. Definitely one of a kind."

I stared at him. No one had ever said that about me before. I'd been called remarkably unremarkable, but never unique. I wasn't quite sure how to react to the label, because I was uncertain whether he meant it as a compliment, an insult, or just an observation.

He grew solemn. "If you're going to succeed at this, and don't get me wrong—in order to go on living, you must achieve the stated goal—you're going to have to trust me. At least a little."

"Kind of hard to do considering . . ."

"I trust you."

"You do?"

He nodded. "If I didn't, I would have never agreed to train you. Just having this conversation with you could ruin my life; destroy everything I've worked for. You talk to the wrong person and poof!" he snapped his fingers. "My family, my career would be devastated."

I hadn't thought about it that way. I'd been so worried about saving my own hide I'd never considered that he was taking a risk. "So why do it?"

"I met you. Looked into your eyes. I'm a pretty good judge of character. I think you're trustworthy."

"I wouldn't . . . I'm not going to . . ."

"I know." He shot me a sidelong smile. "I want you to think about something for the rest of this ride. I want you to think about why you're going to do this thing. What your motivation is. How it'll feel once you get exactly what you want. Can you do that?"

I nodded.

"Good. Lifesaver?" He offered me a roll of round mints.

I shook my head.

"Enjoy the scenery and fresh air." He rolled down the windows of the truck.

The breeze, as we sped along the highway, deeper and deeper into New Jersey's farm country, ruffled my hair. Actually my hair smacked me in the face. It stung.

I do not come from fresh-air stock. My people believe in central air, technologically moderated temperatures, and false lighting. We do not venture outdoors except to go from one hermetically sealed building to another. We have gas-burning fireplaces with realistic, hand-painted, concrete logs that give off no smoke or ash.

I am not a fan of pollen-laden fresh air and the sun that accompanies it.

Of course I didn't tell Patrick Mulligan that. I didn't want to give him a reason to kill me.

I'd never told my parents either, whenever they'd suggested we take advantage of living in the Garden State. I never complained when we went to a pumpkin patch, or apple-picking, or swimming in a local lake that was no doubt full of slimy seaweed, scaly fish, and who knows what else. Fresh air, and all accompanying activity, was something to be endured in stoic silence.

I'd swallowed at least two bugs, and my hair looked like it hadn't been brushed for months, by the time we rolled down a dirt road, pulling to a stop in front of a dilapidated barn.

"We're here," Patrick announced, sliding out of the vehicle.

I followed suit. Squinting at the sun, I tried in vain to finger-comb my hair.

"I'm sorry about this," he murmured softly.

Despite the bright day, I felt a shadow settle over me. I gulped as he moved to stand closer. I had to tilt my head back to see his face. He looked serious.

"I need to pat you down."

"What?"

"I need to make sure you're not wearing a wire."

"I'm not."

"I just have to know for certain."

"I thought you trusted me."

The corners of his mouth quirked. "I do, but I'm also not stupid. I can't go to jail just because a pretty woman says she's not wired."

I blinked at him. Had he just called me pretty?

He moved to step behind me. "Just stay still," he whispered in my ear, his minty breath tickling the sensitive skin.

I jumped a little as his hands cupped my shoulders.

He froze. "I'm not going to hurt you."

Slowly he slid his palms down my arms until his hands covered mine. Grabbing my wrists, he raised my arms so that I was in a T position. "Stay like that."

"Just like when airport security pulls you out of line to search you," I said.

"Exactly like that."

Except it was nothing like that at all. Because at the airport it was usually an unattractive woman waving some sort of wand over me, but now it was Patrick Mulligan's hands skimming my sides. I could feel his body heat through the cotton of my shirt. It was a most inopportune time to remember I hadn't had a date, much less sex, in over a year. I tried to think of something else, while his hands moved lower, but the only thing I could focus on was his touch, gentle, yet determined. I tried to remember if there'd been a ring on those talented hands of his.

I closed my eyes as I sensed him moving in front of me.

"You're trembling," he whispered. "There's nothing to be afraid of."

Keeping my eyes shut, I nodded.

I held my breath as he started at my ankles this time, moving upward with cursory pats. My whole body was tingling. I thought about cold showers, the day the neighbor ran over my puppy when I was eight, and Katie lying in that big hospital bed. Nothing helped. I was enjoying this intimate act.

His hands paused at my rib cage. "The most likely place to hide a wire would be between your breasts."

My face burned. I stopped breathing.

Gently, he traced the curves of my bra. His touch felt a hell of a lot more like a lover's caress than a search for a deadly weapon. I bit back a groan as he patted the valley between my breasts.

I kept my eyes squeezed shut, not wanting to see his expression. It was more pleasant to imagine that he was enjoying this as much as I was, than to see him amused by my stimulated state.

When he was finished, he cupped my shoulders again. I wondered whether it was possible for body heat to incinerate clothing.

"All clear."

"Told you so." Making certain I'd be staring straight ahead, I opened my eyes. I'd expected to be eye-level with his chest, but to my surprise he'd bent down to study my face. Those aquamarine eyes were staring right at me.

"I'm sorry for frightening you."

I blinked. I couldn't very well tell him that the reason I was trembling was because I was turned on. "It's been a rough week. I'm on edge."

Releasing me, he straightened. "Ready to get started?"

I stared at the barn. Maybe he'd meant his earlier crack about a roll in the hay literally? I was starting to think it was a really good idea.

"Rule Number One Is?"

"Don't get caught."

"Good. Now it's time for Rule Number Two: Dead means dead."

Dead means dead didn't sound particularly amorous to me.

Opening the back of the SUV, he pulled out a large, black nylon gym bag. "Ever shot a gun before?"

"Only at carnivals." I regretted the words instantly. Memories that I did my best to keep buried decimated the barriers of my psyche, as they rushed up at me.

The carnival. It was like I was back there. I could smell the popcorn and funnel cakes, hear the screams of the rollercoaster riders, feel the BB gun in my hand as I played the shoot-out-the-star game. Marlene was tugging at my sleeve, like a little kid, despite the fact she was fourteen. She was asking if I'd seen Darlene, but I was more concerned that my mother was in her manic moods and was flirting with the young man running the game. I was afraid Mom was going to get herself into trouble. If I'd paid closer attention to the girls. . . .

I felt dizzy and queasy. I stumbled away, as though there was a way to distance myself from what had happened.

Strong fingers wrapped around my upper arms. It

took me a second to recognize Patrick Mulligan's concerned face as he asked, "Are you okay?"

Wanting to retch, I yanked loose from his grip. Turning my back on him, I bent over double, holding my stomach.

I fought for control. I couldn't afford to fall apart. Not again. Not now. I forced away the carnival memories and the pain that accompanied them. It would be self-indulgent to revisit that place again. Katie needed me to be here. Now. I couldn't have Patrick thinking I was some out-of-control whack job. He'd never trust me, and I needed him to, so that I could do this job. So I could help Katie, even though I'd failed to help Darlene.

Straightening, I turned back to tell Patrick I was fine.

He obviously wasn't.

He was slumped against the SUV, his head buried in his hands. He really didn't look like a killer.

I cleared my throat.

He raised his face to look at me. "I am so, so sorry."

"For what?"

"For upsetting you like that."

I blinked. He thought my mini-breakdown was because he'd patted me down? For a second I tried to figure out how I could exploit his guilt, but he looked so wracked with remorse, I felt obligated to set him straight. "It wasn't you. Really."

I don't think he believed me.

"Too much stress, too little sleep, it's just all catching up with me." That was an easy truth for him to swallow.

"I shouldn't be adding to your . . ." he trailed off.

I wondered what he'd been about to say. Pain? Stress level?

"All this fresh air probably isn't helping matters," I joked.

Receiving a weak smile in response, I bent to pick up the gym bag he'd dropped. It was heavier than I'd imagined, and I almost tipped over.

He took it from me. "C'mon, Dirty Harriet. Let's see what you've got."

Grunting, he pulled open one of the giant barn doors. I'd never been in a barn (that whole nature/fresh-air thing). I pictured horses and tractors, pitchforks and hay. The only thing I was right about was the hay. It was everywhere. Its sweet scent hung in the air, and it crackled underfoot with every step we took.

I stared into the cavernous, shadow-filled space. Patrick flipped on a an oversized light.

I've never been inside a gun range, but I imagine it's a lot like the inside of this barn (minus the bales of hay and Amish hex signs leaning against the wall). There were targets everywhere. Paper targets lined one wall, and empty beer cans lined another.

"A couple things about gun safety," Patrick said, heaving the heavy bag onto a stack of straw. "You know how they say, 'Guns don't kill people; people kill people?' "

I nodded.

"They're half-right. Guns don't kill people. Idiots with guns kill people."

"So I guess this is going to make me an official idiot?"

He grinned. "You and me both." Unzipping the bag he pulled out a big, silver-barreled revolver. "The NRA Gun Safety Rules state that—"

"You quote the NRA?"

"Well, they're common-sense rules, really, but yeah, I believe in credit where credit's due. You have a problem with that?"

I shook my head.

"Okay so rule number one is: *Always keep the gun pointed in a safe direction.*"

"Got it."

He swung the barrel in my direction. "This means you don't point it at others, most specifically meaning me. And you don't point it at yourself. That way if the gun ever accidentally goes off, no one gets hurt. I once grabbed up an idiot robber who'd shot himself in the foot because he'd ignored that basic rule."

"So you're breaking another rule, having that thing aimed at my face."

He pointed the gun away. "Second rule: *Always keep your finger off the trigger until ready to shoot.* See how I've got mine along the side here." Tilting his hand, he showed me.

"Uh huh."

"Rule three: *Always keep the gun unloaded until ready to use.*" He looked at the gun, then back at me. "At least that's what the NRA says. I say: If you're expecting trouble, you should always be prepared."

"Like the Boy Scouts."

"You really are a wiseass. The NRA also says, *Be ab-*

solutely sure you have identified your target beyond any doubt. Which is pretty damn good advice if you ask me because what is Life Rule Two?"

"Dead means dead. Is there going to be some sort of quiz about this stuff later?"

Patrick scowled. "If you don't learn it, you could end up caught or dead. And quite frankly, if you're caught you'll end up dead. This is life and death stuff, Ms. Lee."

"Maggie. Or Margaret if you insist on being formal. You should at least call me by my first name."

He nodded as he fed bullets into the gun's chamber. "In a perfect world, you'd be wearing goggles and ear protection, but I've never shot anyone wearing those, so I want you to learn without them."

He handed me the loaded gun. It felt heavy, solid, real, and right. He gently pushed my arm away from my body so that the weapon wasn't pointed at either of us. A strange sense of calm settled in my chest, snuffing out the on-edge jitters that had plagued me since the accident.

"Okay, so you'll be using a .357 Magnum. It's good for beginners. We'll use the paper targets first."

Careful not to point the gun toward either of us, I turned toward where the outlines of a man's torso hung on the far wall and started walking toward them.

"That's far enough," he said.

"It's too far."

"You're close enough."

I didn't believe him, but saw no point in getting into an argument over it.

Coming up behind me, he took the gun back, inserted

a key, twisted it, and then handed it back to me, murmuring, "Safety lock. It can be fired now."

Using both hands, I raised the gun.

"What's your rush?" He moved even closer. "Stand up straight. Shoulders back."

He rested his hands on my shoulders as I followed his instructions.

I wondered if he could hear my pounding heart. He was standing so close, I wondered if he could feel it.

He slid his hands from my shoulders (since when had they been an erogenous zone?) down to my elbows. His breath tickled my ear as he said, "Just relax."

Easy for him to say.

"You're going to breathe in, focus along the sight, and as you exhale, you're going to squeeze the trigger. You're not going to yank on it or jerk it. You're just going to squeeze with steady, firm pressure. Got it?"

I nodded.

His hands traveled back to my shoulders. "Okay, you're going to take three breaths. The third time you exhale, you shoot."

I breathed in once, trying to focus on the target instead of the man behind me. On my second breath, I managed to use the sight to find the center of the bull's-eye. I squeezed as I exhaled the third time.

I didn't realize it was going to be that loud, and the recoil caught me off-guard. I jerked backward, colliding with Patrick's chest. His hands caught my hips, steadying me. My ears rang, my face flushed, and every nerve in my body sparked. "Sorry."

"My fault. I should have warned you about that." Patrick sounded strained. No doubt I was testing his patience. "Okay, let's try it again, this time with one hand. Turn sideways toward Alfonso."

"Alfonso?"

"Pretend that the target is Alfonso. Ultimately he'll be the one you're shooting at. Better to get used to the idea."

I turned sideways toward the target . . . Alfonso. I imagined his snarling face as he'd attacked me. I raised my arm and was surprised to see my hand shaking.

"Just take your time. Sight down your shoulder and along your arm."

I was mildly disappointed that he didn't trace the route for me. Instead he stayed a few steps away, arms crossed against his chest.

"Squeeze smoothly."

With Patrick's solemn instructions echoing in my ears, I raised the gun, aimed it at the paper version of Alfonso Cifelli, and squeezed the trigger. This time the explosive report didn't make me flinch. The recoil didn't make me jump. I squeezed off the rest of the shots in the chamber with a stable hand.

I'd expected to shake or have sweaty palms, but I was steady and dry. I had thought I'd miss the target altogether, but I knew I hadn't. I watched as Patrick retrieved the paper ghost of the target.

"You've done this before," he accused as he walked back toward me.

"No. Never."

"Your father never . . . ?"

"Taught me the family business? No."

Making no effort to hide his surprise or grudging respect, he pointed at the dark voids clustered at the center of the target's chest. "Then you are an honest-to-God natural."

I ran my fingers over the rough edges of the bullet holes. "I did that?"

"Uh huh."

I'm not sure which of us was more amazed.

A tickle of pride had me straightening my spine and pulling back my shoulders. "Not bad for a first timer, huh?"

Taking the gun from me, Patrick refilled the chamber with fresh ammunition. "You sure as hell don't look the part, but you might have potential after all, Mags."

Chapter Twelve

After shooting at the beer cans with mind-blowing accuracy, and thinking that maybe I'd been some sort of expert sniper in a previous life, I was disappointed when Patrick put the gun away.

"So do you have any kind of martial arts training?" he asked.

"I've got a black belt in stop, drop and roll."

"I remember. Any self-defense training?"

I shook my head.

He frowned.

"That's a problem?"

"What are you going to do if you miss?"

"I won't." I waved my hand in the direction of the destroyed cans. "You saw me."

"But what if you do? What if your nerves get the best of you? What happens if you miss?"

"Run like hell?"

He rolled his eyes. "Hell of a plan."

I frowned. "He's bigger than me, he's stronger than me, and I imagine he's a better fighter than me."

"So what? You're just going to give up? Let him beat the crap out of you?"

"I told you, I'll get away."

"You'll *try* to get away. Try to get away from me."

"What?"

"Now. Try to get away from me."

He lunged toward me suddenly. Fear and adrenaline flooded through me, a mix as potent as rocket fuel and just as combustible.

Shrieking, I scrambled backward away from him, but I wasn't fast enough. Grabbing my arm, he yanked me against him hard. I twisted away, wrenching free of his grasp. I scuttled away, heading for the barn door.

I zigged. He zagged, matching me step for step.

A quick glance over my shoulder showed he was gaining on me.

Turning sharply, I changed course. Abandoning my hope for reaching the door, I clambered up a small mountain of loose hay. He tackled me.

The hit knocked the air from my lungs, but the straw cushioned the impact. The body blow was stunning, but not painful. Thrashing wildly, I tried to roll away from him, but he stayed with me. Before I knew what was happening, he had me pinned, face-down. His body weight pressed into my back, immobilizing me. Trapping my hands with his own, he held them over my head.

I couldn't get any leverage. I couldn't escape.

The dried grass dug into my cheek. The stalks poked

through my clothing. Every nerve in my body was on high alert. Sexual awareness took the place of any fear I'd been experiencing, making me all too aware that both of us were breathing hard, our bodies rising and falling together.

"This is why," he lectured breathlessly; "you need to learn self-defense. So that you don't end up in this exact position."

Personally, I didn't think this was such a bad position to be in. Rolling off, he lay down beside me in the hay. I stayed on my stomach, but raised my head to look at him. He was staring at the ceiling of the barn, his cheeks flushed from the exertion of the chase.

"Just remember: eyes, nose, throat, and groin. Those are where he'll be most vulnerable. That's where your attack should be aimed. And you shouldn't use just your body. Use any weapon that's at hand."

I didn't say anything as I examined his profile. It felt strangely intimate to be lying beside a guy I barely knew. I couldn't figure out why I was so attracted to him. He wasn't anything special to look at. He wasn't ugly, just not handsome. He was, as dear old Grandma was so fond of saying, remarkably unremarkable. So why was I about thirty seconds away from suggesting a roll in the hay with him?

Maybe it was because he was a bad boy. With all the drama of my family, I've always made it a point to date good guys. Guys who were safe. Boring. That might explain why it hadn't really bothered me that I hadn't had a date in ages. I hadn't felt as though I was missing out on anything.

Perhaps the violence lurking beneath Patrick Mulligan's bland surface was what was drawing me to him like a lemming to a cliff.

Turning his head, he caught me staring at him. Reaching out, he plucked a piece of straw from my hair. He tossed it away, and then brushed my hair off my face as though he wanted to get a better look at me.

Who was I kidding? It wasn't the bad boy thing I was attracted to. It was this. The feeling like the only thing that mattered to him in this moment was me. Being the object of that kind of singular attention was a heady experience. I wondered if this was what druggies felt like when they took a hit of their drug of choice. If it was anything close, I suddenly understood the power of addiction.

The unmistakable sound of Sister Sledge's "We Are Family" filled the barn.

Patrick groaned. Putting a finger to his lips to silence me, he glanced at his cell phone as he got to his feet. "Hi Honey." His affection sounded forced.

Leaving me lying there he strode across the barn.

I slowly stood, brushing the straw from my clothes. I should have known he was taken. The good ones always are.

"I might be late, but I'll get home before midnight."

I turned away, more to deal with the crushing disappointment than to give him privacy. I imagined his girlfriend or wife covering a plate of food with plastic wrap and putting it in the fridge for him.

"Okay, bye." He clicked the phone off.

I pretended to be getting the last of the hay off me. I heard his footsteps moving back toward me. Turning, I saw him frown as the gym bag began playing the same song. It didn't make any sense, since his cell phone was still in his hand. Hurrying over to the bag, he unzipped it and pulled out a second phone. I was totally confused.

"Hi honey, I was just about to call you." The note of false cheer in his voice was magnified a thousand percent.

My mouth must have dropped open, because he gave me the universal signal to shut the fuck up again. He shouldn't have bothered. I was speechless.

"I picked up some extra work, and I've got an early shift tomorrow, so I'm not sure I'll make it home."

I gave up any pretense of giving him privacy. I was too busy trying to figure out what hell was going on.

"You're okay staying the night, Sharon?" His voice changed, suddenly all business. "Okay, thanks." He disconnected the call and tossed the phone into the bag with something that resembled annoyance.

He sighed heavily. "So now you know."

"Know what?"

"My secret. I've got two lives."

"You're a cop and a killer, I'd already figured that out."

"Okay, I've got four lives."

"Four?"

"I've got two wives. Two families. Which is why I need the two jobs."

And here, I'd been thinking I was the center of his universe. I sure know how to pick 'em.

"Now that you know means I might have to kill you."

I stared at him, trying to get a read on his expression. I couldn't. "I've got a terrible memory!" I blurted out, the words falling out on top of one another, faster and faster. "Can't remember a thing. Everything goes in one ear and out the other, as my grandmother used to say. She was also big on, curiosity k-k-killed the cat . . ." I was starting to worry she might be right about that one.

"What's Life Lesson Two?"

"D-dead is d-dead."

"And Lesson One?"

"D-don't g-get caught." I'd never stuttered as a child, but I was thinking it might become my standard mode of communication, since I seemed to be spending half my life scared to death.

Patrick pulled a switchblade from his pocket. With a practiced twitch of his wrist, he exposed the blade.

I gulped. I knew he was going to kill me. All because I couldn't mind my own freakin' business. I looked around. There were no weapons in sight. What was it he'd said? I should go for the eyes, the nose, the throat, or the groin. I held up my hands, ready to defend against his attack.

It was pretty much the stance I'd used when Theresa and I played Batgirl and Wonder Woman when we were kids. Back then I'd used my magical Wonder Woman bracelets to ward off the bad guy's bullets. Ping! Ping! Ping! Ping!

"You okay?" The light bounced off his knife.

"I'm not going to let you kill me without a fight."

He cocked his head, staring at me like he thought I'd lost my mind. "I'm not going to kill you."

"But, you said . . ."

"I was just joking, Mags. Geez, you need to lighten up, or the stress of the job will kill you."

"But you won't?"

"Not unless I get paid to. Or if I think you're a threat."

Putting the knife down, he reached into gym bag. I really wasn't feeling any more secure.

"So were you joking about the two wives thing?"

He shook his head. "I wish."

His hand flew out of the bag holding something silver and shiny.

"Don't shoot! Don't shoot!" I screamed.

"I won't! I won't!" he shouted back. "But shut up! Shut up!" He revealed that all he held in his hand was a cell phone. "I was just going to show you a picture of my kids."

"You have kids?"

"I told you, they're in college. You need to listen better."

"I didn't believe you. I can't believe it. *You* have kids?"

"Yes, Mags, even I, who perform the devil's work, has been permitted to procreate by the good Lord above."

"I didn't mean . . ."

"My kids, both of them, are the reason I do this job." He held out his phone. "My daughter, Daria, and her mother, Laila."

I shuffled forward to peer at the photograph on display. Two women, one in her early 20s and the other in her 40s, smiled out, cheek-to-cheek. They were beautiful. Dark hair and eyes set against olive skin gave them an almost exotic look.

"And my son, Russell."

The boy looked more like I'd expected a child of Patrick Mulligan to look, with his light eyes and a smattering of freckles across his cheeks.

He switched off the phone without showing me Russell's mother.

"I can see why you're proud."

"They're good kids. Both of them."

"So you've been married a long time?"

He tensed, and I thought he wasn't going to answer.

"I'm sorry. It's none of my business. I shouldn't have asked."

"I served in the first Gulf War. Operation Desert Storm. I was a kid. Young. Scared. Impetuous. I met a local girl, Laila. She was so different than Mary, my fiancée back home. I thought I was in love." Picking up his knife, he pulled a white paper sack out of the gym bag. He opened it, and plunged the knife in. "I was such a fool. Didn't even use a condom."

"And she ended up pregnant with Daria?"

He pulled the knife from the bag. A blueberry muffin was skewered on the blade. He held it out to me. "Hungry?"

I shook my head.

Holding it up like it was a candied apple on a stick, he took a bite of the muffin. "Yeah, she ended up pregnant. Not that I knew it at the time. We only had sex once. The night before I was shipped back home. I figured I'd never see her again. I just wanted . . ."

"Something different," I supplied. It was a desire I was all too familiar with.

"So I come home after my tour, and I'm feeling guilty because I cheated on Mary. Instead of manning up and confessing, I suggested we elope. She'd been waiting for me the whole time I was gone, so she was more than ready to get hitched." He took another bite of the muffin.

It looked like a dangerous habit to me.

"We go to the justice of the peace, and before I can even adjust to the time difference, I'm on my honeymoon in the Poconos. I'd gone from being covered in sand and grit to taking a bubble bath in an oversized champagne glass in less than a week. A month later, we found out Mary was pregnant."

"So the kids are close in age."

He nodded. "Their birthdays are the same week."

"Wow."

"Yeah, wow. So Mary breezes through the pregnancy. She's happy and glowing and all that crap people say. And I'm miserable, because what I realize during these nine months of living with my wife is that I can't stand her. She's petty, and controlling, and a royal pain in the ass. The reason I was so enamored with Laila was because I wanted something different than Mary, not because Laila was such a prize."

Tipping the knife, he bit off another chunk of muffin.

"So why stay with her all these years?" I asked. "People get divorced all the time." Hell, my Aunt Leslie had done it six times. I was pretty certain she wanted to give Elizabeth Taylor a run for her money.

"Because she had a stroke during child birth. A bad one. She's never recovered."

"So you stayed with her."

He shrugged. "Cops have great benefits."

"And Laila."

He sighed. "Laila, finding out she was pregnant by a GI, fled her country, had her baby, and brought herself and Daria to my front door. She'd given up everything. Her family, her friends, her home. I had to take care of her."

"Do they know about one another?" The logistics of the whole thing had boggled my mind ever since the back-to-back phone calls.

"Laila knows about Mary."

"Does she know . . . about this?"

He shook his head. "I told you. This can't be discussed."

He stuck the knife into his mouth like an amateur sword-swallower, cleaning every last crumb off the blade.

"You really do live four lives."

"And you thought your life and family are fucked up."

Chapter Thirteen

THE MAN CARRIES a metal detector around in a gym bag.

Somehow I found that to be the most disturbing fact I had learned about Patrick Mulligan. Not that he's a contract killer. Not that he prefers to eat his blueberry muffins off the tip of a switchblade. Not that he's got two families, two wives, or four lives. No, what bothered me the most was that he carries around a metal detector.

Apparently the barn which we used as a shooting range is not usually outfitted with paper targets and empty beer cans. Patrick had set everything up that morning before he'd met me at the diner. Once we were done with target practice, we packed up every scrap of paper, can, and bullet in the place.

It took forever. The redhead claimed he didn't want to leave any evidence behind, which was where the metal detector came in. He used the beeping thing to find every last bullet fragment. Did I mention it took forever?

At one point I made the mistake of muttering that it would have been a hell of a lot quicker just to go to a real shooting gallery, and he started spouting Life Lesson One again: *Don't get caught.* Too many potential witnesses at a gun range.

Finally, after he was satisfied we'd removed all traces of our presence, he drove me back to my car at the mall. I was kind of pissed that after all that, he didn't entrust me with the gun, saying instead he'd give it to me "when the time was right." Promising to be in touch, he drove off, leaving me on the opposite side of the shopping center from where my car was parked. I felt like I'd just been out on a first date, hadn't gotten a kiss goodnight, and wasn't sure if the guy would ever call again. Pathetic.

Since I had to walk through the mall anyway, I stopped at the pet store. Ignoring the cute puppies in the window and the brightly colored chirping birds in their cages, I made my way back toward the darkened depths of the shop. It was a world I usually gave a wide berth.

The lighting was muted and the air heavy. It was as though I'd stepped into another world. The world of creepy-crawly things. I did my best to ignore the snakes, lizards, and bugs in their glass enclosures. I told myself that the reason my skin itched was the residual effect of rolling around in hay, but in truth I was grossed out.

I almost turned and walked out, but then I remembered I was soon going to be a bad-ass killer chick. How the hell was I supposed to pull the trigger if I couldn't tough out a couple of uncomfortable moments in a freaking pet store?

"Can I help you?" The store employee lurking in the shadows looked as though he was only a step or two above his charges on the evolutionary ladder. Thick glasses made him look bug-eyed and he compulsively licked his lips.

"I'd like to buy some crickets. They're for my niece's pet lizard." Why did I add that last part? Was I afraid he'd think I wanted them to snack on myself?

"Fresh or freeze-dried?"

I stared at him. "You mean like . . . dead?"

"Either way they end up dead, lady."

"Dead is good!" I exclaimed excitedly. Dead was very good. Dead meant they couldn't crawl on me.

"Okay." He handed me a package. "That should last your little guy for a while." He grimaced. I'm sure he meant it to be a smile, but it was just plain scary looking.

"Thank you."

I hurried away, out of the dark, dank world of reptiles and insects, clutching my plastic container of dried crickets like it was the Holy Grail of petdom.

I was feeling pretty damned pleased when I walked back into my apartment. I'd proved my marksmanship and bought the lizard food. I whistled James Brown's "I Feel Good" as I unlocked the door.

"Oh look who's home," God greeted me snottily. Arrogance dripped from every syllable. "She who forgot to leave the TV on for me."

"You watch daytime TV?"

"It's not like there's much else to do stuck in here. I missed *The Price is Right.*"

I put the container of freeze-dried crickets down on the kitchen table beside his enclosure. "You really have a thing for game shows, don't you?"

"What is *that*?" I hadn't thought it possible, but he sounded even haughtier than usual.

"A game show? It's a contest—"

"No!" he thundered, making the glass of his cage vibrate. "What is that?" He pointed at my afternoon purchase.

"Food for you."

"They're. . . . dead." The distasteful word dripped off his tongue like a drop of acid.

"So?"

"I don't do dead." Turning his back on me, he lifted his snout skyward and shook his head.

Stalking around the table, I bent down so that my face was level with his. "Listen buddy, you're going to *do* dead, or you're going to starve."

"Speaking of doing dead, did you meet your mentor today?"

"I hate that you do that."

"Do what?"

"Change the subject so abruptly."

He shrugged his little scaly shoulders but didn't offer an apology or explanation. He just stared at me with those glossy eyes of his.

"Yes. I met him."

"And?"

"He taught me how to shoot a gun." I sat down on a kitchen chair, so I could conduct this conversation more comfortably. "And you might be surprised to know I happen to be a pretty good shot."

"I'm not surprised."

"You're not?"

"Let me see the gun."

"I don't have it."

"Why not?"

"Patrick said he'd give it to me when the time is right."

"What does that mean?"

"I don't know."

"I think it means he doesn't trust you."

I nodded. That possibility had occurred to me.

"Do you trust him?"

I took a second to mull that one over. "He's a criminal."

"People trust politicians, and they're a bunch of criminals."

I couldn't argue with that logic. "He seems like a decent guy."

"Except for the fact he's a contract killer," God reminded me dryly.

"He's also a cop."

"Which means he's trustworthy?"

I shook my head. I didn't know the answer to that question. Patrick Mulligan had made it clear that if I failed to kill Alfonso, he'd have to kill me. How could I trust someone who was such a threat? "I have to take a shower."

"Now who's changing the subject?" The lizard flicked his tail, signaling his annoyance, as I stood up. "I don't eat dead bugs!" he shouted after me as I walked out of the room.

After I'd taken a shower, dressed in fresh clothes, and

wolfed down two Lean Cuisine meals (with you-know-who bitching the entire time that he was starving) I went to the hospital to visit Katie.

Just like every time I saw her, lying there in that big bed, attached to a myriad of monitors, my breath caught in my throat and a terrible pressure squeezed my chest. I had to force myself to sound cheery as I settled into the visitor's chair beside her bed.

"Hey there, Babygirl." I picked up her hand and began to massage her limp fingers. "It's Aunt Maggie. I just wanted to let you know that I'm taking good care of God. . . . zilla. Godzilla. I'm taking good care of Godzilla. Do you know what he told me? He told me that he doesn't eat dead bugs. All he wants is live crickets. Is that true? Is that all he eats?"

I waited for her to answer.

The silence was like a slap in the face.

I swallowed hard. My eyes burned, but no tears fell. "He also told me he likes *Wheel of Fortune* and *The Price is Right*. Did you know that?"

I carefully put her flaccid hand back down on the bed sheet. Reaching up, I smoothed her hair off her forehead. She was pale. Deathly pale.

"You're going to be okay, Katie. Everything's going to be okay." I hesitated; the next couple of words were stuck on my tongue. "I promise."

I pressed a kiss to her cheek.

"A nice thought," a woman said from the doorway, "but not a promise you can deliver."

I turned to glare at Aunt Susan. I really wasn't in the

mood to have her pragmatism loosen my grip on hope. My grip on optimism was tenuous at best.

"You didn't return my call."

I dimly remembered ignoring the messages on my cell phone as I sat in the mall parking lot waiting for Patrick Mulligan. "Sorry."

"You didn't go to work." When Aunt Susan is annoyed, her eyebrows knit together into a unibrow. It's not an attractive look.

"I took a mental health day."

Her eyes narrowed into slits. For a moment I was afraid she somehow knew where I'd really been.

"Is that smart-aleck remark aimed at your mother?"

Standing up, I strode past her into the hallway and out of Katie's earshot. There was no telling what she could or could not hear in her state, but I saw no reason to expose her to one of Aunt Susan's tirades.

"It was irresponsible of you, Margaret."

"The remark? Or taking the day off?"

"I knew you were too immature to handle this pressure. I'm going to take over the decision-making regarding Katelyn's care." I recognized her tone. It was the same one she'd used the night she told my mother she was having her committed.

Just like then, my stomach flipped nervously, and a chill settled into my bones. When Aunt Susan made a decree like that, her choice was irrevocable. No one had ever stood up to her and lived to tell the tale. Or at least that was how it had always seemed.

"You're still her aunt. You will, of course, be more

than welcome to visit her whenever you wish. You can sign the papers tomorrow night."

"I don't think so." In an effort to sound strong, I spoke a tad too loudly, but I made no apologies. She was lucky I didn't call her every name that was bulldozing through my brain.

Aunt Susan blinked, her jaw slackening with surprise. She wasn't accustomed to defiance. Still, she recovered quickly, her mouth hardening into a line of granite. "Now you listen to me, Margaret—"

"No! You listen to me!" I stood as tall as I could. My right shoulder twinged, a reminder of target practice, a reminder that I could do more, be more, than I'd ever imagined. "I am Katie's guardian. That's what Theresa wanted. For me to take care of her. She is my responsibility, and *I* will make the decisions about her care."

"Margaret! What has gotten into you?"

"I mean it, Aunt Susan. I'm the one in charge, and if you try to undermine me or circumvent my wishes, I will have security toss you out on your Pilates-toned ass." *And if that doesn't work, I'll shoot you*, I added silently.

I expected her to argue. I expected her to rail about what an ungrateful brat I was after all she'd done for me, blah, blah, blah. I put my hands on my hips, readying myself for blows that never came.

Instead she said softly, "Sometimes you remind me so much of her."

"Who?"

A smile softened her lips, but there was no joy in her expression, only crushing regret. "Your mother."

Bending toward me, she pressed a kiss to my cheek before turning and walking away. I watched her go until she'd turned the corner and disappeared from sight.

I could still feel her kiss. Raising my hand, I traced the ghost of the shadow where she'd pressed her lips. Did she really see her sister in me? Was that a good or bad thing?

Before I could puzzle it out, Delveccio passed through my line of sight. With a tilt of his head he indicated I should follow him.

Swallowing hard, I hurried down the hall, hot on his trail. He led the way to the hospital cafeteria. Trying to ignore the siren's call of the chocolate pudding as he settled into a seat near the window, I slid into a seat at the table beside him. Unfortunately it gave me a great view of all those little bowls of chocolaty goodness.

"My guy says he thinks you can do the job."

I tore my attention away from the sugar-laden treat. "That's what you wanted, wasn't it?" I wondered what else Patrick Mulligan had told him about me.

"Yeah. It's what I want. Problem is he's not sure you're ready, and I need the job done fast. Alfonso's out on bail."

"He was in jail?"

He looked at me as though he'd owned gerbils smarter than me. "Yeah. Attempted. You're the one who talked to the police."

I nodded. Of course they'd arrested him. Why hadn't that occurred to me?

"Anyway, he's out now, so I need it done quick."

"Okay."

"Not okay if you're not ready. Someone else has expressed interest in the job. He's already done the prep work for it."

"I'm ready."

"That's not what my guy says."

I tried to swallow the rising anger I felt toward Patrick. Who the hell was he to mess with Katie's future like this? "I'm ready."

Tony/Anthony Delveccio fiddled with his pinky ring. "Here's the deal. You do it by the end of the week or I give the gig to Gary the Gun. If Gary does the job, you become a liability. Capiche?"

Startled, I nodded. I'd never heard anyone except mobsters in movies say *capiche*. He was telling me that if I didn't kill his son-in-law by the end of the week, a contract killer would be sent after me. He meant it as a threat, but it didn't frighten me. Not really. What scared the shit out of me was the idea I might not get the money I needed for Katie. "But when I do . . . perform the chore, you'll pay me, right?"

He nodded. "As soon as you tell me it's done."

Our business concluded, he got up to leavethe cafeteria.

Before going, he shared one last bit of wisdom. "Ya know, I get that you want to blend in and all, but it might not hurt if you flashed those killer gams of yours once in a while."

"Gams?"

"Gams. Sticks. Pins. Show a little leg." He winked at me and strolled away.

I went and bought a chocolate pudding.

Chapter Fourteen

YOU'D THINK THAT with everything on my mind I wouldn't sleep a wink, but I slept like Rip Van Winkle. My slumber was so deep that the only thing that woke me was Godzilla shouting in his most autocratic voice.

"Wake up, you fool!"

I knew bringing him into bedroom had been a mistake, but since he was on a hunger strike, it had only seemed fair to let him watch a late night episode of *Iron Chef* with me before I dozed off. His cage had displaced my reading lamp and alarm clock on my night table, so that he had an unobstructed view of the television. He was *such* a diva.

"Wake up!"

"Shut up," I muttered. "Dead is good. Dead is all you're getting."

"Dead is what you're going to end up if you don't pay attention."

"What are you talking about?"

"There's a man with a gun."

That got my attention. "Where?"

"Here."

I squinted into the darkness. With my clock on the floor, there was even less light in the room than usual. All I saw were shadows.

"Here? Where?"

"Standing in the doorway," God whispered. There was no reason for him to whisper. It's not like my intruder, assuming there was one, was going to understand him.

I didn't move. I didn't breathe. Like the clock, the lamp was on the floor, so it wouldn't make a handy weapon. Somehow I didn't think a pillow fight would take out the prowler. I couldn't just lie here waiting. I had to do something.

I could scream. Maybe I could wake my neighbors and scare him off.

He moved so quickly, I never even sensed him coming. A hand clapped over my mouth as I readied myself to yell.

Instinctively I lashed out. Remembering Patrick's self-defense instructions I tried to gouge his eyes, break his nose, or get my hands on his throat.

"Go for the jugular! Go for the jugular!" God cheered, mere inches from my head.

If I could have reached his cage, I would have used it as a weapon.

"Hey!" My attack caught my late-night visitor off guard and he tumbled on top of me, pressing me into the mattress. I tried to knee him in the groin but he was too heavy. All I managed to do with my heaving efforts was to settle his pelvis onto mine.

"Take it easy, Mags," he said breathlessly. "I didn't mean to scare you."

Patrick! What was he doing here in the middle of the night?

"I'm going to take my hand off your mouth now, Mags. I need you to not scream. Do you understand?"

I nodded.

He removed his hand from my lips. "Don't scream."

"Have you ever heard of knocking?" I asked breathlessly, trying to ignore how good it felt to have his body pressed against mine.

"I didn't want to attract attention."

Fighting the urge to pull him closer, I instead shoved him off of me. He fell to the floor with a thud.

"That's a girl!" Godzilla cried.

Ignoring him, I whisper-screamed in Patrick's general direction, "What the hell are you doing here?"

"Bringing you a gun. I told you when the time—"

"You said you'd be in touch."

"Well, we certainly did our share of touching," he quipped. In the darkness his accompanying chuckle was just about the sexiest thing I'd ever heard. "Not that I'm complaining."

The comment felt like a sensual caress, and my traitorous body responded. Remembering the warmth of his body on mine, how it had felt to have him nestled between my legs, had my blood heating and my heart hammering.

Fortunately, Godzilla chose that moment to pipe up. "Ch-eeeee-sy."

"What is that squeaking noise?" Patrick asked. I could tell from the way the shadows shifted that he was getting to his feet.

It took me a second to figure out what he was talking about. My brain wasn't getting all that much oxygen, what with my blood rushing so much lower.

"That's God."

"God?" There was no mistaking the skepticism in my murder mentor's voice. If he knew that my father was a murderer, he probably knew that my mother was . . . unstable. If he thought I was actually talking to God (the deity) I was screwed.

"Godzilla, God for short. He's a brown anole lizard."

"You have a lizard in your bedroom?"

I sat up. "He . . ." I couldn't very well tell him that God had wanted to watch TV with me. "He's Katie's."

"Oh. I understand."

"You do?"

He sat on the edge of the bed. The mattress dipped under his weight. "Sure. He reminds you of her."

It took concentration to keep my left thigh from rolling into him. "Something like that."

"If that was true, you'd feed me live crickets," God nagged.

I ignored him. The mention of Katie had reminded me that I was pissed off at Patrick Mulligan for more than just his breaking into my place and almost giving me a heart attack. "You told Delveccio I'm not ready."

"You're not."

"That's not your decision to make."

"It's my ass that's on the line."

"No!" I shoved him again, but this time he was ready for me.

He didn't fall off. He didn't even budge. He stayed as still as stone. As still as Katie lying in that big bed.

"This is my niece's life that's on the line. And now Delveccio says that if I don't do it by the end of the week, he's hiring Gary the Gun to take care of Alfonso and any liabilities. *I'm* a liability. So you don't get to say I'm not ready."

"You're too emotionally involved." Standing up, he walked out of the bedroom, leaving me there in the tangle of my sheets and thoughts.

By the time I got up and dressed, Patrick had the kitchen light on.

"Don't you dare leave me in here!" God demanded.

Picking up his cage, I plunked it down right in front of where the infuriating redhead sat at my kitchen table, pawing through my mail.

"You're a runner?" Patrick managed to not sound skeptical, but I noticed he made sure not to look in my direction as he asked the question.

"No. My friend Alice got me subscriptions to both those running magazines. She thinks I should tackle a marathon and raise oodles of cash for charity."

"She's a runner?"

"No. She just thinks I'd be less bitchy if I had a healthy outlet to relieve stress. When we were fifteen I came home to find my bedroom rearranged. She'd read a book on feng shui and wanted to clear my chi. Two years ago she took me on a silent meditation retreat so that I could relax. Do you have any idea how freaking boring a silent retreat is? No talking. No TV. No radio. I was ready to kill someone by the time we left."

"Which brings me to why I'm here. Aren't you going to offer me a drink or anything?"

"You broke in here, but you can't crack the fridge open yourself?" Grabbing two diet sodas, I slid one across the table at him like a deranged barkeeper, before sitting on the other kitchen chair. The table wasn't very wide, and my knee knocked his. The sexual awareness I'd thought I'd tamped down flared back to life.

I inched my knee away from his, but the energy was still there.

I could tell that he felt it, too, by how still he went.

"I'm sorry I knocked you out of my bed," I blurted out. I wasn't sure if I was apologizing for knocking him to the floor, or lamenting the fact we'd missed the opportunity to roll around in my sheets some more.

"Me too." His voice was heavy with regret as his gazed bored into mine.

My mouth went dry. "I . . ."

He broke eye contact and focused on his soda. He cracked open the tab of the can and redirected the conversation back to the business at hand. "You seem tense. Rule Number Three is: Don't get emotionally involved."

I glared at him. Blank-faced, he stared back. It was almost as frustrating as trying to stare down the lizard. "How can you expect me to not be emotionally involved?"

"You've got to get control of your feelings. It's dangerous. They can make you screw up."

"So that's how you do it? You just go around not feeling anything?"

He shrugged. "For me it's a job. It's a business. You don't go getting all upset when someone calls and tells you they totaled their car, do you?"

I shook my head.

"Emotional distance is an asset in this world. You're upset about your niece. You've already lost it once with Alfonso. And now you're worried about Gary the Gun."

"So you've never been emotionally involved with a job?"

"Well. . . . once."

"Tell me about it."

"I'm hungry!" God complained.

"Oh shut up!"

Patrick eyed me warily.

"Not you," I told him. "God . . . zilla." I tapped the glass nearest the pile of freeze-dried crickets on the side of his cage, before draping a placemat over the glass, blocking his view of us.

"That's a petty trick," God grumbled.

Ignoring him, I looked back at Patrick. "You tell me your story."

"I went to confession."

Throwing my hands up in the air, I said, "Okay, fine, don't tell me about it."

"I *am* trying to tell you about it."

"But you're saying you told a priest first? That I'm not your first? I don't understand—"

Reaching across the table he caught one of my hands in his. He stared right at me with those October sky eyes of his and murmured seductively, "You're my first, Mags."

My stomach flip-flopped and my lungs forgot to do their job for a long moment. Patrick Mulligan might be a little old for me, and definitely unavailable, but damn the man was sexy when he turned it on. With just a touch, a look, and four words he had me melting. Heaven help me, if he suggested a return trip to my bed, I would lead the way.

"I went to confession to *do* a priest."

I yanked my hand free of his and rocked back in my chair. Nothing like a cold dose of contract-killer reality to ruin the mood.

"Isn't it some sort of extra bad sin to kill a priest?"

"Dunno."

"So you're okay with killing a priest?"

"Nope. I was good with it. Better than good."

"Why would anyone want a priest murdered?"

Patrick took a long swig of his soda, letting me figure that one out for myself.

"Oh."

"Uh huh. Kid's father tried first, but he was an accountant. What did he know about getting the job done? So the dad, who was only looking out for his kid, he sits in jail, which in the long run was the best thing for him.

While the priest gets away with a couple of flesh wounds, gets discharged from the hospital, and goes back to work."

"And you went to confession."

"Finished the job right. The dad who started it had the perfect alibi. His avenging ass was in lock-up when I did the job." He drained the rest of his soda. A half-smile danced on his lips. I wasn't sure whether it was because he'd enjoyed the drink or if he was appreciating the memory of a job well done.

"Did you get paid for that job?"

He shook his head. "In money? No. But knowing that I'd made the world a better place for that dad and his son and who knows how many others? That, as they say, was priceless."

"So you got emotionally involved and it didn't backfire on you."

"I got lucky. Don't get me wrong, I think that you being willing to do this for your niece is admirable. I think Alfonso Cifelli is a bastard and deserves to die. I just don't want our mutual friend sicking Gary the Gun on you. He's got no honor, no sense of decency. He gets off on hurting and killing people. He tracks and hunts them like they're prey."

An involuntary shiver shook me to my core as I remembered the man from the hospital who'd frightened me so and seemed to enjoy it.

"The guy is scum," Patrick declared.

"I thought you'd . . . take me out, if I don't do the job."

He looked away, suddenly absorbed with studying the drawings Katie had done for me that were plastered all over the fridge. "I just said that to scare you. I don't kill innocent people. I have a code."

"The man's a murderer, and he's going to lecture you about some code of honor?" God called.

Paying no attention to him, I asked, "A code?"

"Yeah. I only take jobs where the victim deserves to be dead. If Delveccio needs to take out a witness in order to affect the outcome of a trial, I'm not the man for the job. Unless the witness happens to be some sort of low-life violent criminal. But if it's just some Joe Schmoe, he knows not to come to me. He gives those jobs to Gary the Gun. *You* would be a job that would go to Gary. Delveccio knows I'd never hurt you."

"Oh."

He leaned toward me, a wide, boyish grin suddenly making him look a decade younger. "Now that we've got that misunderstanding cleared up, do you like me just a little bit better?"

I nodded.

"Good. I hate playing the heavy. I don't get my kicks from scaring people."

"Then you shouldn't have broken in here in the middle of the night."

"I forgot to give you a phone."

"I've got a phone."

"No. I brought you a dump phone. Only I have the number and I'll only call it from another dump phone. That way there will be no record of our calls."

"Ask him if he brought any fucking crickets!" God shouted.

"Geez that thing is loud." Patrick pulled the placemat off the cage and stared at my little reptilian companion. "Why is he chirping like that?"

"He's on a hunger strike. I gave him freeze-dried crickets but he wants the real thing."

"Alive!" God said.

"Live ones," I muttered.

"It must be hard on him." Patrick actually managed to sound sympathetic when talking about the reptile. "He's in a different place, being fed different food."

"See!" God boomed. "Even this gun-toting miscreant understands."

"He must really miss Katie," Patrick mused.

I stared at him. That thought had never occurred to me. I looked down at God questioningly. He had suddenly busied himself with picking up a dried cricket and examining it.

"The least you should do is get him the food he's used to. You wouldn't want him to starve to death."

"I'll think about it," I muttered.

"I'm starting to like this guy," God said. "He's a wise man. You should listen to him."

"But more importantly, Mags. We've got to put together a plan for you to kill Alfonso, and keep you alive."

Chapter Fifteen

THERE AREN'T ENOUGH hours in the day to live a real life and be a killer-in-training. There isn't enough coffee either. That was my conclusion the next day as I sat at my desk at Insuring the Future.

My middle-of-the-night rendezvous with Patrick had left me sleep-deprived, not to mention grouchy. While he'd brought me a gun along with the phone, I didn't have a plan with which to use it. He was convinced that the best way to kill Alfonso was not to go chasing after him, but to figure out a way to make him come to me. Personally I didn't think that kind of thinking made much sense, but the redhead was the experienced professional, so I sort of nodded my head in agreement. He'd promised to call within twenty-four hours with a plan of attack.

Meanwhile, I had to follow Life Lesson One to the letter: Don't get caught, which meant that I had to keep showing up for my crappy job. Barely able to keep my eyes open, I spent the morning taking an inordinate number of calls from people claiming their vehicles had been damaged by hail. I kept a close eye on the clock, watching the minutes roll by, as I waited for my lunch break. I had high hopes I'd be able to run out to my car and catch a quick nap.

Suddenly I smelled pepperoni.

That was never a good sign. Pepperoni meant my boss Harry was lurking nearby. I looked over one shoulder and then the other searching for the department's manager. Sure enough he was standing behind me.

"Hi Harry." It wasn't often that I hoped for more work to do, but I offered a fervent prayer that I'd have to answer my phone. Soon.

"Hello, Margaret. How are you feeling today?" He stepped closer and patted my shoulder, a gesture that was probably meant to seem comforting, but was just downright repulsive.

Fighting the urge to shake him off, I forced myself to stay still. I stared at the phone willing it to buzz. Nothing happened. "Better, thanks."

"Good. Good. You missed a meeting yesterday. I'd like you to come by my office so I can fill you in."

"I read the memo." That was a lie. I'd seen the memo on my desk and folded it up into a small square to tuck under the short leg of my chair to keep it from rocking.

"Good. Good. I just want to go over the details, the finer points with you."

His hand was still on my shoulder, but now he was kneading my tense muscles. I wondered if I could make a case for harassment. Of course if I did that, I'd draw attention to myself, which was probably not a good idea. Patrick had stressed over and over again that I should make every effort to fly under everyone's radar. His example of being the state's hero cop and losing out on making money with his side business was a pretty convincing argument.

I couldn't very well accuse Harry of sexually pressuring me if I was trying to keep up an act of quiet status quo, so I asked, "Can we meet this afternoon?"

"Of course." He sounded exceedingly pleased with himself, as though he knew he'd pressured me into doing something that made me uncomfortable. "Come by my office at two. I'll be waiting for you."

With a last squeeze of my shoulder, he left. He was such a power-hungry little prick. I thought that maybe once I was done with Alfonso I'd turn my gun on Harry.

It wasn't until he was gone that my phone rang. I glared at it. Now that he'd left I had no desire to pretend to work.

After fielding a few more calls, I left my desk. It was finally lunchtime. I'd made it halfway to my car, halfway to a world of uninterrupted slumber, when Armani's voice reached me.

"Hey, Chiquita!"

Grudgingly I turned around. She was sitting at a table under a tree, waving me over to join her. I almost told her to leave me the fuck alone, but then thought better of it. If I pissed off Armani, I'd certainly become the center of attention. Last year a fool in human resources had refused to sit with her at the office Christmas party. She'd "predicted" that he was in for a string of bad luck. Then, in a period of seventy-two hours he ended up with four flat tires, all the screws fell out of his desk chair, and a link to a video of him drunkenly warbling Air Supply's "All Out of Love" spread like wildfire throughout the company.

Pissing off Armani Vasquez was definitely not a good idea, especially when one is trying to keep a low profile, so I dragged myself over to her table.

"You look like hell, Chiquita."

"Didn't get much sleep."

"You're worried about your niece?" For once all her smart-ass attitude was taking a vacation. She seemed genuinely concerned.

"Among other things."

She nodded sympathetically. "What did The Jerk want?"

The Jerk was Harry. "To have a private meeting."

Armani rolled her eyes. Everyone knew what that meant. He'd sit too close. Touch too often. Get way too chummy. "You should report him."

I shook my head. "Probably. But I've got way too many other things to worry about. I can't handle an H.R. issue on top of everything else."

"I missed you yesterday. Were you really sick?"

"Needed a mental health day."

"Good for you." She unzipped her lunch bag and took out two plastic containers. "You should eat something. You look pale."

Sleep-deprived, I'd been too tired to pack myself a lunch, and I wasn't in the mood to make a mad dash for fast food now. "Not hungry."

She pushed one of the packages across the table at me. "Peanut butter and raspberry jelly. Made it this morning. It's your favorite, right?"

I stared at her like I'd never set eyes on the woman before. She knew what my favorite sandwich was? She'd made one for me? I pried off the lid and peeked inside. It definitely looked like PB&J. "What's the catch?"

"No catch . . . except . . ."

I waited for it. I knew such a generous act wouldn't come without a steep price tag.

But the sandwich looked and smelled awfully good. I found myself saying, "Except what?"

"I need you to be straight with me."

"About what?"

"About whether or not you're looking for another job."

"Your Scrabble tiles haven't told you?"

She tossed that magnificent head of hair of hers, signaling she wasn't amused by my crack.

"No. I'm not looking for another job."

"You swear?"

I nodded.

"Good. You being here is the only part of this job that keeps me sane."

Opening the container, I took out half a sandwich and bit into it. I considered pointing out that I probably wasn't the best barometer of sanity, what with the fact I was holding regular conversations with a lizard and I was gearing up to kill a man.

"If you left, I'd lose my mind."

Something I'd apparently already done. "Which would make you different . . . how?"

"I'm starting to think your inner Chiquita is a real bitch," Armani complained. But she was smiling.

Chapter Sixteen

NOTHING TESTS ONE'S grip on sanity like a family dinner.

That was the conclusion I reached before we even sat down. It was Aunt Leslie and Loretta's birthday. A celebration that had been scheduled long before the car accident. Aunt Loretta loved, loved, loved her birthday. She adored being the center of attention. She felt like she deserved to be showered with gifts. As her twin, Aunt Leslie just sort of went along for the ride.

Aunt Susan called and left a message to remind me that dinner was that night at seven. I had just enough time to run over to the hospital after work to visit with Katie for an hour, before heading on over to the B&B for what should have been a birthday bash, but had morphed into a family dinner. Meaning me, the three aunts, Alice, and Loretta's latest paramour, the one Alice had warned me about. Claiming to be suffering from jet lag, Lamont had the good sense to hide out in his room, which was too bad; everyone might have been on better behavior if he'd been there.

Luckily I had their gifts in the trunk of my car, where they had been for weeks. I am a woman of many faults, but I am actually an awesome gift buyer. I pride myself on finding the perfect gift for each recipient. I shop often and early. And I always have the presents wrapped by professionals, because yet another thing I suck at is gift wrapping. The average five-year-old does a way better job than me. I can't cut in a straight line, I can't fold for shit, and the tape sticks to everything but where I'm actually trying to place it.

As a general rule, I actually like most of Aunt Loretta's suitors. Usually the poor guys are besotted with her. It doesn't seem to matter if they're forty or ninety, she's got them wrapped around her little finger—poor saps. But I took an instant dislike to her latest man, even before we were introduced. Just the smarmy way he was talking to Alice from across the room had me on edge. He was standing a tad too close to her. His suit was almost too well-cut for him to be called dapper. His smile seemed too wide to be real.

After Aunt Loretta had showered me with air kisses, so as not to muss her make-up, she dragged me across the sitting room to introduce us. "Templeton, this is my niece, Margaret. Margaret, this is Templeton."

Alice, stepping away immediately, seemed grateful to be offered the chance to escape from the old coot.

So far the only thing Loretta's date had going for him was that he was actually age-appropriate for my aunt. He extended a tanned hand toward me, a twinkle in his eyes. "Your niece? Why you two look like sisters!"

Loretta giggled girlishly at the compliment, while I grit my teeth. His words taken another way meant that I looked like I'd already passed the half-century mark.

"It's a pleasure to meet you, Margaret." He pressed his lying lips to the back of my hand.

"I'm sorry," I said with my most charming smile, "Did she say your name was Templeton?"

He nodded.

"Like the rat?"

Taken aback, he dropped my hand as though he'd just realized I carried the bubonic plague.

"Margaret!" Aunt Loretta gasped.

"The rat in Charlotte's Web," I explained smoothly. "I'd never heard anyone except the rat called Templeton before."

"There's a first time for everything." Aunt Susan said archly from behind me.

I flinched. I hadn't noticed her enter the room.

"Dinner's ready. Margaret, will you help me serve?" Susan requested.

"Of course."

Obediently we all filed into the dining room. Aunt Leslie was already seated at the middle of the table. Swirling the water in her drinking glass, she seemed to be studying it intently.

I noticed that Alice sat down next to her immediately. Sad when the best company at the table is stoned. I saw Templeton maneuvering to sit beside her, so I called out, "Save me a seat, Alice?"

Flashing a smile of gratitude in my direction, she

offered a silent shrug of an apology at Templeton, who had the good sense not to reveal any disappointment he might have been experiencing.

Following Aunt Susan into the kitchen, I said, "Smells good."

Glancing over her shoulder, she asked, "Since when do you say any form of seafood is appetizing?"

My dislike of anything that comes out of the ocean is legendary in my family.

I shrugged. "I smell garlic."

"Shrimp scampi." She busied herself with stirring one of the steaming pots on the stove. "Would you put the salad on the table?"

Opening the fridge, I pulled out the bowl of crisp greens. I never understood why she made such gigantic salads. She was the only one who ever ate them.

"A rat," Susan muttered.

I braced myself. I'd known this was coming. "It was the first thing that popped into my head."

Susan put the wooden spoon down on its rest and turned to look at me. "I doubt that."

I didn't argue with her.

"That was your favorite book when you were a girl. You went around greeting everyone with 'Salutations!' for about six months. You were a precocious child."

I squeezed the sides of the dish. "Who matured into a disappointing adult?"

She shook her head. "Now you sound like your grandmother."

I wondered what she meant by that. I realized she was

right, but still I wanted to know exactly why she'd said it.

"The balsamic dressing is in the crystal pitcher. It's already on the table. If you'll have Alice dish that out. . . ." Turning away from me, she resumed stirring.

Dismissed, I carried the rabbit food to where the ravenous diners were poised to devour it.

Aunt Leslie was humming "Puff the Magic Dragon" when I burst into the dining room.

I was holding the bowl so tightly that my hands ached. As I put it down, Alice caught my eye. She looked worried. The problem with having a friend for over twenty years is that she can read me like a street sign. I offered her a weak smile to let her know I was okay, turned on my heel, and headed back into the kitchen for round two.

"How much was Aunt Leslie puffing today?" I asked.

Susan frowned. "Why?"

"She's singing about the Magic Dragon." I grabbed the oversized, handmade clay bread basket. It was filled with an assortment of dinner rolls.

"Tread gently tonight, Margaret. It's a hard day for them."

"I guess getting older *is* a bitch."

Aunt Susan was rummaging around in the refrigerator, her back to me. "They miss your mother."

"Uh huh."

She handed me the crystal butter dish. She was using all the good stuff tonight. "For most of their lives, those three celebrated their birthdays together. Mary's birthday is next week you know."

"I knew that!" I left the kitchen before my aunt could

call my bluff. Before she could guess I'd forgotten when my own mother's birthday is. I'd blocked it out.

I practically threw the bread and butter on the table. Not that anyone noticed. Loretta and Leslie were in the midst of an argument about a long-dead relative who might or might not have killed himself depending on whose version of family history you believed, while Alice was pretending to be enthralled by some tall tale Templeton was weaving about a baseball and a kangaroo . . . or was it a koala bear? I always get those two mixed up.

"Can I ask you something?" I asked Aunt Susan as I swung back into the kitchen.

"Of course."

"When did you know?"

"Know what?"

"That Mom was . . ." Remembering God berating me for my lack of sensitivity, I purged the words *loony*, *nuts*, and *crazy* from my tongue. "Different."

"The day she brought Archie home." Susan made no effort to hide the hostility she felt for my father.

"Really?" If associating with dangerous men was the first sign, then I must be well on my way to the nuthouse, since I'd found myself enjoying the company of Patrick Mulligan.

"No. Not really."

I breathed a sigh of relief. "What was the first sign?"

"It was a long time ago. I don't remember."

"Did she start talking to things . . . animals?" If she confirmed that was my mother's first symptom, I was going to book myself a suite at the funny farm.

I didn't know Aunt Susan could move so quickly. Before I knew what was happening, she'd crossed the room, grabbed both of my upper arms and was shaking me. "Is this because I said you reminded me of her?"

"I . . . no." It wasn't like I could tell her my real reason for asking. "Geez, chill out, Aunt Susan."

"You're nothing like her, Margaret. Nothing. You're strong. You're pig-headed sometimes—a lot of the time—but you're stronger than she ever was. Tougher. Don't you forget that." Her voice wavered at the end, and I thought I saw her eyes glistening with tears, but I couldn't be sure because she yanked me into her. Hugging me tightly, she murmured. "You're a fighter, Margaret. This family needs more fighters."

Aunt Leslie is a big hugger. Aunt Loretta is a kisser. Aunt Susan was never one to demonstrate warmth. But this embrace of hers felt surprisingly like . . . affection. The day must have been hard on her, too.

Feeling bad for upsetting her, I patted her back. "I'm sorry. I—"

"And for the record," she whispered in my ear. "I think you're right about Templeton being a rat."

Chapter Seventeen

NOTHING EARTH-SHATTERING HAPPENED because Aunt Susan and I agreed about something, though I spent the entire meal expecting it to.

Alice and I took over the clean-up duties, which gave us a chance to catch up while the witches and the rat chatted in the sitting room. By the time the last glass was dried, I knew about her latest adventure, including the details of her relationship with her baby-daddy, Lamont.

"You seem . . . preoccupied," Alice said, as I tied up the garbage bag reeking of shellfish. "You must have a lot on your mind."

Busying myself with finding a fresh trash bag, I muttered, "I do." I'd spent a good part of the evening waiting for the "dump" phone in my pocket to buzz, signaling that Patrick had come up with a plan for me to kill Alfonso Cifelli.

It had been a surreal experience to sing "Happy Birthday" while knowing that with every passing moment I was getting closer to killing a man.

"Do you want to talk about it?"

I shook my head.

"She's going to be okay," Alice said with an eager smile. "I have a good feeling about Katie."

"Thanks. Every positive thought helps." I didn't really believe that bullshit, but I knew saying it would make my old friend feel better. The only thing that was going to help Katie right now was dollars. A lot of them. That was why Alfonso had to die. Soon.

Using the excuse that I had to be at work bright and early the next morning, I said my good-byes and made as early an escape as I politely could. I checked my cell the moment I got into my car. Patrick hadn't called.

Laying the phone on the seat beside me, I headed for home. Two minutes later it rang. Snatching it up, I pressed it to my ear as I coasted through a yellow light.

"Hello?"

"Hey, Mags."

No one besides him had ever called me Mags. It made me feel all warm and tingly inside when he said it. I felt special.

"So, I've got a plan," he continued. "Can you meet me at the McDonald's on Washington Street tomorrow morning?"

"I've got to work. Remember, Rule Number One?"

"You start at nine. Be at Mickey D's at eight."

I groaned. I am not a morning person. "Okay."

"And wear comfortable shoes."

"Why?"

"Because it's part—"

A siren wailed, interrupting him. A glance in my rearview mirror had me nearly blinded by flashing lights.

"Oh crap. I'm getting pulled over."

"Stay calm, Mags. Keep your hands on the wheel and just act normal."

He hung up before I could ask what "acting normal" looked like.

Tossing the phone on the seat, I grabbed the steering wheel with both hands. I coasted onto the shoulder of the road and pulled to a stop. The police car followed me.

"Oh crap. Oh crap. Oh crap." Was I going to end up in prison before I'd even committed a crime? Thankfully, the gun Patrick had brought me was still under the mattress in my apartment. What evidence could they have on me? What cause did they have to even stop me?"

"License and registration," a no-nonsense male voice demanded.

I squinted up at his shadowy figure, but his flashlight was shining in my eyes so I couldn't see much.

"License and registration, please, ma'am."

"Of course."

Leaning across the car, I popped open my glove compartment. A cloud of napkins from fast-food joints spilled out. Sifting through the remaining papers, I found my vehicle registration. I handed it to the police officer before picking up my purse to find my driver's license. Finding it, I gave that to him, too.

"Could you please step out of the vehicle, Miss Lee?" He opened my door.

Fumbling for the seat belt release, I stuttered, "Is s-s-something wrong, Officer?"

"Are you aware that it's against the law in this state to talk on a cellular phone while operating a moving vehicle without a hands-free headset?"

Freed from the safety device, I climbed out of the car. "I am." There was no point in lying about it. There were signs everywhere reminding drivers of that very fact.

"Please wait here."

He walked back to his vehicle. I stood by the side of the road, watching the traffic whiz by. I tried a deep-breathing exercise Alice had taught me once. It was supposed to relax me. It didn't work.

I was too busy worrying that this routine traffic stop would somehow be connected to Patrick or Delveccio. I couldn't let that happen.

"Maybe I should explain," I called out to the cop sitting in his car.

He waved me to approach. The overhead dome in his vehicle was on, and I could finally see him. Thirty-something, dark hair and eyes, a strong chin.

"You see, my sister was killed in a car accident, and my niece is in the hospital, and I thought it might be the hospital calling."

"Was it?" He climbed back out of his car. He wasn't that much taller than me. I also couldn't help but notice that his biceps were barely restrained by the sleeves of his uniform.

"Ummm . . . no. It was . . . a wrong number."

"Your driving record is clean."

"Yes sir."

"Don't."

"Don't what?"

"Don't call me sir. It makes me feel old." He flashed a smile so pearly white that I blinked.

"My apologies, Officer . . ."

"Kowalski. Paul Kowalski." He handed me my license and registration. "I'm going to let you off with a warning, ma'am."

"Ma'am makes me feel old."

"Miss."

I knew that he was baiting me, but I was kind of enjoying the flirtation. "Maggie."

"It really isn't safe to talk on the phone and drive, even with a headset. Some studies claim it's even worse than driving drunk. Which isn't to say you should start driving drunk."

I chuckled. "Of course not. Thank you for your understanding Off—"

He held up a finger to interrupt me. "Paul."

"Paul."

"On the other hand, one drink does not a drunk make. My shift ended five minutes ago. Care to join me?"

"Join you?"

"For a drink."

"You're asking me out?" This was almost as strange as talking to a reptile, or dining with a hitman.

Paul Kowalski raised his hands defensively. "I wasn't

trying to pressure you or use my position to influence you. I just thought a drink with an attractive woman would be a nice way to end my day. My shift is over. I meant no offense. Have a safe evening Miss Lee."

I briefly wondered if my wanna-be hitwoman status was giving me some sort of glow. Two different men had called me attractive in the past week. Or maybe I was subconsciously following Armani's advice and had freed my inner-Chiquita. Either way, I'd just been asked out for the first time in a year.

"Are you single?" I blurted out as he turned back toward his cruiser.

He turned back around. "Yes."

"You're sure? No wife. No mistress. No girlfriend?"

"Not unless you count my job." He walked back toward me. "Does that mean you'll join me for a drink?"

I nodded.

He smiled. A breath-taking, heart-breaking smile that would make me the envy of every girl in whatever place we ended up.

"I have to turn in my car. Change clothes. How 'bout we meet up at Shenanigans over on Lincoln Ave in about thirty minutes?"

"I'd like that." I particularly liked that he'd chosen a place a block from my apartment which meant I'd have time to run home and freshen up.

"It's a date." With a wink, he headed back to his car.

I jumped in mine, set a land-speed record for getting home (something the officer probably wouldn't have approved of), changed clothes, and applied some smoky eye make-up that I hoped made me look alluring and not like a victim of domestic violence.

"What on earth are you doing?" God demanded haughtily.

"I've got a date."

"A date?" He sounded as though he'd never heard of such a concept.

"Yes. A man. A woman. A drink. Romance."

"I know what a date is. I just didn't think you went for that sort of thing."

"Why not?"

He didn't answer me.

I poked my head into the kitchen to see why not. He was lying on his back on the bottom of his cage, all four feet sticking straight up in the air.

"God? Godzilla?" Panicked, I ran over to his enclosure and lifted the lid. "Please don't be dead. Please don't die."

I couldn't tell whether he was breathing. I did notice that the pile of freeze-dried crickets appeared to be untouched. What if I had starved him to death? Katie would never forgive me. I'd never forgive myself.

"God?"

"What?"

Screeching, I stumbled backward, knocking my toaster to the ground as I tripped.

"What grace," he drawled snottily, standing up on his hind legs.

"Why'd you do that?"

"To get your attention."

"Well it worked; you almost gave me a heart attack."

"You can't even starve a reptile to death. How are you ever going to kill a man?"

I frowned at him. "I don't need you putting doubts in my head, Little Guy."

He flicked his tail, unhappy about being reminded of his diminutive stature. "You must have asked yourself the same question."

Scooping up the remains of my toaster, I made sure not to look at him. "Why do you think I haven't brought you fresh bugs? You're my dry run. If I can kill you . . ."

I stole a quick look at him. His tiny lizard jaw had dropped open. It was nice to have shocked him for once. Grinning, I dumped the ruined appliance in the trash. "I'm going to be late for my date."

"Don't do anything I wouldn't do!" God yelled after me as I strode out of the apartment.

I tried not to imagine what a lizard would do . . . if it could do something.

Chapter Eighteen

A LITTLE WHILE later I was sipping a drink with a paper umbrella stuck in it. I wondered if God would like the miniature parasol. It was the perfect size for him.

It had been forty minutes since Officer Paul Kowalski and I had gone our separate ways. I was starting to worry I was being stood up. I was also starting to worry that the weathered old guy at the end of the bar was starting to ogle me like a starving man eyes a steak.

Old Dude had just slipped off his chair and was stumbling toward me when Paul walked into the place. I gave a big wave, hoping to attract his attention. The plan backfired when Old Dude waggled his fingers in reply and gave me a toothless grin.

"Hey, Gorgeous. Sorry I'm late." Paul cut right in front of Old Dude and placed a kiss on my cheek. Instead of sitting in the seat opposite me in the booth, he squeezed in beside me, throwing an arm around my shoulders. Claiming me as his own, he shot Old Dude a warning look.

The old guy shrugged as if to say *can't blame a guy for trying*, and shuffled away.

"Sorry I'm late. My sergeant . . . never mind." He took his arm off my shoulders.

I expected him to move to the other seat, but he stayed where he was, his thigh practically welded to mine. He picked up my drink and sipped it, an oddly intimate act, considering we'd met less than an hour before. I'd left a lipstick print on the glass, and his lips overlapped the exact spot where mine had just been.

"Pineapple juice, coconut rum, and raspberry chambord." He brought the glass to my lips inviting me to drink. Staring into my eyes as I sipped, he said, "Sex in the Bedroom."

I almost choked on the alcohol. Instead I spluttered. Not an attractive look.

Not that Paul Kowalski seemed to mind. "An interesting choice of drink."

Getting my coughing under control, I told him, "It's the drink special of the night."

"I'm going to get a beer. Do you want another of those?"

I shook my head, not trusting myself to speak. What I wanted was real sex in the bedroom. Too bad this was only our first date. I have rules about these things. No sex on the first date. Or the second. If I still liked the guy by the third, then he had a chance of getting lucky. Unfortunately, I'd found myself bored or aggravated by most of my first and second dates, which explained the current drought I'd experienced.

Sliding out of the booth, Paul smiled at me before crossing to the bar. He'd changed into tailored jeans and a polo shirt that stretched tight across his massive shoulders. Other women in the bar, even some who were with dates, watched his progress.

It was kind of thrilling to find out he only had eyes for me when he turned back around. My heartbeat, which had almost returned to normal, sped up again as he drew near.

Putting his bottle down on the table, he grabbed my hand and pulled me out of the booth. "Dance with me, Maggie."

Shennanigans wasn't really a dancing kind of place. No one else was dancing. "I'm not much of a dancer."

Ignoring my protest, he pulled me closer. Looping my hands around his neck, he stared into my eyes as he rested his hands on my hips. Unlike Patrick Mulligan, Paul Kowalski was an easy man to read.

He wanted me. Specifically, he wanted sex.

No one had ever regarded me with such undisguised, unrepentant lust before in a public place. Usually the guys I dated practiced a modicum of decorum. They at least pretended to be further evolved than their caveman forefathers.

Not Paul. His need was primitive, raw, and he was making no effort to mask his desire.

I knew nothing about the man, including whether or not I even liked him, but I was already calculating how long it would take to get back to my place, when he captured my mouth with his, sealing my fate. This was no getting-to-know-you kiss. It was hot. It was wild. It promised—no, demanded—sex.

My knees buckled, but Paul had a tight grip on me, imprinting the length of his body against mine. After assaulting my senses and decimating any judgment I might have had left, he lifted his head, letting me up for air.

"Let's get out of here," he growled.

I couldn't speak. All I did was nod my head like some wind-up sex doll. Somehow I'd completely forgotten my rule about no sex on the first three dates. Hell, I was about to have sex with a guy I'd met ninety minutes earlier.

We practically ran out of the bar to Paul's car. It was like him. Dark and strong and powerful. A muscle car. He opened the passenger door for me, but before I could climb in, he yanked me back toward him, our bodies colliding, my nerves combusting.

"I don't usually do this," he rumbled, his excitement evident as our bodies collided.

"Me neither." I panted, tugging his shirt free from his jeans and slipping my hands beneath. His muscles rippled beneath my touch.

Mirroring my actions, he slid his fingers beneath the hem of my shirt, stroking the sensitive skin of my abdomen, before sliding his hands around me to cup my butt.

Usually I didn't enjoy being manhandled like this, especially not in a parking lot where anyone could see, but I decided to go with my inner Chiquita and enjoy the moment.

He practically shoved me into the car, though he

made sure I didn't hit my head on the way down. That must be a cop thing.

Hopping into the driver's seat, he started the engine. The vibration of the motor seemed to shoot right through me. Powerful. Fast. Dangerous.

"Which way?" he asked.

It took all my concentration to direct him to my place even though it was just down the block. Once he parked, we raced to my front door. Somehow I unlocked the door, and we stumbled inside, groping each other.

"That was a quick date," God grumbled from the kitchen.

I ignored him. Paul was pulling my shirt over my head.

"What are you doing?" God asked from nearby.

Startled, I looked around. He was loose! The lizard was perched on the back of my couch. I must have left the lid off his enclosure. Crap!

"This is a very bad idea, M&M."

I glared at him while Paul tried to unbutton my jeans. Drawing himself up to his full height, the lizard shook his head disapprovingly. He was really killing the mood. I wanted to tell the lizard that I was about to have sex for the first time in over a year. And it was going to be good, passionate sex. With a guy who'd just met me. A guy who found me so attractive he was ready to rip my clothes off.

"It's cheap and tawdry, and you deserve better than this," God lectured.

I waved for him to go away. He didn't budge. He just stayed there staring at me.

"Bedroom," I gasped. Grabbing Paul's hands, I pulled him after me as I headed for my bed. I could close the door. That would keep the lizard out. It would keep him from watching us.

We were halfway down the hall when God reminded me, "The gun is under the mattress."

That stopped me cold. There was no way I could have sex knowing the gun was there and that Paul Kowalski could find it at any moment, like some twisted version of "The Princess and the Pea." Crap!

"I can't . . ." I said breathlessly. "I can't." I pushed him away from me.

He stared at me uncomprehendingly. I'd caught him off guard. The poor man probably wasn't accustomed to a woman putting on the brakes so abruptly.

"I can't do this. It's too much. Too fast." *And I've got a Magnum under the mattress.*

He blinked.

I could practically see the gears in his brain spinning. He was trying to figure out how to change my mind. He reached for me and I jumped back.

My brain was in charge again. I couldn't afford to let my body control my choices, and I knew that if I let him touch me, I'd make decisions driven by lust, not logic. I couldn't afford to do that. Too much was riding on my actions. I had to remember Life Lesson One: Don't get caught.

Having a cop catch me with a gun was a definite no-no.

No matter how much I wanted him.

Chapter Nineteen

I MUST HAVE looked pretty ragged when I pulled in beside the Golden Arches the next morning, because the first words out of Patrick's mouth were, "You look like hell."

"You're a charmer."

"Come for a ride."

I parked my car and climbed into his truck. It smelled like coffee. Hot, strong coffee. I stared longingly at the large cup in the cup holder.

"That's for you." Patrick pulled away from McDonald's as I greedily gulped down the java juice. "You can have one of those breakfast-sandwich-things, too, if you want."

"Thanks." I ripped the wrapping off an egg sandwich. It smelled almost as good as the coffee. The man was awfully good to me.

"I was worried about you."

"Why?"

"You got pulled over."

"You thought I'd tell them about you?"

He shook his head. "I thought you'd call back."

"I got busy."

He glanced over at me, frowning. "What did they stop you for?"

"Talking on the phone with you."

"Did you get a ticket?"

"Nope."

"So you don't know who stopped you."

"Paul Kowalski."

"You know his name?" If it was possible, Patrick's voice got even softer than usual.

"He told me."

"Why?" He didn't sound happy that I was on a first-name basis with a cop other than him. I guess I couldn't blame him.

"He asked me out."

"Kowalski asked *you* out?"

"You don't have to make it sound quite so unbelievable." I knew I wasn't the most attractive Barbie in the dollhouse, but even I could occasionally land a date.

"Did you accept?"

I nodded. Remembering how I'd accepted everything else he'd done to me, I felt my face grow warm.

Patrick Mulligan has the observational skills of a detective. He didn't miss my tell-tale blush. Putting the truck into park, he twisted in his seat to get a better look at me. He pressed the back of his hand to my burning cheek, before sighing heavily.

"What?" I said defensively. "I'm not allowed to date?"

"Just be careful. Kowalski doesn't exactly have a reputation for *dating*. This job . . . it can make people reckless. Do things they wouldn't normally do."

I took a giant swig of coffee to keep myself from saying, *Like have sex?*

"Let's walk and talk." Patrick climbed out of the truck before I had a chance to tell him I was pretty darn comfortable sitting right there with my coffee and breakfast.

I scrambled out after him, only to freeze when my feet hit the ground.

We were smack dab in the middle of a cemetery.

I eyed the graves wondering if one was about to become mine. Maybe Patrick had decided I was too much of a liability, what with my getting pulled over by the cops the night before.

His footsteps crunched along the gravel as he rounded the vehicle and came toward me. I readied myself to throw the remains of my lukewarm beverage in his face. It wasn't much of a weapon, but it was all I had. The gun he'd given me was still in my house. I'd wrapped it in a sweater and placed it in the washing machine, just in case Paul Kowalski returned for another visit.

"I like this place," Patrick said, putting his hands in his pockets and surveying the land like an old-time rancher surveying his spread. "It's always so quiet. And there's history here. Real history."

It didn't sound as though he was ready to kill me, so I took another bite of the sandwich.

"Do you have any phobias or superstitions I should know about?"

I thought about it for half a second before I ruled out my preternatural aversion to anything that involved Tom Hanks. I decided not to mention it. "No."

"Are you afraid of dogs?" Patrick began weaving his way between the headstones.

I followed. "Not particularly."

"The number thirteen?"

"My lucky number."

"Afraid of heights?"

That made me smile. "Nope."

Glancing back at me he cocked his head. "Why the grin?"

I scowled at him. I was not in the mood to be hassled.

"Your face is going to stick like that if you're not careful, Sourpuss. I take it you're not afraid of heights."

"Said I wasn't."

"Are you into bungee jumping, or cliff-diving, or some other adrenaline-junkie shit?"

It took me a second to answer him because I was swallowing the last of the breakfast sandwich. "I like to climb trees."

"You what?"

"I like to climb the trees in my aunts' backyard." It was pretty much the only time I enjoyed the whole fresh-air thing.

Patrick planted his butt on a gravestone. Leaning against it as though it were a chair, he watched me carefully. "Like a monkey?"

I grinned, there was something exciting about this verbal sparring of ours. It made me feel alive. "Like a lumberjack."

"You think of yourself as a lumberjack?" The redhead made no effort to hide his amusement. I got the impression he, too, was enjoying our ridiculous repartee.

"That's somehow worse than thinking of myself as a monkey?"

"Hey, at least we're evolved from monkeys."

Draining the last of my coffee, I looked him in the eye. "Maybe I'm a creationist."

"A creationist?"

"Yeah, maybe I don't accept evolution. Maybe I believe that God Almighty in his infinite wisdom created us in his image."

"So you're thinking that God is a fucking lumberjack?"

Laughing, I shook my head. "Nope. I was just saying I'm not afraid of heights. And for the record, I'm a damn good climber."

"Now that," Patrick said thoughtfully, "might come in handy someday. But for now we're going to focus on your hiking skills."

The plan Patrick had come up with was simple. So simple that there wasn't much chance that even I could screw it up. It seemed that besides being a child-beater and connected to organized crime, Alfonso Cifelli had a softer side. An artistic side.

Specifically, he considered himself to be a nature photographer. Every morning, at around the same time, he hiked into one of the nearby state parks, trekked up the same "mountain" and took a photograph of the same spot, thereby recording how the scene changed each and every day.

There was a note of respect in Patrick's voice as he described Alfonso's artistic pursuit. I, though, was unimpressed.

The plan was simple. The next morning I'd hike up Cifelli's favorite hill before he got there, lay in wait, and blow him away as he prepared to snap his picture.

Foolproof, right?

Yeah, right.

Chapter Twenty

I'M NOT A morning person. I'm not an outdoorsy person. And I don't have a killer's personality.

At least I don't think I do.

I didn't get a wink of sleep the night before the hit. I spent most of the darkened hours pacing my halls and generally driving God crazy as I second-guessed myself. It sort of went on an endless loop that went something like this:

Was I really going to take another human being's life?

It sounded crazy.

Was I going crazy? Is that why I'd agreed to murder for hire?

Was I already crazy? If I was indeed insane, would I wonder if I was?

Did my mother know she'd lost it?

Did she talk to animals?

Would she ever consider killing someone, even in her current mental state?

Maybe I'm just evil.

Evil people kill people.

But I'm going to kill a very bad man. For a very good reason.

Don't evil people justify their wicked deeds? Don't crazy people?

Maybe I'm crazy and evil!

I really wasn't cut out for this line of work, but I couldn't back out now.

I'd picked up the framed family photograph that I'd knocked off the wall a couple of days earlier. Looking at the picture caused me physical pain. My chest ached and my eyes burned. We looked so . . . normal.

You know those before and after pictures they're so fond of using on makeover shows? This was our "before" picture.

My family. Mom, before she lost it. Dad, before he got locked up. Theresa flashing a the-world-is-my-oyster grin. Toddlers Marlene and Darlene, standing so close you'd think they were Siamese twins instead of fraternal. And me, gap-toothed and pigtailed.

Aunt Leslie had taken the picture. She hadn't smoked so much pot back then, so her hand had been steady, and there isn't a hint of fuzziness in the photograph. She captured us all; she commemorated that moment with unflinching clarity.

I think that's why the picture makes me so sad. Because while a quick glance might seem to reveal a picture-perfect family on a summer day, a closer look would reveal that it was the beginning of everything falling apart.

Mom's eyes aren't focused. Dad's wearing a gold chain around his neck that he shouldn't have been able to afford on a store clerk's salary. Theresa's smile is strained. Marlene and Darlene are too close, each hanging on to the other like she's a lifeline.

And me? I look at this picture and try to remember what I was thinking that day, what I was feeling. But I can't. I'm eleven in the picture, but I can't even remember it being taken. It's as though I'm looking at a rendering of someone else's life.

Around three in the morning, as I tossed and turned in bed, waiting for my alarm to go off so that I could get up, God made his suggestion.

"You should take me with you."

"What?"

"I can help."

"How?" It wasn't as though he was big or strong enough to actually pull the trigger. That unpleasant task fell fully on my shoulders.

"I can offer moral support." He actually managed to sound sincere for a change, instead of sneering.

I considered the offer. I could use all the help I could get. I was already worrying that I wouldn't be able to go through with it, even though I knew I was a dead woman if I didn't.

"And," God sweetened the pot, "I could be your lookout."

"My lookout?"

"Uh huh. I could wait on the trail and let you know when he's coming. But it'll cost you."

I rolled my eyes. I'd known this was coming. There are no free rides in life.

"You have to get me some live crickets."

The promise of bugs seemed a small price to pay, so I agreed.

A few hours later, not long after the sun had risen, I perched behind a boulder. Gun in hand, I waited for Alfonso Cifelli to come take his daily photograph. While I waited, I stared at another picture. This one had been taken only a week or so before the accident. Katie grinned up at me, a drop of chocolate cake icing on her nose and a devilish gleam in her eyes.

"Did you disable the safety?" God asked from where he was sunning himself on the rock.

"For the third time, yes."

"Excuse me for making sure your I's are crossed and your T's are dotted."

"I's dotted and T's crossed," I corrected.

"Excellent! You *are* paying attention after all."

"Of course I am. Listen, I know you're working on your tan and all, but shouldn't you be going down the path, getting ready to do your job?"

He stretched lazily. "You don't have to snap at me."

"Excuse me for being on edge." I shoved Katie's photo in the pocket of my jeans.

"As long as you do exactly as your murder mentor instructed, everything will be fine." With a flick of his tail, Godzilla scampered off the rock and disappeared down the trail.

I hoped he was right. I hoped Patrick was right. This had to work. It had to. Katie's life depended on it.

"Here he comes!" God chirped.

I swallowed convulsively, as my stomach churned. I tightened my grip on the gun. It was heavier than I remembered.

I pressed my back into the boulder as Alfonso Cifelli's footfalls approached.

"Ready or not, here he comes!" God called.

I didn't answer him. I waited, replaying Patrick's shooting instructions in my mind. *Breathe in, focus along the sights, and as you exhale, you're going to squeeze the trigger. You're not going to yank on it or jerk it. You're just going to squeeze with steady, firm pressure.* I imagined it was him standing behind me, offering support, instead of the rock.

Alfonso stopped at the cliff's edge. I understood why he'd chosen this place. The view was breathtaking. I'd admired it myself before I'd settled into my hiding place.

"What are you waiting for?" God asked, scrambling up beside me. "He's not going to stand there with his back to you forever."

I knew that. I knew that all it would take to end a man's life was three breaths and one bullet. What I didn't know was whether I could do it.

"If you don't do it now, the job will go to someone else," God reminded me. "Then what will happen to Katie?"

There's nothing more inspiring than a reptile doling out a guilt trip. I stirred just to get him to shut up. Swallowing hard, I willed my body to move. Slowly, carefully I crept out from behind the rock.

Focused on fiddling with his camera, my mark gave no indication he even knew I was there.

Three breaths and then I'd fire.

"Just do it!" God urged.

Despite the pounding of my heart and the pressure building in my chest, I made myself take my first breath.

I wondered if this was how my dad had felt before he pulled the trigger. I forced the thought away. I wouldn't be distracted by thoughts of him. I couldn't afford to compare myself to him. Not now.

Exhaling shakily, I inhaled again.

"Thatta girl!" God applauded. He was really taking this support thing a bit too far. I wondered if my mother had her own cheering section for her delusions. Maybe Aunt Susan was right. Maybe I was just like her.

Behind me on the trail, a twig snapped.

Like an idiot, I turned to see what had made the noise.

So did Alfonso Cifelli.

By the time I'd realized my mistake and turned back toward him, he'd seen me. He'd seen the gun. He didn't seem afraid.

"If it isn't the bitch from the hospital." He stepped toward me.

"Stay r-right there!" I ordered. Even I didn't think I sounded convincing, so I wasn't surprised when he kept coming toward me. I backed away from him on rubbery legs.

"Shoot him!" God yelled.

"What are you going to do with that thing?" Cifelli asked derisively. "Do you really think you're going to shoot me? Do you even know how?"

"I d-do." But my body felt weak, and I was suddenly afraid I wasn't physically strong enough to pull the trigger. The gun was so heavy and my heart was pounding so hard. I broke into a cold sweat.

He was almost upon me. I could see the madness in his eyes. It distorted his face, revealing his inner monster. I knew that one of us going to die. I just didn't know which of us it would be.

He grinned smugly. "Knowing how to do something and actually doing something are two different things. I'm going to make you sorry we ever met."

He lunged at me.

"Shoot! Shoot!" God screamed.

I pulled the trigger. I didn't think about it. I didn't aim, or breathe, or smoothly squeeze. I just pulled the trigger. Twice.

You'd think that when you do something as monumental as shooting another human being it would be a shock to your system, but I felt . . . nothing.

Both slugs caught Alfonso Cifelli in the gut. Neither of them killed him immediately. Instead he fell to his knees about a foot in front of me.

I took a step back, watching as he swayed unsteadily before doing a face-plant into the dirt. I knew he still wasn't dead because he was making an awful gurgling noise, sort of like when you've only partially cleared a clogged drain.

"You did it!" God stood on his hind legs, clapping.

I didn't feel victorious. I didn't feel anything. Except queasy. Skipping breakfast had been a wise move, otherwise I was sure I'd be bent over puking. Instead I just stood there feeling nauseated.

I kept remembering Patrick's admonishment that I had to be sure Alfonso was dead. After he'd stopped gurgling and his body had gone limp, I knelt and placed a hand on his neck, feeling for a pulse. I couldn't find one. Not that that meant much. Half the time I can't even find my own pulse.

I rolled Alfonso over and laid my head on his chest, listening for a heartbeat. There wasn't one.

"Now what?" God asked.

Patrick had hypothesized that the cops wouldn't do much of an investigation into the death of someone as scummy as Alfonso Cifelli, but I kept remembering Life Lesson One: Don't get caught.

I decided to dump the body.

With a lot of straining, grunting, and cursing I dragged the corpse over to the edge of the cliff and pushed him over. As I watched the body plummet, it felt like I was the one who was falling.

Chapter Twenty-One

God is a backseat driver. Or in this case, a front-seat driver. After killing Alfonso Cifelli, I made the mistake of buckling Godzilla's terrarium into the front passenger seat for the ride home. He second-guessed every turn I made, every touch of the brake. I was ready to kill the lizard by the time we got back to the apartment.

I almost did, when I dropped his enclosure the second I walked into my place, but that wasn't my fault.

"Hey, Mags."

Expecting to walk into an empty apartment, I shrieked and almost let go of the cage as I registered the outline of a man standing just feet away.

"Don't you dare drop me!" God boomed.

"Easy! Easy. It's just me." Patrick said. He'd been examining the family photographs lining the wall when I walked in. "I didn't mean to startle you."

"Well you did!" I shoved the glass container into his chest. "What the hell are you doing here?"

His face revealed nothing as he stood there examining me, running his gaze over me from head-to-toe and then back up again.

"Have him put me down," God demanded.

"Put that down on the kitchen table." Somehow giving an order to the redhead helped to slow my racing heart.

Moving toward the kitchen, Patrick peered inside the clear box. "You brought it with you?"

"Inform him that I am a him, not an it."

"Him," I muttered. "He's a him."

Carefully placing the enclosure on the table, Patrick bent over so that he was eye-to-eye with the little guy. "He looks pissed."

"What do you expect? You called him an *it*."

Straightening, Patrick stared at me. I recognized that wary expression. It was the look people gave my mother the moment they realized she's bat-shit crazy. I hated that look when it was directed at her. I hated it even more now that I was caught in its spotlight.

"That was a brilliant move," God drawled haughtily.

I had to bite my tongue to keep from telling him to shut the hell up. If I did that, Patrick would know for sure I'd lost it. Instead I did my best to sound outraged. "What the hell are you doing here?"

"I was worried about you."

"Worried about me?"

"It went okay?" He moved toward the kitchen sink and turned on the water.

"If by *okay* you mean that a man's dead, than yes, it went okay."

"And you're okay?" He wet the edge of my dish towel.

"Well, if you mean by *okay* that I've just killed a man and haven't gone running to the police to confess my crime, then yes, I'm okay."

"Did he hurt you?"

Shuddering as I remembered the destruction in his eyes as he lunged at me, I shook my head.

Turning off the water, Patrick crossed the room so that he was standing right in front of me. Grabbing my chin, he tilted my head up so that he could see my face.

Cold fear skittered down my spine. Now that I'd done his dirty work, was he going to kill me? Like an idiot, I'd stashed the gun under the front seat of my car. I didn't have anything to defend myself with.

He raised his other hand toward my face. He was going to smother me! I knew I should move away, fight back, but I couldn't. I couldn't even breathe.

He dabbed the wet towel along my jaw line. I hadn't been aware that my face was burning, until I felt the cool water against it. The chilled dampness snapped me out of my near catatonia. Knocking down his hand holding the soaked cloth, I tried to spin away, but he tightened his grip on my chin. The pressure was insistent, but not painful.

"You've still got some on you." He wiped at my fiery cheek.

"Some what?"

"Blood." He whispered the syllable as though he somehow knew that would lessen the force of the blow to my psyche.

"B-blood?"

"On your face and in your hair." He swabbed at my face a bit more vigorously. "It's not too bad."

"Oh yes," God piped up. "I'd been meaning to tell you about that. It looks like you practically bathed in the stuff."

Screaming, I shoved Patrick away and made a mad dash for my bathroom so that I could look in the mirror.

God had exaggerated. It wasn't as bad as he'd said. On the other hand, Patrick had definitely downplayed the mess I'd made. Cifelli's blood covered almost half my face and matted my hair. Basically I looked like a horror-movie reject.

I retched into the sink, but since I still hadn't eaten, I wasn't actually sick. It was pretty much the only break I'd caught.

"It'll come off." Patrick was standing in the doorway of my bathroom watching me dry heave. Yeah, the day really wasn't going my way.

Without thinking (or undressing) I jumped into my shower and turned the water on full blast. It was ice cold. "Fuck!" I screamed. "Fu—"

My air supply was cut off by a hand slapped over my mouth. My scream was stifled too.

"You can't go around screaming, Mags. Neighbors remember that kind of thing." Standing in the shower behind me, Patrick scolded gently before taking his hand away.

"I have to get it off!" I whimpered through chattering teeth, raising my face into the stream of water. I wasn't sure if I was shivering because I was cold or upset.

"I know, Sweetheart. I know."

"This is all your fault!"

I felt every muscle in his body tighten, but he didn't argue. "How do you figure that?"

"Goddamn Life Lesson Two. Dead is dead. I listened for his heartbeat. That's how I got his blood on me."

"Good girl. Nice to know you were paying attention." Reaching around me, he snatched up my bottle of shampoo and squirted some on top of my head.

"Hey!" I spluttered as soap got in my eye. "What the hell do you think you're doing?"

"Washing your hair."

You know all those movies where a man is washing a woman's hair and it looks like one of the sexiest things ever? They're all a lie. Trust me, there is nothing remotely sexy about having a man standing behind you, rubbing your scalp like he's scrubbing a stain in the kitchen sink.

The water warmed as we stood there, soaking into our clothes. Suds flowed down into my eyes. It stung, but I didn't cry. I couldn't.

"You're going to blind me," I muttered. "Just let me do it myself."

Squeezing my eyes tightly shut, I raised my hands to my hair and began methodically rinsing the lather away. I was barely aware of Patrick stepping out of the shower and leaving the bathroom.

The only thing I could hear over the roar of the pounding water was God singing. In Italian.

I wondered whether it would be difficult to drown a lizard.

Chapter Twenty-Two

"You lack empathy."

I glared at Harry while I counted to ten to keep from telling him that he lacked hair, a personality, and the basics of dental hygiene.

He was unaware that I was giving him a look that could kill. He was too busy studying his copy of the printed-out report he'd given me.

I was having a crappy day, even by my standards, which, let's face it, aren't set all that high. First I'd killed Alfonso Cifelli and gotten his blood smeared all over me, then the damn lizard harangued me mercilessly and Patrick practically gave me a heart attack. Now, to make my misery complete, I'd been called into my boss's office for my quarterly review. It wasn't even lunchtime yet.

"Yes, you definitely lack empathy." Harry clucked like a disapproving schoolmarm. "There will be no way I'm going to be able to approve you for a raise on your hire anniversary if you don't improve those empathy scores."

I really wished Patrick hadn't taken the gun I'd used to kill Alfonso. It would have come in handy right about now. I knew damn well that Life Lesson One was: Don't get caught, but eradicating Harry might be worth it.

"Do you understand what I'm telling you?"

"But my other numbers are off the charts," I argued. "My call volume. My accuracy. My problem-solving."

Harry shook his head sadly. "But we can't tolerate employees of Insuring the Future being heartless."

"I'm not heartless!" Sure I hadn't shed a tear for Theresa or Katie, and I hadn't felt much of anything when I'd pulled the trigger and ended Cifelli, but that didn't mean I was a cold-hearted bitch. Did it?

"All you have to do is stick with the script, and your scores will go up." Standing, Harry walked around from behind his desk to sit in the chair beside me. "And if you could refrain from calling people stupid . . ."

"People *are* stupid. If you're talking about that call last week with the guy who left his keys in the ignition of his car while he ran into the sporting goods store to buy a new nine iron . . . he *is* stupid."

"But it's not our place to tell the customers that."

"His kid was strapped into the carseat in the back seat! He left him and the key in the car so he could get a new golf club, and then he has the nerve to complain that the jackass who stole his car . . . and his kid, let's not forget the kid was in there too . . . the jackass smashed the front fender when the police chased him down."

"Our job is to take the claim. It's not our place to judge."

"If you ask me, somebody should have taken the nine

iron to the guy's skull!"

"That's not my concern. All I'm worried about is the fact that you called him stupid. According to the transcript of that call, Mr. Balch said, 'Isn't that awful?' And you replied, 'Awful? No. Stupid? Yes.' You can't go around saying that kind of stuff to customers. If you do, I'll have no choice but to let you go."

Harry let what he perceived to be a threat hang in the air. Personally, I thought getting let go from this hellhole would be a blessing.

Leaning in close, Harry laid a hand on my knee. I eyed the stapler on his desk. I was pretty sure I could use it to both shatter his creeping fingers and bash in his head.

"I know you've been through a lot, Maggie." Sitting this close, his pepperoni breath threatened to trigger my gag reflex. "That's why I'm willing to overlook this."

He squeezed my knee.

I envisioned grabbing the stapler and swinging it through the air. I closed my eyes as I imagined the satisfying thunk it would make as it bounced off my boss's skull. It made me smile.

"I'm glad you appreciate that I'm looking out for you."

Jolted out of my pleasant daydream, my eyes snapped open.

"Just try to remember when someone tells you that something has happened that was upsetting to them, you're supposed to say, 'I'm so sorry to hear that.' Let me hear you say it."

I stared at him.

"Go ahead. Say it."

"I'm so sorry to hear that." My delivery was flatter than a pancake.

"Okay. Okay. Needs a little work, but you've got the general idea. Let's practice a couple of scenarios. I'll be the customer."

"Do we have to?" I was thinking another root canal would be preferable to role-playing with Harry.

"You're my responsibility, Maggie. I want you to be the best that you can be."

I'd have been willing to bet he'd learned this lousy pep talk at one of his manager-training meetings.

"Oh," he said in a falsetto that would have given Mickey Mouse a run for his money. "I'm so upset. My car was rear ended."

"Really?"

"No! You're not supposed to say *really*. You're supposed to say . . ." He waited for me to fill in the blank.

Desperate to get away from him, I did my best to sound sympathetic. "I'm so sorry to hear that."

"Better. Much better! Let's try another." He looked at me expectantly, like he was waiting for me to indicate that I was into this stupid game we were playing.

"Okay."

"I had a little too much to drink, and I crashed my car into my house."

This time I didn't miss a beat. "I'm so sorry to hear that."

The vermin actually clapped his hands. "Now, for good measure, you could always add, *Are you ok?* Let's try one more."

"If you insist." It wasn't like I had any choice in the matter. If it was up to me, he'd be lying on the floor of this office with his mouth stapled shut.

"I ran a red light and mowed down an old lady trying to cross the street."

I swallowed convulsively. Sadly, I'd had a call just like that a couple of weeks earlier. I knew for certain I'd offered no empathy to that driver. This one was the ultimate test. Forcing myself to smile, I said, "I'm so sorry to hear that. Are you okay?"

"Excellent! Now just remember that when you're back on the phones." He patted my knee.

I stood and walked out before I made a grab for the stapler.

—#—

At lunch Armani offered to help me perfect my bullshitting skills. "Pretend it's a game," she encouraged, pushing a peanut butter and jelly sandwich across the table toward me. "Imagine you're an actress, giving the performance of your life."

I looked from her to the sandwich, unsure of which made less sense.

"Try it," she urged.

I picked up the sandwich.

"Not that! Try the line."

"Why?"

"Why? Cuz I'm not going to let you get your Chiquita-lite ass fired. I'd miss your swollen face."

"Sullen."

"What?"

"Not swollen. You'd miss my sullen face."

"Damn right I would!"

"Is that why you brought me the sandwich, to sweeten my disposition?"

"Naah . . . that there is a bribe."

"A bribe for what?" I asked even though I knew I wasn't going to like the answer. I tried not to think about what it meant that my friend thought I could be bribed with a sandwich.

"I need you to go shopping with me."

"For what?" The last time we'd done the retail thing she'd taken me to a sex shop where she insisted on . . . sampling everything, much to the amusement of the clerk and my humiliation.

"Bibs and clothes. Baby shit."

"You're pregnant?" I gasped.

Armani threw back her head and laughed. "I'm as likely to get pregnant as you are to get laid any time soon."

I BARELY MADE IT through the work day, and all I really wanted to do once I was done was to go home and sleep. Instead I drove to the hospital. While there under the pretense of visiting my beloved niece Katie, I would talk to the mob boss Tony/Anthony Delveccio. I couldn't wait to tell him I'd done the dirty deed and he had no reason to worry about his ne'er-do-well son-in-law ever again, and every reason to hand over a hundred grand.

Of course, my life being the clusterfuck that it is,

things didn't exactly turn out that way.

Before I even passed through the doors of the hospital, I heard a familiar voice calling my name.

"Maggie, oh, Maggie, Darling!"

Hoping that this was just another of my ill-timed hallucinations, I turned around slowly.

Nope, not a hallucination, just a nightmare come true. Aunt Loretta came tottering toward me on her five-inch stilettos.

"I'm so glad you're here!"

That made one of us.

"A terrible thing happened, just terrible." As she grew closer, I could see that her mascara had run down her face. She'd been crying.

Something had happened to Katie.

Something terrible.

The world around me tilted and swirled. Overcome by sudden vertigo, it was a struggle to remain standing.

Katie.

A shadow fell over everything, and I was suddenly cold.

Not Katie.

My sisters were gone and now my niece.

I'd never in my life fainted, but I was pretty sure I was going to. Maybe if I was lucky I'd hit my head as I fell and would die too.

"It's poor Templeton!"

I swayed unsteadily as I tried to make sense of what she was saying.

"So much blood. So very much blood!"

She charged into me, almost knocking us both to the ground. "I'm so glad you're here, Maggie," she gasped on a hiccupped sob.

"What?" I had no idea what she was trying to tell me. I'd thought she'd meant something had happened to Katie, but now I wasn't so sure.

"Templeton's hurt!" Loretta wailed.

"What happened?" Now that I knew for sure that Katie was okay, well, as okay as someone in a persistent vegetative state can be, I had to sort out why Aunt Loretta was so upset. And she was upset. This wasn't her being overly dramatic for attention. Her whole body was shaking. Hugging her tightly, I led her to a bench beside the hospital doors. "Take your time, Aunt Loretta. Just tell me what happened."

"We were . . . getting frisky," she sniffled. "And I was on top and—"

Ewww. The image scarred me more than that of Alfonso Cifelli keeling over in front of me. I hurriedly interrupted her before she could give me any more details about her lovers' tryst. "You said something about blood?"

"The portrait above my bed, the one in that heavy oak frame, you know the one."

I nodded. I'd never known anyone else who kept an oil painting of themselves hanging in their bedroom.

"It fell and broke Templeton's nose!" She cried. "So much blood!"

I almost started to laugh hysterically. Here I'd been thinking Katie was dead, and all that had happened was the rat had gotten his snout dented. I didn't think Aunt Loretta would take kindly to my being amused by her boyfriend's fate, so I fell back on my professional training.

"I'm so sorry to hear that. Are you okay?" There was no way my aunt could say I wasn't empathetic.

Chapter Twenty-Three

I SAT WITH Aunt Loretta for almost thirty minutes. That was when my ration of sympathy pretty much ran out. Then we went inside and found Templeton waiting to leave. He'd been patched up and had his discharge papers signed. Even I felt a twinge of sympathy for him, when I saw the size of the bandage they'd used on him.

"That must hurt." Sometimes my brilliant observations amaze even me.

"My pride's the thing that took a beating." He sounded as though he had the world's worst head cold.

"He hadn't finished getting dressed when the paramedics arrived," Loretta confided. "All he was wearing were his hot pink LOVE MACHINE boxer shorts."

"Too much information, Aunt Loretta. It does answer the age old boxers-or-briefs question, though."

Templeton chuckled. At least I think that's what the noise—like a pig snuffling out wild truffles—was supposed to be.

It's hard not to like someone who deals with a painful and embarrassing situation with humor. I found myself wondering if my instant dislike of the man had been misguided. Maybe he wasn't all that bad.

Finally, once the two love birds were safely on their way home, I went looking for Delveccio. He wasn't in his grandson's room, or the waiting area, so I took a chance he was in the cafeteria and headed that way. Okay, okay, I was hedging my bet. Even if he wasn't there, I'd probably find some chocolate pudding. A treat I richly deserved after the day I'd had.

Delveccio was there. Sitting at a table in the back, studying what appeared to be the sports section of the newspaper. I tried to remember whether he'd been charged with illegal gambling as I headed toward him.

"Mind if I join you?"

He glanced up and blinked, as though he was surprised to see me. "It's a free country."

I slid into the seat opposite him, noticing for once he wasn't wearing his ubiquitous pinky ring. "How's your grandson?"

"No change." He folded up the paper and placed it on the table between us.

"Well, at least you'll be relieved to know that you won't have to worry about any . . . outside interference with his recovery." I'd never realized how much work it was for criminals to talk in euphemisms.

"I know."

"You do?" That caught me off guard.

"Of course. He told me."

"Of course." Patrick must have told him. "So when do I get paid?"

"You?" He squinted at me disbelievingly.

"Who else?"

"Are you trying to tell me that *you* took care of that particular problem?"

I really didn't understand why everyone seemed to be talking in riddles. "Yes. I fulfilled my end of the contract. When do I get paid?"

Leaning back in his chair, he considered me thoughtfully.

I gulped. It probably wasn't the best of ideas to shake down the head of a crime syndicate for money, but I was desperate. I needed that cash for Katie.

"Where'd you do it?"

"Washington Park."

"How?"

I glanced around nervously to make sure no one was within earshot. Leaning as close as I could, I whispered. "I shot him. Twice."

"The body hasn't been found."

"That's because I pushed him off a cliff."

"Why'd you do something like that?"

"For the sake of my alibi."

"Somebody's lying to me. I don't like to be lied to. It makes me angry. You wouldn't like me when I'm angry."

For a split second I imagined the mob boss morphing into the Incredible Hulk. It was not an attractive picture. "I'm not lying to you, Mr. Delveccio."

"Maybe, maybe not."

"Are you trying to welch on our deal?" I asked. I couldn't believe this. I'd killed a man, and I wasn't even going to get paid for my trouble? This was officially the crappiest day ever.

"Keep your voice down."

I fought for control. I couldn't afford to let my emotions get the best of me. Feelings led to screw-ups. I imagined my internal submarine hatches slamming shut, closing off my anger, my desperation. "Why are you doing this to me?"

"I'm a businessman, Miss Lee."

"Then why won't you honor our deal?"

"Because someone else has already claimed credit for the job."

Patrick. It had to be. "Son-of-a-bitch! I'll kill him!"

Delveccio tilted his head to the side. "You do that and you'll collect the fee for the first job."

"You mean that?"

"It's a deal." He extended his hand.

I shook it, but I wasn't happy about it. I'd made a deal with this particular devil before, and he'd screwed me. Besides, I wasn't so sure I could kill Patrick Mulligan even if he had stolen my money. Alfonso Cifelli was a monster. Killing him had been a service to society, but for the most part the redhead seemed to be a pretty decent guy.

"But either way," Delveccio said, "you're still on the hook for our mutual friend's cut."

I stared at him, trying to make sense of what he was

saying. Our only mutual acquaintance was Patrick. If he was getting paid for killing Alfonso, why the hell would he need a cut?

"You can't expect me to cover your expenses," he said. "It would be bad business."

"What expenses? What cut?"

"What? You didn't think he was helping you out of the goodness of his heart did you? That you were getting somethin' for nothin'? Trust me, lady, you're okay looking, but you're not the kind of a woman a pragmatic man like our friend is going to turn himself inside-out for, if ya know what I'm sayin'."

I nodded. That, at least, was something I could understand.

"So I told Gary the Gun that I wouldn't pay up until I had confirmation that the bastard Cifelli is dead."

I looked around nervously. There was no one else in the cafeteria. No one to eavesdrop on this bizarre conversation we were having. "Gary the Gun claimed credit?"

Delveccio nodded.

I did my best to ignore the surge of relief I felt, knowing that Patrick hadn't betrayed me and that I wouldn't have to kill him.

"Now, once the body turns up, I'm going to have to fork over the cash to Gary. Unless . . ."

"Unless I kill him first."

Delveccio nodded. "You do that, and you get the payoff that'll keep your niece here. How's she doing by the way?"

"She's the same."

"That's too bad." For a moment that mobster almost sounded human. "She's a cute kid."

"There's something I don't get."

"I get the feeling there's a lot you don't get, lady."

I couldn't argue with him there. "This Gary, he's a long-term employee of yours, isn't he?"

He shrugged. "More like a consultant. He gets paid to come in and do a job, and then he leaves."

"So why do you want him dead?"

Delveccio considered me thoughtfully. I got the impression people didn't usually ask him too many questions. "You ever hear of honor among thieves?"

I nodded. My father had ranted about it when his wheelman ratted him out and sent his murdering ass to prison.

"Everybody's gotta have a code to live by. Gary doesn't respect the code."

I nodded as though it made sense that a man who lived and breathed organized crime would be giving me a morality lecture.

"If I were you, I'd be real careful with this one. Gary's a sneaky bastard. And nasty. Guy's got a mean streak longer than any I've seen. And trust me, I've known more than my share of really bad guys. You get a chance to take him out, don't screw it up, or there will be hell to pay."

Since he was in a sharing mood, I decided to push my luck a little further. "Any suggestions on the best way to do it?"

He chuckled. "I like you. You're a ballsy one. That's not my department. Ask our mutual friend."

"The one I can't afford to pay."

"It's business, Miss Lee. Tell him if he doesn't help you, he's got zero chances of getting paid. He'll come around. It'll cost you, though. You should know that nothing in life that's worth having is free."

I nodded. That I understood.

"Remember, the clock is ticking. Once Cifelli's body has been found and officially identified, Gary the Gun will show up looking for his money. If you can't take care of him before then . . ."

The loaded, unspoken threat that he'd send Gary after me, hung in the air like a guillotine waiting to fall.

"It's my head that'll be on the chopping block."

"Exactly. I'm glad we understand each other."

He picked up his newspaper and began studying it again, letting me know I'd been dismissed.

I eyed the chocolate pudding on the far counter wistfully, but I knew there wasn't time for it. I had to figure out how to kill another man.

Chapter Twenty-Four

I WENT TO the pet store and bought live crickets for God. At least I could afford his cut for helping me to kill Cifelli. The bugs made a racket in the car on the way home. By the time I walked through the front door of my apartment, I was happy to feed them to the lizard, if only to get them to shut up.

"Ah, music to my ears!" God trilled as I stomped into the kitchen. "I can't tell you how pleased I am that you're honoring our deal."

"I told you I would," I muttered, shoving the lid of his habitat aside and dumping the jumping insects inside. Slamming the lid shut, I picked up the enclosure and carried it into the bedroom. Without being asked, I turned on *Wheel of Fortune* so that the lizard could eat in front of the TV.

"Very kind of you. Very kind indeed," he crowed, chowing down on one of the bugs.

"I realize that it can't be easy to live in a cage and rely on others for food and entertainment."

He cocked his head to the side and stared at me suspiciously. "What are you up to?"

"I'm being empathetic."

"Hmmmm."

I don't think he believed me, but he was too busy stuffing his face to pursue the matter further. I went back into the kitchen and heated myself a Lean Cuisine meal. I stood watching the plastic tray spinning in the microwave. When had my life turned into this? What could be more pathetic than subsisting on TV dinners and talking to one's pet?

Oh wait, I know: killing a man and having someone else claim the credit for it.

"How's Katie doing?" God called from the other room.

At least that's what I think he said. It came out a garbled mess. "I told you, no talking while your mouth is full."

Leaving my plastic dinner in the microwave, I shuffled into the bedroom and collapsed on the bed.

"My mouf—isn't full," the lizard replied. "It's only half full."

"I'm not in the mood for your smart-ass shit," I muttered.

"Why not? What's wrong? We took care of that distasteful business this morning, earning—"

"*We?*" I asked incredulously. "I don't remember you doing any of the heavy lifting, buddy."

He ignored my interruption. "—the money to pay for Katie's care. You should be overjoyed, but instead you're moping around like a kid who's had her bicycle stolen."

"This is much worse than that." I knew what it felt like to have your bicycle stolen. In my case, the culprit had been my father, who'd pawned it for some cash so that he could bet on a racehorse. I still remember how sucky that felt, but this was definitely worse.

"What are you going on about?" Apparently sated, he leaned back and patted his bulging belly.

"I didn't get the money."

"What do you mean you didn't get the money?" The lizard sounded alarmed.

"Someone else claimed credit for . . . you know."

"Who? That sneaky redhead?"

"I thought you liked him. I thought you said he was wise and I should listen to him."

He glared at me. "Is that your pathetic attempt to be clever?"

I shook my head. "Another hitman . . . hitperson, Gary the Gun."

"How? Why?"

"How the hell should I know?" I exploded. "It wasn't like I was there when it happened."

"So what's going to happen to Katie?" When the lizard wasn't complaining about his food, he seemed to have a one-track mind regarding my niece. I decided his concern for her well-being was his one redeeming quality.

"I can get the money."

"How?"

Sighing heavily, I burrowed my face in my pillow. All I wanted to do was sleep.

"How, Maggie?"

"If I kill Gary before Delveccio pays him."

"Which is when?"

"When Cifelli's body turns up. Once Delveccio has proof that Alfonso is really dead, he'll hand over the cash."

"So then that's what we'll do. We need a plan."

"We?"

"You're not in this alone, Maggie. I'll help you."

It felt oddly reassuring to know that I didn't have to shoulder all the responsibility for this mess.

Even if the other shoulders lightening the load were awfully small.

Chapter Twenty-Five

IT WAS GOD's idea to call Patrick. Personally, I wasn't too enthused about the suggestion, since I was afraid he'd demand his cut of the fee Delveccio owed me. A cut he'd failed to mention throughout our dealings. It made me worry about the other secrets he must be hiding.

Patrick told me to meet him at an address on the other side of town at midnight, so I curled up and napped a few hours before our rendezvous. I didn't even have to set an alarm. God woke me at 11:15, just as he'd promised.

Driving to the address Patrick had provided, I was surprised to find myself outside a little boutique. Even in the dark I could see sparkly party dresses displayed in the window.

"Crap!" I must have gotten the address wrong. I shouldn't have been surprised. I'd screwed everything else up. Frustrated, I kicked the front tire of my car.

"Did it do something to offend you?" Patrick's familiar voice seemed to come out of nowhere.

I whirled around. All I saw was shadows. "If your shin was handy, I would have kicked that."

Stepping out of the darkness, he approached me warily. "Why's that?"

"You never mentioned I was going to owe you a cut."

He shrugged. "I figured our boss had explained it to you."

"He hadn't!"

"Let's go inside and talk about this." Placing his hand in the small of my back, he propelled me toward the store.

"I don't have your money." If he was going to get angry at me, I preferred for it to happen out here on the deserted street instead of inside the empty building.

"We'll work it out. Come on inside."

I stopped in my tracks. "We can't work it out. I can't pay you."

His palm slid from the small of my back up to the base of my neck. I stopped breathing.

"I got a pizza. Do you like pizza?"

"Everybody likes pizza."

"C'mon." Stepping in front of me, he led the way down an alley that ran parallel to the store.

I hesitated, debating whether I should go after him or run for my life. I ended up following. The man knew where I lived and worked. There wasn't much chance I could hide from him successfully for long.

Unlocking a door, he guided me inside the building. He switched on an interior light. To my surprise we didn't end up in the shop or a storeroom. We stepped into a small, studio apartment, complete with a couch and a big-screen TV.

"Welcome to my man cave," Patrick joked as he grabbed a pizza box off the kitchen counter. "I don't usually have visitors. Hell, I've never had anyone here before, so I'm afraid we're kind of limited in terms of seating space. The couch is it." He thrust the pizza box at me. It was still warm, and the aroma wafting out of it was heavenly. "Have a seat on the couch."

Obediently, I sat on the sofa and balanced the cardboard container on my knees. I watched as Patrick grabbed a handful of paper napkins and a stack of paper plates. I wondered how many people he was expecting to feed with this single pie.

"Beer or soda?"

"Soda, please."

Grabbing a couple of bottles, he joined me on the couch. "I wasn't sure what you'd like, so I got half plain and half with olives."

"Olives are my favorite."

He grinned. "I kinda guessed that."

"How?"

"I am a detective you know." Sliding an olive-laden slice onto a pile of plates, he chuckled. "You have like six different kinds of olives in your fridge."

I'd forgotten he'd peered into my fridge during his unannounced nocturnal visit. I wondered what else he'd noticed.

"I know I owe you, but I can't pay you."

"So you've said." He took a bite of pizza and chewed it thoughtfully. "How come? You don't think I earned it?" There was no challenge in his tone, just quiet curiosity.

"Delveccio didn't pay me."

Putting down his pizza with deliberate carefulness, his eyes narrowed at that, his features suddenly growing hard. "Why not?"

I hung my head, suddenly ashamed by my failure to collect the money owed to me.

"Talk to me, Mags." Cupping my chin with the tips of his fingers, he applied gentle but insistent pressure, forcing me to look up at him. "What's going on?"

I shook my head, causing his hand to slide up my cheek. It felt so much like a lover's caress that my breath caught, and my eyes drifted closed. Instinctively, I leaned closer to him, wanting nothing more than to lose myself in his touch.

"Mags." There was no mistaking the desire in the usually unflappable detective's tone.

My eyes fluttered open as he swept his thumb over my lower lip. I'd never in my life wanted to be kissed as much I did in that moment. And he wanted it, too. I could feel it in the possessive weight of his hand on my face and see it in his eyes.

I waited for him to close the small gap between us.

But he didn't.

Instead he pulled his hand away, as though burnt by a flame. Leaning away, he picked up his pizza. "Why didn't Delveccio pay you?"

The slap of rejection had me sitting back in my seat,

trying to make sense of what had just happened. Or, more importantly, what hadn't happened.

"Delveccio must have given you a reason."

"Gary the Gun claimed credit before I got to the hospital tonight," I mumbled, suddenly numb.

"Oh crap." He frowned at his slice. "Bad news. I told you that guy is bad news."

"But there is good news." I sounded way too chipper.

Patrick eyed me suspiciously. "Oh yeah? What's that?"

"If I kill Gary before Delveccio pays him, the Cifelli money is mine."

"That bastard!" Tossing his plate of pizza on the floor, the redhead jumped to his feet and began pacing.

"If you help me come up with a plan—"

"Are you out of your mind?" For the first time since I'd known him, Patrick seemed to be on the verge of losing his grip on that constantly cool façade of his. It probably should have frightened me, but I was fascinated. "Gary's going to know you're pissed about him taking your money. He'll be expecting you to come after him. He'll be ready."

"So what am I supposed to do? Just let it go. I can't do that. I can't let Katie down. I can't . . . I've lost them all . . . everybody . . . I can't . . . I didn't save . . ." My fear of failure had my words tumbling on top of each other like the cars of a train in a wreck.

"Who have you lost?"

The question was asked with a deceptive casualness that morphed my panic into anger almost instantaneously. He wasn't asking a polite question; he was forcing me to address an issue I couldn't bear to examine. "Are you really going to pretend you don't know, *Detective*?"

My sarcasm could have peeled paint, and he flinched.

"I didn't mean . . ."

"What?" I spat. "You didn't mean to pretend that you don't know that my father is rotting in prison or that Theresa died in that car accident?"

Patrick said nothing. He stayed very still, watching me carefully.

His reaction, or, more accurately, lack of reaction, enraged me. Unable to sit still, I jumped to my feet, balling my hands into fists. "Or maybe you'd like me to believe that when you were checking up on me, you didn't find out that my mother is locked up in the loony bin."

"Take it easy."

"Is it in the official police report that when my younger sister Darlene was taken by the animal who eventually killed her, I was too busy watching my mom, making sure she didn't get into trouble? I should have been watching the kids but I was too busy baby-sitting my parent. Does it say that? Does it say that it's my fault?" I was screaming at a man who could easily kill me, but I didn't care.

Instead of retreating, he took a step toward me. "None of what happened is your fault, Mags." The pity in his voice softened his words to just a whisper.

I couldn't decide whether it made me want to cry on his shoulder or punch him. My emotions were getting the better of me. I couldn't afford to let that happen. I hadn't gotten through everything I'd endured by indulging in freakouts. Taking a deep breath, I made an abrupt turn in the conversation, bringing us back to the business at hand. "You have to help me kill Gary."

Patrick halted mid-stride. "I can't."

"You mean you won't." Suddenly deflated, I sank back down onto the couch.

"Alfonso Cifelli was a thug. Gary the Gun is a killer. Chances are he'd get to us before we ever got near him."

"So you're afraid of him?"

"Damn right, and you should be too!"

It occurred to me that if a cop/hitman was scared of this guy, and a mob boss wanted him whacked, that I was probably going after a genuine badass. "I'm in over my head, aren't I?"

Sitting down heavily on the seat beside me, Patrick buried his head in his hands. "Sweetheart, you're in so deep, you're not going to be able to figure out which way is up."

Chapter Twenty-Six

I MAY HAVE felt like crap when I showed up for work the next morning at Insuring the Future, but Armani looked even worse than how I was feeling. Her inner Chiquita had gone into hiding. There was no spark to her as she limped past my desk. She didn't even acknowledge my deadpan greeting of "Good morning."

Something was really wrong, but I didn't have the time or energy to wonder what that might be. It took all of my concentration just to get through my calls. I'm pretty sure I forgot to say, "I'm so sorry to hear that" on multiple occasions, but I really didn't give a shit. All I cared about was figuring out a way to get Gary the Gun before he got me.

Patrick had made it abundantly clear that I was on my own with this one. I'd asked him for a gun, and he'd refused, saying I'd just end up getting myself killed. So I was all alone. Except, of course, for God, who'd insisted I leave the TV set to the true-crime station, in the hopes that he'd find us some inspiration.

I'd taken a quick inventory of the possible weapons in my home. My choices seemed limited to kitchen knives and copious amounts of pain relievers. And of course I had my car . . . maybe I could just run him over. Sure, I probably wouldn't get away with it, but how much time could someone with no criminal record get for vehicular manslaughter? At least I'd be alive and I'd have gotten the money for Katie. Prison couldn't be that much worse than Insuring the Future.

"Have lunch with me," Armani ordered as soon as our lunch hour rolled around. Something was definitely wrong. She had no sparkle, no edge.

We walked over to our favorite picnic table in silence, a first for us, since my work-friend usually chattered incessantly. I noticed that her limp seemed more pronounced than usual.

I was the one that broke the oppressive quiet. "Are you okay? Are you sick or something?"

Lowering her butt onto the bench with more care than usual, Armani shook her head. I wasn't sure if she was signaling that she wasn't okay, or that she wasn't sick.

"You're freaking me out. What's going on?"

"You don't believe."

"Believe what?" I sat on the seat opposite her.

"That I'm psychic."

"Is that what this is about? You're pissed at me?"

"I'm not pissed. I'm worried about you."

This conversation wasn't making any sense. I tried to get a look at her face, but her expression was hidden behind the sheet of her dark, glossy hair. "You've lost me."

"The Scrabble tiles, all that crap, it's a gimmick, but you have to believe me that I have a gift."

"A gift?"

"An ability. Sometimes I sense things before they happen." She pushed her hair off her face so that she could stare at me intently, as though that would make me believe her. "The problem is that I usually interpret things incorrectly. Actually always. I always misinterpret what I've seen. It isn't until afterwards that things make sense, but by then it's too late."

I stared at the woman before me. I didn't know this stranger. It was like all the badass bravado that made her unique had been sucked right out of her; only her meek, mousy shell was left. No doubt if she'd had two hands she would have been wringing them. Instead she was compulsively shredding a leaf that had the misfortune of ending up on the tabletop.

"I'm sorry, Armani, but I'm having trouble following you."

"I had a dream."

"Seriously? You're this bummed out over a dream?"

"But before I tell you about last night's dream, I have to tell you about the one I had the day before . . . before your accident." She looked away as though she felt guilty.

My spine stiffened. Had she known what was going to happen and failed to warn me? Was Theresa dead and Katie in a coma because of her?

My logical self dismissed the notion, but the part of me that needed to make sense of the horror was quick to latch onto the idea that Armani was somehow to blame for all my problems. It would be a hell of a lot easier to hold her responsible for my misfortune than to just accept that it was a cruel twist of fate.

"The dream was about a spider web," she said.

I exhaled. I hadn't even realized I'd been holding my breath. I almost laughed out loud at my foolishness. Had I really expected her to reveal some sort of psychic vision that had foretold of a drunk running a red light and colliding with us?

"Does that make any sense to you? A spider web?"

I shook my head automatically, but something tickled the back of my consciousness.

"There was music, singing, I think, and the web was silver, but then it turned green, and then red. The music stopped, and it broke apart, all those strands, they just snapped."

I was starting to think that Armani had just snapped. I could see no other reason why she'd be so upset by a dream. I told her as much. "It was just a dream, Armani. Maybe you're suffering from arachnophobia or something, but it was just a dream."

"Iraq-what?"

"Arachnophobia. A fear of spiders."

"You think I'm afraid of bugs?" She said it like it was the craziest thing she'd ever heard.

I refrained from pointing out that getting upset about a dream about a cobweb was one of the nuttiest things I'd heard in a while . . . and I was conversing with a lizard on a regular basis.

"I'm not scared of bugs. You need to listen to my story."

She pounded her good hand on the table for emphasis.

"Okay, okay, I'm listening." I was already on the bad side of Gary the Gun and on the verge of pissing off Tony/Anthony Delveccio. I wasn't in any position to cross Armani Vasquez.

"Okay, so the web breaks apart, but then the weirdest thing happens, it re-spins itself."

I found myself asking, "With or without a spider?"

"Without. It re-forms into a crystal version. I didn't know what it meant at the time. I would have told you if I did. I should have told you."

I could tell by the intensity of her gaze and the uncharacteristic pleading note in her voice that she was looking for some kind of absolution from me. "It's okay," I told her. And it was. After all it was just a dream. A dream that didn't make any sense.

She pulled paper out of the pocket of her pants. "When I woke up, I drew it. The crystal spider web." She tried to smooth out the sheet, a tough task with one hand and a steady breeze blowing.

Reaching across the table I helped her. "Hey, this is pretty good." I hadn't known that my favorite Chiquita was an artist, but her sketch, done in pen, proved she was.

"You don't recognize it?'

I couldn't name it, but something niggled at me like an itch demanding to be scratched. It did look familiar. "Don't all spider webs look pretty much the same?"

"No two webs are exactly alike."

"I'm pretty sure that goes for snowflakes, not webs."

"Webs too."

I shrugged, conceding her point.

She pulled another piece of paper from her pocket. This one was a folded-up newspaper article. "I should have told you. Warned you. I hope you can forgive me." She extended the clipping across the table.

A chill skittered down my spine as I took it from her. Slowly, with a sense of foreboding I unfolded the paper.

I gasped when I saw the spider web.

Of course it wasn't really a spider web, rather it was glass that had cracked, its splintering crystalline lines spinning out in a web-like pattern. It also happened to be a photograph of the windshield of Theresa's car.

The newspaper clipping consisted of the picture of the wreck and the headline: DEADLY ACCIDENT CLAIMS THREE – TWO OTHERS GRAVELY INJURED.

The remembered terror of the accident welled up within me like a black cloud of smoke, blurring my vision and cutting off my air supply.

"Are you okay?" Reaching across the table, Armani shook my arm as though she was an on-stage-hypnotist bringing me out of a trance.

Blinking, I forced myself to take a breath. The darkness dissipated but the scent of fear still hung in the air.

"You there, Chiquita?" She knocked on the table three times. Maybe she thought that would allow her entry to my psyche.

"I was unconscious at the scene," I whispered. "I never saw . . ."

"I shoulda warned you."

"You think?" I would have glared at her, but she

looked pathetically miserable huddled on the opposite side of the table.

"Now do you believe I'm psychic?"

I looked from her sketch to the photo of the cracked windshield. They were remarkably similar. "I'm willing to admit there might be a possibility," I said carefully. After all, I believed I was able to converse with a lizard, not to mention I'd killed a man. Something I would have thought impossible not that long before. The idea that a coworker was psychic wasn't that far-fetched in my new reality.

Armani perked up a bit. "Good, because I need you to pay attention to what I have to say." She paused to make sure I was listening.

"Which is . . . ?"

"You need to meet the guy."

"Meet a guy?"

"No. Meet *the* guy. It's important. I'm not sure why, but it sort of feels like a life-or-death kind of thing."

"Meeting a guy is a matter of life-or-death?" Even in my new warped world that made no sense.

She shrugged. "I suck at interpreting them. That's why I don't usually act on the premonitions." She lifted her handless arm. "Do you know what the sign for this was?"

I shook my head. I wasn't sure I wanted to know.

"Hearing Vanilla Ice crooning, 'Ice, ice, baby,' every time I closed my eyes for two weeks straight!"

I laughed. I couldn't help it. The idea of Vanilla Ice delivering a psychic warning was just too much. "I'm sorry!" I wheezed through a gale of laughter. It wasn't right to laugh at Armani's gift, or her disfigurement. It wasn't right, but it was damn funny.

She chuckled along with me. "It's funny now, but when I was lying on the ice at the arena with that damn Zamboni coming at me, I was pretty pissed."

"I bet."

She grew serious. "But I mean it, Chiquita. You've got to meet the guy. Have you met anyone lately?"

I nodded. The image of Paul Kowalski, half-naked in my kitchen, sprang to mind. I hadn't heard from him since I'd abruptly kicked him out of my place, when God had reminded me that I had a gun stuck under my mattress.

"Tell me about him."

"He's a cop." And a hell of a kisser.

"That funny-looking redhead?"

The memory of Patrick staring at me with undisguised desire had every muscle in my body tensing.

"The hero cop? What's his name? I'll do his number for you."

I shook my head. Even I wasn't dumb enough to get involved with a guy with two wives and a sideline assassination business, no matter how much I found myself attracted to him. "A different cop."

"You think he's the one?"

"The one, what?"

"The one you have to meet."

I considered that for a moment. "When did you have your dream?"

"Last night."

"Then I don't think so, seeing as I'd already met him."

She thought about that for a second. "Maybe you've got to meet him for a date."

"I doubt it. He hasn't called."

"Well, keep an open mind and just keep telling yourself that you have to meet the man. Work on your . . . what's the word for it? It starts with *man*?"

"Man-catching?"

"That's not a word!"

"Manhunting?"

She cocked her head to the side and eyed me like I'd lost what little mind I might have had.

"What?" I asked defensively. "You're the one who can't think of the word."

"Manifestation skills."

"What?"

"Manifesting. Believing in a wish strongly enough that it comes true. Oprah did a show about it a few years ago."

I tried to manifest that this conversation had never occurred. My wish didn't come true.

Chapter Twenty-Seven

I'd have thought that while Armani was busy showing me pictures of cracks in glass and telling me my life depended on meeting "the" guy, that she could have at least given me a heads-up that Aunt Susan would be visiting Katie when I got to her room that night.

In true Aunt Susan fashion she wasn't reading to or talking to the little girl in the giant bed; she was working on her laptop. The only sound in the room was the steady beeping of Katie's monitors. I guess it would have killed her to show some kindness to the silent, helpless child.

Swallowing my anger toward my heartless aunt, I focused on doing what I'd come here for, visiting my niece. It was important that she knew she was loved, even if I was the only one to tell her.

I walked into the room and planted a kiss on my niece's cheek. "Hi there."

"Hello." Aunt Susan didn't look up as she spoke.

"I was saying hi to Katie."

Raising her penciled-in brows, my aunt didn't take

her eyes off her computer screen. Clearly she thought that my greeting a comatose child instead of her was an insult.

Closing my eyes, I counted to ten. I had enough problems, not to mention a tension headache. I really didn't need to get into an argument, too.

"Have you heard?" She managed to pack disapproval into those three words like it was gunpowder in a cannon.

"What?"

"About my sister."

I bit back a groan. If Mom had wandered off from the nuthouse again, my day would be complete. It was selfish of me, but I really hoped that the sister Susan was annoyed with was one of the twins. "No," I said slowly. "I haven't heard."

Aunty Susan banged away on her keyboard, hitting the keys harder than she would have had to if it was a manual typewriter. I felt a twinge of pity for the poor machine.

"She's gone and done it again."

I held my breath, waiting to find out if the laptop was being abused because of my mother or aunt. That wasn't much of a clue. Mom could have made a run for it, Leslie could have gotten nailed with another charge of Driving Under the Influence or Disturbing the Peace, or . . .

"She's going to marry that slimy bastard." Susan slammed the screen shut and glared at me.

For my part, I exhaled a shaky sigh of relief. My mother was still wed to my father, a slimy bastard for sure, but it meant she couldn't be getting married. She had to be talking about Loretta. Aunt Susan stared at me, waiting for me to say something.

"To Templeton the Rat?"

The corners of her mouth quirked. "Of course."

In most families when someone announces they're engaged, a round of congratulations is offered. In our family we say, "My condolences." And then start a betting pool to guess how long it will be until the happy couple files for divorce.

"They're moving out."

"At least you won't have to see him every day." Personally, I thought this was a huge positive, but my aunt scowled.

"He's trying to convince Loretta that I should buy her out of her share of the B&B."

"You're kidding me." Aunt Loretta always returned to the B&B every time one of her marriages disintegrated.

"He's a tricky one. I tried to talk to her, but she wouldn't let me. It's like he's brainwashed her against me." Aunt Susan tried to sound outraged, but I heard the undercurrent of sadness flowing through her words.

"Can you afford to buy her out?" I asked as gently as I could. The bed and breakfast was not only part of her livelihood, but her home. I wasn't sure that even my leather-tough aunt could survive losing that and her sister.

She nodded slowly. "But if I buy her out, I won't have much left for Katie's bills. I don't know what to do."

And I felt like shit. Lower than shit really. Here I'd been judging her, and she'd been worrying about Katie.

I would have given anything to be able to tell her not to worry about it, that I'd earned enough to keep Katie in quality care, but I couldn't. Not with Gary the Gun out there, ready to swoop in and claim my payday.

"Aunt Loretta's not going to make you buy her out no matter what The Rat says," I told her with what I hoped was a reassuring smile.

"I don't know . . . you didn't hear her . . ."

She sounded so pitiful I needed to say something to make her feel better. "I have an investment," I said slowly. "Hopefully it'll pay off soon, and we won't have to worry about her bills."

Susan cocked her head and stared at me like I was some bizarre museum display that she'd never seen before. "*You* have investments?"

Yeah, she was right, I wasn't the type to make investments. But it wasn't like I could just go and tell her I'd killed a guy for money. "Don't look so surprised."

Shaking her head, she considered me thoughtfully, "You've surprised me lately."

Something in her tone annoyed me, and I snapped, "That's because you set the bar so low for me."

"Perhaps."

I waited for her to launch a counterattack, but none came. Instead she got to her feet, put her computer aside, stepped up to Katie's bedside, and took her hand. "I know you have a lot on your plate right now, Margaret, more than any one person should have to bear, but do you think you could try talking to Loretta?"

It was my turn to tilt my head with surprise. Aunt Susan was asking for my help? That was almost as bizarre as my talking to a lizard and definitely weirder than Armani's psychic visions.

When I didn't answer her, she raised her gaze to meet mine. "Please?"

"Of course, of course," I practically babbled. "I'll try. I mean I don't know what I'll say to her, and I don't know if it'll do any good, but of course I'll talk to her."

"Thank you." She bowed her head. "You're a good girl, Margaret."

For a moment, I felt like I was seven years old again. That was the first time I'd realized that the reason my Daddy had to go to jail was that he was a bad man. I'd told Aunt Susan that I was afraid that meant I was a bad girl and she'd hugged me tight, saying, "You're a good girl, Margaret."

I'd forgotten about that. Probably like I'd forgotten or taken for granted a myriad of other kindnesses that she'd bestowed on me for the past thirty-two years. I wanted to tell her that I was grateful for all she'd done for me and my sisters. I wanted to tell her I was sorry.

But just then my phone rang.

I glanced down at my display. The number was unfamiliar.

"Take it," my aunt urged. "I'd like a few minutes alone with Katie."

So I walked out into the hall and took the call. "Hello?"

"Maggie?"

The man's voice was vaguely familiar, but I was only half-listening, since I was trying to hear what Susan was murmuring to my niece.

"Maggie? Are you there?"

I gave up trying to eavesdrop. "I'm here. Who is this?"

"It's Paul. Paul Kowalski."

Paul Kowalski, the cop I'd almost bonked. How long ago had that been? I tried to do some quick calculations. Only a couple of days. It felt longer. Back then I hadn't been a killer.

"Listen," Paul said hurriedly, probably taking my silence as a way of signaling annoyance, "I'm sorry I didn't call. I've been working crazy shifts."

"Uh huh."

"I was hoping maybe we could meet for drinks, maybe dinner."

"I don't know," I said slowly. My life was complicated enough. I really didn't need to be getting involved with a new guy . . . let alone a cop.

"Look, I know this is awkward. Things got a little . . . intense last time. I really like you, Maggie. I'd like to start over. Take things slow. What do you say?"

Meet the man! Meet the man! I could practically hear Armani screaming.

"Okay."

"Have you had dinner yet?"

"No."

"I'm off duty in thirty minutes. Maybe we could meet in an hour or so?"

I glanced toward Katie's room. Visiting hours were

over in an hour. "Can it be a little later? Figure ninety minutes from now?"

"Perfect. Do you know Angelo's?"

I quoted their slogan. "Best Italian in the States."

"I'll see you there in an hour and a half."

"It's a date."

He ended the call. I stared at my cell phone, wondering if I should call Armani to ask whether she'd had any more psychic wisdom to impart before I went on this dinner date.

Aunt Susan interrupted my thoughts. "I'm leaving now."

"Okay. I'll swing by tomorrow and will try to talk some sense into Aunt Loretta."

"I appreciate that. Did I overhear that you've got a date?"

I nodded.

"Not with a rat I hope."

I shook my head. "With a cop."

"That's wonderful! Have a good night." Carrying her computer case, she strode away.

I think Aunt Susan was always afraid that I'd end up with someone like my father. I wondered what she'd think if she ever found out that I was the one who'd ended up being like my father.

Chapter Twenty-Eight

I WENT BACK into Katie's room and spent the next hour reading to her from a book of nursery rhymes.

Have you ever read nursery rhymes? They're way too violent for kids. Mice getting their tails cut off with carving knives, Jack cracking his head open, and Humpty Dumpty falling to pieces. It's a wonder there aren't more serial killers running around.

When I was done, I kissed Katie's cheek. "See you tomorrow, Baby Girl."

The parking lot of Angelo's was packed, and I worried that I'd have trouble finding Paul inside the restaurant. Fortunately he was standing at the bar, near the front door.

Smiling, he walked over. He looked better than I remembered. Maybe that was because I wasn't seeing him bathed in the glow of a streetlight, or hidden in the shadows of a semi-seedy bar. Or maybe it was just because he was single and available, as opposed to the other man in my life. "Our table should be ready in about five minutes. Can I get you a drink?"

Knowing that I needed to keep my wits about me in order to maintain a modicum of control, I asked for a Pepsi.

By the time the bartender had drawn the soda, the hostess was batting her fake eyelashes at Paul and letting him know that she was ready to seat him.

I was pretty sure she was ready to do other things for him too, but I tried to control the twinge of jealousy I felt when Paul winked at her. I centered my attention on the surroundings. Candlelight, soft background music, he'd asked me to dinner at a romantic place. He wasn't interested in the hostess. He was interested in me.

Practically the moment we were seated, Paul ordered.

For both of us.

Maybe if I'd been on top of my game, I would have gotten in a cutting, witty remark and chosen my own damn food, but as it was, I was a little slow on the uptake. No one had ever had the audacity to order for me before. I stared at him, no doubt with my mouth hanging open like the village idiot.

Leaning across the table, he grabbed my hand the moment the waiter left. "About the other night."

I expected him to apologize for not calling sooner. I thought he might say he was sorry that things had moved so quickly. I sure as hell wasn't expecting the words that came out of his mouth.

"I need to know why you kicked me out."

"What?"

"No woman's ever done that before."

"There's a first time for everything."

"It was like a body blow to my ego."

I watched the candlelight flickering across his features. Did he really think he was all that? I mean, he was okay. All right, better than okay, but did he really mean to tell me that no other woman had ever refused him?

Did the rest of my life really depend on meeting *this* guy? Or had Armani and I misinterpreted her dream?

"It's not that I think I'm some great catch," Paul said.

"You don't?" It sure as hell had sounded like he did.

"No. It's just that . . . our chemistry . . . you were amazing . . . on fire . . . and then all of a sudden you turned into an ice princess, and I don't know what I did wrong."

"It wasn't you." That was the truth. It had been God, shouting about a gun under the mattress, who had doused the passion. "It was me. I've just got a lot going on."

"Want to tell me about it?" He flashed his most charming smile.

I would have loved to unburden myself to someone, but I didn't think sharing my problems with a cop was the best of ideas. "Actually, I'd like to escape from my troubles for a little while, if you don't mind."

"Okay. Do you mind if I talk about my problems? Specifically my crazy family?"

I chuckled. "Of course not. As they say, misery loves company."

And speaking of misery, I could have sworn I could have heard its siren's call.

Then I realized that it was just Aunt Loretta. "Yooo-hooo, Maggie!"

I turned and there she was, mincing across the restaurant toward us, with Templeton the Rat trailing behind, the giant bandage still covering half his head.

"I am so sorry," I muttered to Paul. "Family."

"Imagine running into you here," Loretta practically cooed. "How lucky is that?"

I was not feeling lucky.

"Have you heard the news? Templeton proposed." She waggled her bling for emphasis.

Instead of congratulating them, or admiring her ring, I asked, "Why?"

Aunt Loretta blinked at me, as though I'd spoken in a foreign tongue. "What?"

"Why?"

"Because," Templeton inserted smoothly, "Your aunt is a wonderful woman and I want to spend the rest of my life with her."

I looked him dead in the eye. "So it's not because you're trying to get your hands on her money?"

"Margaret!" Aunt Loretta sounded horrified that I'd even think such a thing, let alone suggest it. "How dare you?"

I have to give Templeton credit, though. He didn't even flinch, let alone respond with anger. Instead he smiled benevolently. "Your niece loves you, Letty. She's just looking out for your best interest. Perhaps in an overzealous, overprotective manner, but she means well."

"How sweet!" Loretta bent and planted a kiss on my forehead. Not one of her usual air kisses, she actually made physical contact, risking messing up her lipstick.

Have you ever seen a politician screw up during a televised debate, and there's that moment when it's written all over their face that they know they've just lost the election? That's how I felt at that moment. Like I'd lost. I'd been outmaneuvered by the man with a busted nose. I should have stuck with my first impression of him. I'd never talk sense into Aunt Loretta now.

"We're interrupting your date," Templeton said to Paul. "Sorry about that."

"Why don't we join you?" Loretta said, sliding into an empty chair.

I looked at Paul helplessly. He seemed a bit overwhelmed by it all.

"I'm Loretta, Maggie's aunt. And you are?"

"Paul. Paul Kowalski."

"Maggie's *date*," I supplied dryly. The hint that I wanted my aunt to leave sailed right over her head.

Templeton sat down too.

"Have you two been going together long?" Loretta asked Paul.

"We've already ordered," I told them before Paul could answer.

"That's okay," Templeton replied breezily. "We were only going to get soup and salad anyway." He waved over our waiter.

"Do stop interrupting, Maggie." Loretta frowned at me. Then she smiled at my date. "Tell me how you met."

Paul blinked, and looked to me for guidance. I shrugged.

"A routine traffic stop," Paul said slowly.

"You're a police officer?"

"Yes, ma'am."

"How wonderful!" She clapped her hands. "I bet you look quite dashing in your uniform. He does, doesn't he, Maggie?"

"He does," I admitted grudgingly.

Paul grinned at that.

"And tell me, Officer, did you feel it? That magic spark the moment you met?"

"You have got to be kidding me." I grumbled. "We're on a date. It's not like we're soul mates."

"First date?" Loretta asked.

"Yes," I said.

"Second," Paul countered.

I frowned at him. I didn't think that a drink at a seedy bar and groping in my kitchen counted as a date. Apparently he did.

Loretta tittered. "Bickering like old love birds already."

I glared at her. "We're not bickering. We're not old. And, we're not love birds. We're just two people who are trying to get to know each other. Something which is proving difficult since we've been joined by uninvited dinner companions."

Aunt Loretta patted my arm. "You'll have to forgive our Maggie for being a little grouchy. She's been through a lot, poor thing."

"Like what?" Paul asked with a sly grin in my direction.

I could have kicked him for encouraging her.

"Well, a few weeks ago her sister, my niece Theresa, died." Tears welled in her eyes. Snatching up her napkin, she blotted them away. "It was terrible loss. So senseless."

"A drunk driver," Templeton murmured.

"I'm sorry for your loss, Loretta." Paul swung his gaze over to me. "That must have been devastating for you, Maggie."

I nodded, unable to speak because of the lump that had lodged in my throat the instant I'd spotted my aunt's tears. I tried not to compare Paul's condolences to Patrick's, but it did occur to me that my date's sounded canned, while Patrick's had seemed genuine.

"And Theresa's daughter, Katie, she's three, is in a coma. And we're all hoping and praying that she'll wake up . . . but the waiting . . . the uncertainty . . . it's so hard." Loretta needed a moment to compose herself before she could go on.

I took a sip of water, trying to get control over my own emotions.

"Not to mention the fact that her father is rotting in prison."

Choking mid-swallow, I sputtered like an outboard motor.

Templeton clapped me on the back. "Easy now."

"Are you all right, dear?" Aunt Loretta peered at me, her eyes wide with concern.

Gasping for breath, I shook my head.

"What's wrong?"

"Do you need the Heimlich? I bet Officer Kowalski here knows the Heimlich."

"I do," Paul said.

"I don't need the freakin' Heimlich!" I practically shouted. Aware that other diners were swiveling in their seats to see what was going on, I lowered my voice to a whisper. "I just don't know why you had to tell him about Dad. It's our first date."

"He said it was your second."

"First, second, fifty-seventh, I don't care. It's not your place to tell my date that my father's a felon!"

Aunt Loretta shook her head sadly. "You've always been so touchy about this, Maggie. There's no reason for you to be ashamed. It's not your fault that he was a bank robber and killed someone."

Paul watched the exchange like it was a Wimbledon tennis match.

I wanted to crawl under the table. I wanted to kill Loretta. Okay, maybe not kill, but definitely muzzle. A muzzle for that rabid mouth of hers sounded like a damn good idea. Instead I said, "Paul, my father is serving a life sentence. And my mother is—"

"Don't say it!" Loretta shrieked.

Restaurant patrons and staff turned to see what all the commotion was about. Her reaction was so intense that even smooth-talking Templeton looked alarmed.

I looked her in the eye while I made the pronouncement. "My mother, Loretta's sister, is locked up in the loony bin!"

Yeah, it was bitchy of me, but she drove me to it, horning in on my date and then telling him about my father.

Bursting into tears, Loretta fled the table.

Thankfully, Templeton followed her, but not before chastising me. "You should be ashamed of yourself."

And I was . . . later on. In that moment, all I felt was victory.

His mouth hanging open, Paul stared after them. "I take back what I said earlier; my family doesn't seem nearly so crazy now."

"Gee, thanks."

"Your dad is really a bank robber?" He sounded a tad too excited about that particular nugget of information.

I frowned. "You think that's a good thing?"

"You have to admit that it's kind of cool."

"Definitely not cool."

He shook his head. "Girls. I bet you never played cops-and-robbers when you were a kid, did you?"

"Nope."

"Well I did. A lot. And the thing about cops-and-robbers is that sometimes you're the cop, and sometimes you're the robber. The cops usually win, but the robbers, they get to do all the cool stuff like blow up vaults and lead police chases."

"So you're saying you think you made the wrong career choice?"

He laughed. "I'm saying I think I made the boring career choice."

I pursed my lips to keep from blurting out, "Where do you stand on contract killers?"

Chapter Twenty-Nine

"You're late," God complained the moment I unlocked my apartment door.

Instead of answering him, I turned around and waved good-bye to Paul, who had insisted on accompanying me home.

I had insisted on his not coming in with me, despite his tempting kisses.

I still had a modicum of sense left, and I knew getting involved with a cop was a bad idea. That said, I agreed to another date with him. After all, what if he was the guy I was supposed to meet? It didn't make sense to shut him out of my life entirely. Besides, he was a damn good kisser.

"Where were you?" God asked.

"On a date."

"On a date? Have you forgotten you're supposed to be killing someone?"

"How could I forget?" I switched off the television in

the bedroom and flopped down onto my bed, so that I was eye level with the lizard's terrarium perched on my night table. "How'd your research go?"

"Well, most women seem to prefer using poison."

"Great, now all I have to do is study *Arsenic and Old Lace*. Hey, do you believe in psychics?

"Pyschics?'

"You know, people who have a gift. Who can see the future."

"No." He tapped his foot impatiently while he delivered his answer. "There are no such things as psychics."

"Like there are no such things as talking animals? You'd seem to disprove that."

He stared up at me with those unblinking glassy eyes of his.

"My friend Armani claims to be a psychic. She gave me a message today. Want to know what it was?"

"Not really." He yawned just to emphasize his disinterest.

"She gets messages. She just doesn't know how to interpret them," I continued stubbornly.

"And I should care about this because . . . ?" Disdain dripped from his every syllable.

I refused to let it annoy me. "She told me I have to meet the guy."

"What guy?"

"She didn't know."

"Well then that's the most helpful advice I ever heard." He buried his little brown head in his scaly . . . hands.

"It wasn't advice. More like a warning. She said my life depends on it."

"Have you lost your mind?" He shouted loudly enough that the top of his enclosure rattled.

"That's a possibility. I mean consider the evidence. One–I'm talking to you. Two—I've killed a man and am trying to figure out how to kill another. Three—Cuckoo for Cocoa Puffs runs in the family."

He twitched his tail impatiently. "I'm worried."

"About what?"

"You."

"Aw, that's sweet. You think I'm going to wind up in the nuthouse?"

"Only if you're lucky. I watched *Women Doing Hard Time*. You'll never survive in prison."

I couldn't argue with that theory. I had enough difficulty just visiting my father. Getting locked up in a cell would probably do me in. "That's why I can't get caught."

"Which is why poison won't work."

"I don't follow your logic."

"In order to successfully poison someone, you have to purchase a poison, administer it, and sneak away. You just don't have the time or the resources to do that."

"So what do you suggest?"

"Shooting him."

"I don't have a gun."

"Why not?"

"Patrick took it back. He said he'd dispose of it."

"And you believed him? What if he's framing you?"

"He's not framing me."

"How can you be so sure?"

I shrugged. I couldn't be.

"Something else occurred to me today. Maybe it's good news."

"I could use some of that."

"Delveccio got what he wanted. His son-in-law is dead. I really don't think it makes good business sense for him to pay someone to kill you."

"He doesn't have an MBA," I told the lizard. "He's in the M-O-B mob. I'm not sure good business practices are high on his list of priorities."

"Think about it. He's got no reason to want you dead. He just doesn't want you and Gary the Gun bickering about who should get paid for services rendered."

"Which should be me," I reminded him.

"Yes, yes, yes. But is it worth having a cellmate for the rest of your life?"

I rolled over and studied the ceiling, imagining I was lying on a bunk in a cell.

"Maybe you should just let Gary have the money."

"And what about Katie? What happens to her?"

"Maybe you should just try to come up with the money for Katie's bills another way."

"How?"

"You could ask your father for the money."

I closed my eyes. "He won't do it."

"You won't know until you ask. Just explain it to him."

"You don't know him."

"You don't have any other options."

Yes, I was having a lizard tell me that the only chance I had to save my own butt and my niece's life lay in the hands of the guy who'd pawned my bicycle. I wasn't feeling hopeful.

Chapter Thirty

STILL, GOD HAD been right about other stuff, which is why the next morning I stopped by the Galaxy Diner in the hopes of running into Patrick.

Sure enough, he was there at the counter, a pile of jelly packets stacked up like a game of Jenga. I wondered if that was some kind of signal and he was waiting for someone to join him, so I took a seat at the opposite end of the counter and waited for him to him to make eye contact. It took a while, because he appeared to be lost in thought, staring into his coffee as he stirred it.

He finally did look up, sweeping his gaze over the entire place, slamming to a stop when he saw me. When he didn't offer a greeting of any kind, I inferred that he was waiting for someone, so I threw a couple of bills on the counter to cover the coffee I'd just ordered but hadn't even sipped and walked out.

I considered tucking a note under his windshield wiper, but I couldn't figure out a euphemism for my question, which was: Is Delveccio going to have me killed?

"Lifesaver?"

Turning around, I found Patrick standing behind me holding out a cylinder of foil-wrapped mints.

I shook my head. "I have a question for you. Will—"

"Do you remember how to get to the cemetery?"

I nodded.

"Okay, I'll meet you there." Without another word he climbed into his truck and drove away.

I watched him go. If Delveccio did want me dead, the cemetery would be a good place for Patrick to do the deed.

I slowly climbed into my car, wondering if showing up to the Galaxy had been the brightest of ideas. Still, I needed an answer to my question, because that would determine if I'd go ask my father for the money. At the moment I wasn't sure if dying or begging was worse.

A couple of minutes later I rolled to a stop behind Patrick's truck. He'd left the vehicle. Crouching to read the epitaph on a headstone a few rows away, he seemed oblivious of my arrival.

I got out of my car and waited beside it. It was bad enough that I'd driven to my own execution, if that was in fact what I'd done; I sure as hell wasn't going to just stroll over to the proverbial hangman's noose.

After a moment, the redhead straightened and headed toward me. "What do you want your tombstone to say?"

I swallowed hard. I should have listened to my own gut and ignored the urgings of that stupid lizard.

Looming over me, Patrick tilted his head, waiting for my answer.

"Same shit . . . different asshole."

He threw his head back and laughed.

And when he wasn't looking at me, I hit him.

In the gut.

Which, if I'd paid any attention during his self-defense lesson, I would have known was a mistake. I should have gone for his balls.

He gasped, and the air whooshed out of him when I socked him, but he stayed on his feet. "What the . . ."

I tried to yank open my car door to make my escape, but he reached over me and slammed it shut.

"What—"

I drove my elbow backward, trying to do more damage, but he was ready for me this time. Grabbing it, he swung me around so that I was facing him. Faster than a ninja he captured both my hands and held them at my sides. I flattened back against my car. He followed, pinning me with his body weight. It was both frightening and intimate.

"What's going on?" Slightly breathless, he spoke as casually as if we'd been discussing the weather. "Did Delveccio tell you to kill me too? Because if he did, he shouldn't have sent a little girl to do the job."

I shook my head. I didn't know which was stranger. The idea that he thought I'd been sent to kill him, or that he seemed so freaking unperturbed about it.

"Then why did you hit me, Mags?"

"I . . . I thought you were going to kill me."

"Why the hell would you think that?"

"You asked me what I wanted on my tombstone!"

Okay, I'd been paranoid before that, but that little question was what had driven me over the edge. "You're hurting my wrists." That complaint wasn't true; he was holding onto me firmly, but he hadn't caused me any pain. I just needed some space.

"Sorry." As if he understood that, he released me and backed away a few paces. "I didn't mean to."

Feeling guilty for the lie, I looked away.

"I was just wondering if you were going to have the usual family relationship stuff or a philosopher's quote, or if you were going to go for something original."

"Oh." When he put it that way, it didn't sound all that menacing.

"I should have known you'd already have something unique picked out."

I looked back at him, trying to figure out what that cryptic statement meant, but as usual his expression was unreadable. "I don't like the 'beloved' or 'in loving memory' crap. I've already buried two sisters, my third's probably dead too, and I just want anyone who reads my stone to know that life is crap."

"She's not."

Working at Insuring the Future, I had heard people call their cars, boats, motorcycles, and jet skis *she*. I'd never heard anyone refer to life as one before, but it kind of made sense in a "life's a bitch" sense. Not wanting to get into a philosophical argument with a guy who ended lives as a side gig, I just sort of shrugged.

"You don't want to talk about it?"

"Not particularly."

"Okay, but if you ever do . . ." He seemed puzzled by my reaction, but I didn't elaborate.

My sisters were gone, my mom was a lost cause, and my dad was locked up. All I had left was my comatose niece, a crappy job, my wacky aunts, and a job I hated. There was a good chance I'd run over the next person I saw wearing one of those ubiquitous Life is Good shirts.

"You had a question for me?" Patrick prompted gently. "That's the reason I had you meet me here. It wasn't because I had some violent end planned for you."

"So G—" Holy crap! I'd almost told him God had been theorizing. If I did that, he might think I was cracking under the pressure and might have to actually kill me. "So . . ." I started again, more deliberately, choosing my words carefully. "So guess what I was thinking?"

"What?"

"It doesn't make sense financially for Delveccio to have me killed."

Patrick nodded slowly. "As long as you don't go opening your mouth, there's no reason at all."

"So if I let Gary the Gun keep my fee for killing Cifelli, no one should want me dead, right?"

Patrick nodded enthusiastically.

"Then maybe I'll do that."

"Really?" A pleased smile stretched Patrick's features. Approval sparkled in his eyes.

"Maybe. I've got to look into an alternative method of funding Katie's care, but if it works out . . ."

"That's great, Mags. Really great. It'll keep you safe."

I felt badly that he seemed so excited about the possibility. There was always a chance my father wouldn't go for the plan. If that was the case, I'd definitely have to try to take out Gary the Gun.

And that could turn out to be very dangerous, indeed.

Chapter Thirty-One

BECAUSE I HAD to make a decision about how to proceed before Cifelli's corpse showed up, I feigned getting sick, just before my lunch break. In all honesty, it wasn't much of a stretch, considering the call I'd gotten was from a guy who wanted to know if Insuring the Future was going to cover the cost of removing the bloodstains from his passenger seat.

Apparently his wife had mouthed off to him, and he'd slugged her, breaking her nose, and "the bitch had the nerve to bleed on my seat."

Like I said, pretending to feel sick wasn't a challenge.

So I left work early and drove out to the prison to make my plea. I'd mentally rehearsed what I was going to say, but my well-constructed speech was forgotten the moment he walked into the visiting room.

I gasped when I saw him, and I immediately felt sick to my stomach. For real.

His face was one giant bruise, one eye was swollen shut, and a line of fresh stitches zipped his forehead closed.

"Not looking my most handsome today," he quipped, his speech slightly impaired by the fat lip he sported.

"What happened?" I was surprised at how upset seeing him like this made me. I'd made the decision long ago not to care about him.

"You should see the other guys."

That wasn't an answer, but obviously he wasn't going to tell me. Maybe he figured that when a guy in prison looked like someone had beaten the crap out of him, chances were that was exactly what had happened.

"Why are you here, Maggie? Is Katie . . . ?"

"She's fine. The same. Actually that's the reason I came to see you." I took a deep breath to fortify myself before taking the plunge. "I need money for her hospital bills."

He nodded, almost smugly. "Told ya the insurance would only be a drop in the bucket."

"You were right." That admission didn't come easily to me, but I thought it might help to soften him up. "Can you help?"

"I'm sorry, Maggie May, but my prison salary doesn't add up to much at all."

Rage burned in my gut. This was his granddaughter we were talking about. I closed my eyes for a second imagining my submarine doors slamming shut, containing my anger. "They're going to move her to a state-run facility."

"I live in a state-run facility," he reminded me, like I wasn't fully aware of the concrete walls, uniformed guards, and jumpsuited prisoners surrounding us.

But you deserve this, I wanted to say. *Katie doesn't.* Instead I took another slow, deep breath, just like Alice had taught me. I didn't feel any calmer. I was starting to think this stress-reduction technique of hers was a load of shit. "I've been told that Katie's best chance at recovery is to continue receiving treatment where she is. The doctors she's seeing now are the best in treating cases like hers."

An alarm sounded in another part of the prison, causing the convicts and their visitors to shift uncomfortably in their seats, but Dad and I pretended not to notice.

My father waved his hand in front of his battered nose as though to dispel and unpleasant scent. "Legal robbery! That's what doctors have figured out how to do."

I nodded. Delveccio had said something pretty similar.

"She needs to stay there. I need the money to keep her there." I looked him in the eye. "I need you to give it to me."

"I told you, Maggie May, I—"

"What about the jewels?" I hissed, having had enough of his pauper act.

Sitting back in his seat, he crossed his arms over his chest. "You do know that I pleaded not-guilty, don't you?"

"Yeah, I know. Just like I know that they convicted your lying, thieving, murdering ass."

A flush spread up his face, darkening his bruises. He didn't like being talked to like that, certainly not by his daughter.

I, however, wasn't in the mood to give a flying shit about his feelings. "It's not like you're ever going to get a chance to use whatever you've got hidden away."

"Allegedly hidden away, and you don't know that."

I rolled my eyes. "You really think you're going to escape again?"

"I've filed an appeal."

"Yeah? Good luck with that." I used my most sarcastic tone and was rewarded by him jumping up out of his chair, fists clenched and eyes wild.

A guard bellowed, "We've got a situation. Everyone's got to get out of here."

I spotted the violent monster lurking in him, and it frightened me, but I was more scared for Katie. "Where are they?"

"They're a popular topic this week."

"What the hell is that supposed to mean?"

He pointed at his face. "I get jumped and drilled about the stash and then you show up asking about it. You expect me to believe that's a coincidence?"

"You think I had something to do with your getting beaten up? I didn't. I just want to help Katie."

"You have a strange way of asking for help."

"Everyone up and out," the guard ordered.

Ignoring the instruction, I stared down at my sandals, noticing that the strap on the right one was frayed. Like everything else in my life it was on the verge of coming undone. "Please," I whispered. "Will you please help me to save Katie?"

He was silent for so long that I started to think maybe he was considering it. I looked up at him hopefully.

"I can't." He sounded almost sad about it.

"You mean you won't," I shouted, knowing full-well

the reason he wasn't helping me was that he didn't want our recorded conversation to be used against him when he filed his appeal.

Everyone in the room, despite the fact that they were saying good-byes to their loved ones, turned to look at us. I glared at them defiantly.

"I mean I can't, Maggie May." Dad sounded choked up about it, but I dismissed that as a side-effect of the beating he'd endured. "I'm sorry."

"If she doesn't wake up, it's your fault!"

"No, it's not. And it's not yours either. It's the fault of the drunk driver who ran the red light."

"You keep telling yourself that."

The guard grabbed my arm and yanked me to my feet. "You've got to get out of here, ma'am. It's not safe."

Without another glance in my father's direction, I stalked out.

I knew full well how "not safe" I was. I also knew that somehow, some way, I was going to have to kill Gary the Gun.

Chapter Thirty-Two

It's really hard to come up with a plan to take out a killer when no one will leave you the hell alone . . . including him.

After my disastrous confrontation with my father, I went to visit Katie.

Okay, that's a lie. I went to the nearest donut shop, bought a dozen assorted and one of those giant cups of coffee you practically need two hands to lift to your lips, sat in my car, and threw myself one hell of a pity party. I wolfed down nine of the donuts in the hope the sugar and fat would make me feel better.

They didn't. I mean I ate *nine* of them . . . one right after the other like I was loading coal into a furnace. All I felt was overwhelming nausea.

And sticky. I was definitely sticky. I'd managed to get powdered sugar, jelly, chocolate frosting, sugar glaze, sprinkles, cream filling, vanilla icing, and strawberry frosting all over myself.

That was the condition I was in when I stumbled

into my niece's room: ready to vomit and looking like a confectionary shop had puked its contents on me. "Hey there, Baby Girl."

She of course didn't respond.

I sighed and glared at the stuffed toy on the bed beside her. Dino, the one her grandfather had been so concerned she had with her. The reason I'd allowed myself to believe he might actually pitch in and help with her bills.

Sinking into the seat beside the bed, I took her tiny limp hand in mine. If I could have cried I would have done it then.

"Your niece is such a cute kid."

The guy who'd frightened me so badly days earlier stood just feet away, his face a malevolent mask that caused a knot of dread to lodge in my throat.

My gut churned as I got to my feet, watching warily as he rounded Katie's bed, taking up position on the side opposite me. Something felt wrong, and I didn't think it was just because I'd binged on doughnuts.

"Do I know you?"

He smiled, a spiteful grin that left me feeling cold. My heartbeat, turning into a frenzied tribal drumbeat, thundered in my ears.

"We haven't been introduced, but I've seen your work."

And I knew with a certainty that changed the donuts in my stomach to lead who he was. Gary the Gun.

When he reached for his pocket I made a mad grab for Katie's IV pole, the only weapon at hand.

"Easy there, Margaret," he chuckled. "I'm just taking out my phone."

On guard, I watched as he pulled it from his pocket. "What do you want? Why are you here?"

"You are an impulsive one. You really should get that under control. I just wanted to show you some pictures I have." He held out his phone so that I could clearly see the image of myself pointing the gun at Alfonso Cifelli.

"It's a whole slideshow. Want to watch it?"

Not only had I killed a man, but now the guy who was claiming credit for the job I'd done was telling me he had photographic evidence of my crime. I hadn't thought it possible, but my life had suddenly gotten even worse. I shook my head. "How?"

"I was following him. Getting ready to make my move. I like to do that, follow people, get to know their routines."

"That's you who was here at the hospital that day."

"Of course." He showed me another picture."Pretty good shots, don't you think?"

I studied the picture fascinated by the snapshot of Cifelli's anger and my fear. "What do you want?"

He shrugged. "A hundred grand."

"You're already getting that from Delveccio."

"I want another."

"I don't have that kind of money."

"I know. I know. That's why I'm going to be generous and offer you a payment plan. You can pay me ten grand a month for the next twelve months . . . that'll get me what you owe me plus a little interest."

"I don't—-"

"If you don't accept my more-than-generous offer," he

interrupted harshly, turning off his phone and stowing it in his pocket, "the photographs will go to the police . . . and I'm not talking about that redheaded freak. And you will go away for a very long time."

I had no doubt that he'd carry through on his threat. "Okay."

"You've got seventy-two hours to get my first payment to me." He reached out to run a finger down Katie's cheek.

From across the bed I slapped his hand away. Grabbing my wrist he twisted it brutally. A white-hot pain zipped up my arm. I cried out.

With a fierce tug he pulled me toward him so that I half-hung over the bed. "Listen you little bitch, I don't know why the hell you thought it would be okay for you to horn in on my job, but if you don't pay up, I'm going to make your life a living hell. It's not a coincidence I'm here today. It's all part of a plan. My plan. I'll go after every member of your family. Do you understand me?"

I nodded. The searing pain was making it hard to breathe. To think.

"Glad we understand one another." He released my wrist and I almost fell on top of Katie. "Let's meet here again in, say, seventy-two hours. And don't forget to bring the cash."

Struggling to regain my balance, I watched as he slipped out of the room, flashing me a smug smile.

Weak-kneed, I collapsed on the bed beside Katie. If I could have cried, I would have sobbed hysterically. Instead, rubbing my throbbing wrist, I struggled for breath like a hooked fish knowing death was imminent.

Chapter Thirty-Three

"YOU SAID I had seventy-two hours!" I screamed when I saw her body lying in front of my apartment door. Throwing my car into park, I raced toward her, my heart in my throat.

She was lying at an odd angle, her body splayed on the ground, her head almost perpendicular against the doorframe.

"Aunt Leslie?"

I dropped to my knees beside her. I couldn't see any bullet holes or knife wounds. Maybe Gary had snapped her neck. Oh god, this was all my fault. "I'm so sorry," I told my dearly departed aunt.

"Do you know her?"

I let out a scream that could have shattered an elephant's eardrum, scrambling away on all fours from the unidentified male that had snuck up behind me.

He laughed at me.

I turned to look up at him.

That was when Aunt Leslie sat straight up.

I screamed again.

My dead aunt had come back to life!

She let out a shriek of her own, albeit not as impressive as mine, but still fairly decent.

It's a wonder the neighbors didn't call the police, what with the two of us screaming our heads off. Maybe that's because the cops were already there. At least one was.

Bent over double, tears streaming down his reddened face, Paul, in uniform, leaned against the door jamb for support as he laughed his ass off at us.

"What the hell is going on? What are you doing here?" I turned my attention to Aunt Leslie, who had stopped screaming and was looking around as though she was trying to figure out where she was. "And why were you playing dead on my doorstep? I almost had a heart attack. No, a stroke! No, an aneurysm!"

"Get melodramatic much?" I heard Godzilla drawl from inside my apartment.

Getting to my feet, I planted my hands on my hips. "An explanation from both of you is required. It's not an optional exercise, so get talking!"

Paul had the good sense to go first. Straightening up, and adopting a more serious expression, he pointed to Leslie. "When I got here, your door was open and she was sitting beside it." He stepped closer so that he could whisper in my ear. "I'm pretty sure she's stoned."

I was pretty sure that Aunt Leslie had been stoned for a good portion of her adult life, but it probably wasn't a good idea to tell that to a law enforcement officer. Instead I deflected the attention off my chemically-altered aunt and back onto the man who could haul her ass off to jail. "I know why my aunt is here." That actually wasn't a lie. The reason was clasped in her hand. No doubt the glass-enclosed four-leaf-clover necklace was meant for me. "What are you doing here? And what the hell were you doing inside my place?"

Paul backed up a step and held out his hands defensively. "The door was open."

"So you decided it was okay to just waltz right in?"

"I didn't want them to die."

"What?"

"The flowers I brought you. The door was open so I figured I'd put them inside."

"And you just left her out here? Lying on the ground like a goddamn corpse?"

He blinked. "She wasn't lying down when I went inside. She was sitting up and humming." He reached for my hand. "Come see what I brought you."

"Help me get Aunt Leslie inside first."

Together we lifted, cajoled, and dragged my aunt all the way to my couch. I was shocked that once we got her lying down on the furniture that Paul took off her shoes, covered her with throw, and tucked a pillow under her head. Aunt Leslie beamed up at him, obviously enjoying the special treatment.

Once he'd gotten her settled, he led me into the kitchen.

"You're pretty good at that," I muttered grudgingly.

"You're not the only one with a family of characters, Maggie. You'll have to meet my mom. She alternates between being a miserable dry drunk and a two-bottle-a-day drinker. I've had lots of experience tucking in."

"So you're not going to take her to jail?"

He laughed. "Jail is for people who do bad things, not someone who indulges in some weed now and then. Besides, from what your other aunt said, your family's been going through a lot lately."

"You don't know the half of it."

"Which is why I brought you some flowers."

"Don't trust him!" God shouted from his terrarium in the bedroom.

"I thought they'd cheer you up. Do you like them?" Paul waved at the pitcher of lilies he'd put on my kitchen table.

I hated them. "They're beautiful."

Lilies remind me of funerals.

And they stink.

Which is probably while they're so popular at funerals—one stink covering up another.

Anyway, I hate them. "They're perfect!"

"The florist told me they symbolize a beautiful lady."

The man was a charmer, I had to give him that, even though he'd put the smelly flowers in my own chipped pitcher.

"Maybe I should have asked him which ones work with a sweet woman."

Now don't go thinking he was some silver-tongued Romeo, as I did for a split second.

It didn't take me long to realize he was referring to the fact that I was still covered with powdered sugar, jelly, chocolate frosting, sugar glaze, sprinkles, cream filling, vanilla icing, and strawberry frosting from my donut binge.

Thankfully, Aunt Leslie picked that precise moment to call out, "I've got the munchies!"

That allowed me to kick Paul out using the excuse that I had to take care of her. I walked him to the door, thanking him profusely for the flowers I hated.

"We should go to dinner again."

"Why?" I asked. Chances were good I was either going to be dead or in jail in another seventy-two hours. I wasn't in the mood for making long-term commitments I wasn't going to be able to keep.

Instead of answering me, he kissed me. As usual his kiss was hot, hard, and demanding . . . and as usual it set me on fire.

"Oh, get a room," God snarked from his enclosure around the corner.

I ignored him.

It occurred to me that even prisoners on death row were entitled to a last meal. Why shouldn't I have mine?

"Tomorrow night?" He asked when he finally came up for air.

I nodded, too breathless to speak.

With a victorious grin, he walked away.

"You didn't really fall for that act of his, did you?" God asked.

A quick glance told me that Aunt Leslie had either passed out or fallen asleep. Walking into my bedroom, I pulled the door shut behind me before flopping down on the bed beside God's cage. He seemed more agitated than usual, scurrying from one end to the other.

"Are you okay?"

"Of course I'm not okay. That hooligan broke in here."

"By hooligan I assume you mean Paul?"

"Yes! He broke in and ransacked the place!"

"Or," I suggested mildly. "He came in after Aunt Leslie had unlocked the door and put the flowers in water."

"That stench is horrible." The little guy covered his snout for emphasis.

"I noticed."

"So throw them out."

"I can't."

"Why not?"

"As you well know you little eavesdropping monster, I've got a date with him tomorrow."

"With a hooligan!"

"Or with a guy who brought me flowers, helped me take care of my aunt, and wants to take me out for a third time."

"He was looking for something. I could hear him banging around. Opening and closing things."

"A vase. For the flowers. He couldn't find one since I don't own one."

"Who doesn't own a vase?"

"Me."

"Why not?"

"I broke it."

"How?"

"It was Alice's fault."

"Who's Alice?"

"My best friend. You'd like her. She's normal."

"Normal?" He said the two syllables as though he couldn't even imagine the concept in relation to me.

"The closest thing to normal I've ever had in my life."

"But she made you break a vase?"

Okay, confession time. Remember when this whole thing started, and I sort of painted myself as a nonviolent person? Well most of the time I'm not, but if you threaten someone . . . "I broke it over Alice's ex-boyfriend's head."

"Oh." Apparently the lizard wasn't quite sure how to react to this revelation.

"Trust me, he deserved it. Dumb jerk breaks down my door and tries to drag my best friend out by her hair . . . what else was I supposed to do?"

"I'm sure you did the right thing," he soothed. "Speaking of dumb jerks . . ."

I jumped up from the bed. "I need a shower." And I needed a break from his constant criticism of Paul.

The pounding of the water offered only a brief respite from God's diatribe.

"I don't trust him," he said as soon I'd finished de-stickying myself.

As he ranted, I made a mental note that I was putting on my last clean pair of underwear and would have to buy some more for the next day.

"He's a little too sneaky. A little too smooth. Are you listening to me?"

"Uh huh," I replied absentmindedly. In truth I was trying to figure out what to do about Aunt Leslie. Obviously the easiest thing would be to let her sleep it off on my couch. I knew the responsible thing to do was to call one of my other aunts to tell them where she was. Therein lay my problem. I hadn't spoken with Aunt Loretta since she'd fled the table in the middle of my date with Paul, and I hadn't yet told Aunt Susan that I'd failed to talk any sense into her wayward sister.

I had to do something, though, because I needed to find Patrick to tell him that Gary the Gun was blackmailing me.

"He's dangerous, Maggie. You should stay away from him," God said.

"Patrick?"

"Patrick? Have I been talking about Patrick all this time?"

"Because I really don't think he'll hurt me. He's had plenty of opportunities and hasn't yet." There was a ringing character endorsement.

"Not Patrick, you nincompoop!" The lizard's shout seemed to echo off the bedroom walls.

I wondered if the neighbors could hear him chirping.

"I'm talking about Paul!"

"Okay, you've had your say. You think Paul is bad news. Message received. Now will you please shut the hell up so that I can figure out what to do about Aunt Leslie."

"Let her sleep."

"I have to go out."

"Where?'

"To find Patrick. I have to kill Gary the Gun."

"Your father wouldn't help with the money?" The lizard sounded genuinely surprised by this.

"I told you he wouldn't."

"Is that why you're in such a rotten mood?"

"Maybe I'm just in a mood because you won't stop bugging me."

Crossing his little legs over his chest, he tapped his foot, indicating he didn't believe that. "What happened?"

My cell phone buzzed at that moment, saving me both from telling him about Gary the Gun's blackmail threat, and from having to make a decision about what to do regarding my slumbering aunt. "Hey Aunt Susan, I was just about to call you."

"I'm sure you were, Margaret." Obviously she didn't. "I heard about your . . . interaction with Loretta."

"Is it about Katie?" God asked.

Shaking my head, I raised a finger to my lips to silence him. "Sorry about that, Aunt Susan."

She spoke with quiet resignation. "One can only win so many battles."

I wasn't sure what she meant by that, but I knew I didn't want her to elaborate. "Aunt Leslie's at my place."

"That's nice, dear."

"She's passed out."

There was a long silence.

"I have to go out, so I was just going to let her sleep it off."

Another long silence.

"Unless there's something you want to suggest?"

"Leave her there. Let her sleep. Live your life."

I thought I detected a note of resentment in her flat tone.

"Okay."

"Are you going with us to visit your mother for her birthday?"

"I don't know if I'm going to be around." That was the honest truth. I might be dead. Or incarcerated.

"Well, think about it." She sounded inordinately pleased, probably because I hadn't refused outright. Just the possibility that I'd even consider going was a high point in my aunt's life. "Have fun tonight!"

She hung up.

"What happened that's got your disposition so dour?" God asked.

"This is all your fault," I told him. It felt good to say that, to blame someone else for the galactic fuck-up that had become my life.

"What's my fault?"

"If only you'd been a better lookout."

He drew himself up to his full height. Which is really not such an impressive feat when you're only inches tall. "*I* was an excellent lookout. You're the one who took your sweet time pulling the trigger."

"There was someone else there."

He opened his mouth to respond, but hesitated, as though a thought occurred to him. "The branch that broke. The reason you looked away from Alfonso Cifelli."

"That's my guess."

"Who was it?"

"Gary the Gun."

"Your competition? That explains how he was able to tell the mob boss that the job was done."

I nodded. "It also explains how he threatened me with blackmail today."

"Blackmail?"

"He's got pictures of me and Cifelli."

"Pictures?"

"You know, for a guy who thinks he's so smart, you're pretty slow on the uptake."

I left him to chew on that, changed clothes, and went in search of Patrick.

Chapter Thirty-Four

I DIDN'T HAVE a phone number for my murder mentor and he wasn't at his man cave behind the boutique. I had no idea how to find him.

It did occur to me that I could call the police and ask for him by name, but I figured that would be in direct violation of his Don't Get Caught rule. For all I knew, all calls placed to a Police switchboard would be recorded and maybe traced.

Eventually I decided to see if Delveccio was at the hospital. I reasoned that his employer must have a way of getting in touch with him. Since I was going to ask Delveccio favor, I made a point of wearing my black dress and heels. I figured *flashing my killer gams* wouldn't hurt my chances of gaining his cooperation. I made a tottering beeline for the cafeteria.

Sure enough, my favorite mobster, excuse me, "alleged" mobster was there, deep in conversation with a pretty brunette. I decided that interrupting him wasn't the best of ideas considering I was going to impose on him for his help, so instead I got myself a chocolate pudding. Okay . . . I got two.

I'd finished one before the woman got up and walked away. As soon as she was gone, Delveccio waved me over, his pinky ring glittering like a disco ball in the drab cafeteria. His gaze narrowed appreciatively as he surveyed my *sticks*.

"My daughter, Antoinette. She was asking if I knew what happened to her good-for-nothing-mother-fucking-scumbag husband."

And I thought the conversations I had with my family members were loaded with landmines.

"You here to tell me you did Gary?" He sounded hopeful.

I shook my head. "I need your help"

"I told you. I can't help you with this thing. It's all you or it's nothin'."

"I just need to get in touch with our mutual friend."

He stared at me for a long, uncomfortable moment. I did my best to project confidence and to hide my fear.

"You gonna eat that?" He pointed at my remaining pudding, which I'd carried over with me.

"You gonna give me a phone number?" I said with false bravado.

He chuckled, scribbled some digits on a napkin and pushed it toward me. I slid the dessert in his direction.

"Good luck."

I nodded. I needed it. So badly, in fact, that I'd taken the four-leaf-clover Aunt Leslie had brought with her, and put it on before I left the house.

It just so happens that a hospital is one of the few places around that still has pay phones, so I used one to call the number Delveccio had provided. Rubbing the necklace for luck, I held my breath as the phone on the other end rang three times.

"Hello?"

"Please don't hang up, it's me," I begged Patrick breathlessly.

"Mags?" He sounded surprised.

"Uh huh."

"How'd you . . . never mind, I can guess. What's up?"

"I'm in trouble."

"Are you in a safe place?"

"Is any place safe?" I countered.

I heard a crunch and figured he was chomping on one of his mints. "Can you meet me at my place?"

I nodded.

"Mags? Did you hear me?"

I'd forgotten he couldn't see my nod. "Yes. Yes, I heard you. Yes I can meet you there."

"Okay, I'll be there within the hour." He hung up.

I drove over to the street the apartment was on, parked under a streetlight, and double, triple, quadruple-checked to make sure my car was locked up tight, though I wasn't sure what kind of protection I expected my windows to provide if Gary the Gun took a pot shot at me.

The street was deserted. And creepy. Fortunately I didn't have to wait long. Within five minutes of my arrival, Patrick's truck slid into a parking spot.

I leapt out of my car. "Thank you so much for coming," I said as he slid out of his vehicle.

"What did you say to convince Delveccio to give you that number?"

"I gave him my chocolate pudding."

He cocked his head. "Is that a euphemism for something I don't want to know about?"

I laughed. "No. I just told him I needed your help and he traded me the number for a chocolate pudding. I think I got the better end of the deal."

"That's because you're assuming I'm going to help you. Come inside."

I followed him into his man cave. It was obvious that he hadn't been expecting company. He hadn't cleaned up.

An assortment of handguns and ammunition were laid out on the couch like produce at a farm stand.

Just what I needed to kill Gary, a shiny new gun. I stepped toward them.

"No touching," Patrick warned. "Do you want something to drink?"

"Okay."

I didn't touch, but I did bend over to examine the weapons. I didn't spot the Magnum I'd used to kill Cifelli.

"Soda, right?"

"Beer if you have it, I could use one," I muttered, still studying the instruments of death, wondering which one could be used to bring about the end of Gary.

I heard Patrick open two beers and then a crinkling of a cellophane bag which I took to mean there'd be a snack served with the drink. I was up for that . . . as long as it wasn't donuts.

"Here you go." Handing me my beverage, he put his own down on the floor and started gathering up the guns to make a place for us to sit. When he was done with that, he sat down and patted the cushion beside him.

I looked around for the snack. A bag of pretzels remained on the counter.

"Okay, so tell me about this trouble you're in."

Refusing to sit, I instead paced the length of the couch nervously. "It's Gary the Gun."

"You promised you weren't going to go after Gary."

"I didn't 'promise'."

"All right. You told me you weren't going to."

"I wasn't."

"So what's the problem?"

I took a big swallow of alcohol for courage. "He has pictures."

Patrick took a long swig of his beer, sat all the way back in his seat, and closed his eyes, as though this conversation with me was giving him a headache. "What kind of pictures?"

"I screwed up."

"Will you please sit down? You're making me nervous pacing like that."

Obediently, I perched on the edge of the cushion beside him. "I'm sorry."

"What kind of pictures, Mags?" I got the distinct impression he was being deliberately patient with me.

"Of me pulling the trigger," I admitted in a whisper.

His eyes snapped open. "Did you not pay one whit of attention to me? Did I not tell you right off the bat what Rule Number One is?"

"Don't get caught." Even though he'd stayed perfectly still and hadn't raised his voice, I could tell he was steamed. I couldn't blame him. "He's blackmailing me."

Tilting his head back, he chugged the rest of his beer without coming up for air.

"He wants me to pay him ten thousand dollars."

He put the bottle down with exaggerated care beside the couch. "That's not so bad."

"A month. For a year."

"Greedy bastard."

"Or he'll turn the photos over to the cops . . . not you."

"Not me?"

"He said *that redheaded freak*. I assumed he meant you."

"You think I'm a freak?" He sounded hurt. "Cuz I'm not such a bad guy. I mean sure, I do some bad things, but I'm a pretty good guy."

I wondered if he'd been drinking before he'd met me, because I sort of doubted that one beer could make someone ramble like that. "I just assumed he meant you because I don't know any other redheads."

"I'm just trying to do what's best for my family . . . families," he said sadly.

"And," I said, trying desperately to return his attention to my plight, "he threatened my family. I mean he confronted me in Katie's room. He was waiting there. Studying my routine. Hunting me just like you said he would."

Patrick shook his head. "I told you he was a bad man."

"So now you understand why I have to kill him, don't you?" Placing my beer on the floor, I twisted in my seat so that I could look him in the eye while I pled my case.

"I can't let you do that, Mags."

"You have to!"

"If I let you go after him alone, he'll kill you for sure. I'm going to have to help you. You have to agree that we'll do it together."

"You're going to help me? I wasn't sure I'd heard him correctly. I was pretty sure that was in violation of a number of his rules.

He nodded.

"Really?"

His mouth twitched as though he was holding back a smile. "Really."

I threw my arms around his neck. "Thank you! Thank you! Thank you!" This was more than I had dared to hope for. I thought I might have had a chance to convince him to arm me, and maybe an outside chance he'd help me hash out a plan of attack, but I'd never imagined he'd actually offer to help me.

For the first time in weeks, something was finally going my way.

Leaving my hands looped around his neck, I leaned back and searched his face. "You mean it, right?"

His stared at me, soaking up my expression. "I've never seen you happy before." Gently, his touch as soft as a feather, he brushed the hair off my face with his fingers.

He didn't bother to hide his smile as he tucked it behind my ear.

I knew he was going to kiss me, and even though I knew it was probably a bad idea, I wanted him to. I let my eyes drift closed, inviting his approach.

"It's a good look on you," he whispered, before he touched his lips to my . . . forehead.

Yes, he pressed a chaste kiss to my forehead like I was a five-year-old. Pushing away from him, he jumped to his feet, stalked into the kitchen and dug into the bag of pretzels.

For my part, I just sat on the couch, too stunned to move. How had I misread his intentions so badly? I felt like the world's biggest idiot.

"You want another beer?" he asked through a mouthful of crunch, opening the fridge and staring into it.

"Still working on this one," I managed to choke out, snatching it up.

"Did he give you a deadline for getting him the money?"

"Seventy-two hours."

"So we'll have to work fast." He was still standing in front of the open refrigerator, leaving me to wonder if he was memorizing the contents or trying to get what he really wanted to magically materialize. I found that I did the latter myself quite often when I was home.

A cell phone buzzed. Pulling it from his pocket he glanced at the caller ID and frowned.

I wondered which of his wives was calling. Even if

he'd only had one spouse, it seemed to me that the man was never home.

"Hello?"

He closed the fridge door. "Yeah . . . okay."

He held out the phone toward me. "He wants to know if I'm with the ballsy broad."

I took it, trying not to notice that it was still warm from his body heat. "Hello?"

"So you asked for my help," Delveccio boomed.

I held the phone away from my ear. "Yes . . . we made the trade . . . the number for the pudding."

"I like you, Miss Lee."

"Um . . . thanks?"

"Which is why I'm going to give you some more help."

I waved Patrick over to sit beside me so that he too could hear the conversation. "What kind of help?"

"I've got . . . friends in the Coroner's office. Word is some teenagers were messing around in the park and found a body."

My breath caught in my throat. That meant it was time for Gary the Gun to collect my fee for killing Delveccio's son-in-law.

"The thing is . . ." Delveccio continued, "they're kind of swamped. There was a bus accident on the highway. So I've asked my friends to sort of stick the guy from the park in a back drawer, as it was. You get what I'm saying?"

I did. Tony/Anthony Delveccio was buying me some time.

"They figure they won't get to that particular stiff for about two days. You get my meaning?"

"Yessir." That meant I had two days to get rid of Gary the Gun, collect my fee from Delveccio, and save Katie.

The mobster chuckled. "*Yessir* . . . I could get used to that. You've got two days, Miss Lee."

He ended the call. I handed Patrick's phone back to him.

"I take it you didn't tell the boss that Gary's blackmailing you."

I shook my head.

"Smart girl."

Chapter Thirty-Five

It is impossible to feel that you are anything but the world's biggest idiot during Insuring the Future's quarterly staff meetings. It's not because the information they're passing along is difficult to understand, but rather it's because they deliver it to you as though you're a kindergartner.

Who's been kept back.

Twice.

Patrick had insisted that I stick with my regular routine, meaning showing up for this mind-rotting, soul-sucking day at work, while he drew up a plan to deal with Gary the Gun.

While I sat in the World's Most Boring Meeting Ever, I kept myself entertained by coming up with different ways to kill Harry, the World's Most Annoying Boss Ever. My favorite so far was rigging that damn laser pointer he was so fond of to explode in his hand. I wasn't certain that would kill him, but I did think it would be pretty damn satisfying to watch him screaming and bleeding.

Armani of course, strolled, or more accurately limped, into the meeting late, so we didn't get to sit together. Midway through the first hour, she got up and walked out for a potty break. This pleased me because it was obvious that it irritated Harry, who followed her painfully slow progress out the door. When she came back in, she whispered something in the ear of one of my co-workers seated near me . . . Laura? Laurie? Lauren? . . . one of those, and handed her a folded up piece of paper.

What happened next made me feel like I was back in junior high, as the note made its way down the aisle in my direction, with every single person communicating to the next who it was meant for. When it finally reached me, there was silence.

I stared at the folded up sheet of paper remembering the time Alice had slipped me a note in homeroom telling me that she had a date with . . . funny, but I couldn't remember the guy's name, but he'd been my secret crush for most of the school year . . . and that she hoped I wouldn't be mad at her. I had been. Furious.

Even worse than her betrayal is that Kurt, my teenage nemesis, and Alice's second-best friend, had offered me his condolences when he'd found out. I wasn't sure who I'd hated more at that point in time Alice or Kurt. The memory made me squeeze the paper as though I was wringing the life out of it.

Harry said something about "customer satisfaction" which felt like a cold slap across the face, bringing me back to the present.

I unfolded Armani's note and read the three words she'd scribbled down: Doomsday is coming.

I considered crossing it out and sending it back to her with a note of my own which would have read: "WTF???". Instead I spent the rest of the morning session wondering if she was commenting on the state of the meeting, or if it was another premonition she'd had.

If it was a premonition, then things weren't looking up for my take-down of Gary the Gun. When we finally broke for lunch (meaning Harry said, "You're dismissed") I headed straight for our favorite picnic table to wait for Armani. While I sat there I gave my cell a quick check to see if Patrick had called. He hadn't.

Aunt Leslie had. She apologized for being such a poor guest (which insinuated she'd been invited over, which, for the record, she hadn't) and had, as I'd requested in the note I'd taped to the shirt she was wearing, left her key for my place on the kitchen table. She sounded hurt that I didn't want her having free rein to invade my privacy any time she felt like it.

I think it's important to mention that I never gave Aunt Leslie, or the other two, the key to my place. My sister, Theresa, bless her almost-saintly soul, took it upon herself to do that after I gave *her* the key in case she ever needed to get away from Dirk the Jerk.

"Hey there, Chiquita," Armani greeted me with such a fake note of cheeriness, I winced.

"Hey there yourself, Queen of Doom and Gloom." I waved the paper she'd had passed to me. "What's this about?"

Settling into the seat opposite me, she tossed her mane of dark hair dramatically.

I wasn't impressed.

"I had another dream. In it, I kept hearing those three words. Doomsday is coming. Doomsday is coming."

"And you know for sure they're a warning for me?"

"They could be for the entire world, but I was thinking I should keep that, if that's the case, to myself. I probably shouldn't go around telling a whole lot of people because there would just be worldwide panic and chaos."

"I never knew you were such a humanitarian," I told her.

"Seriously though, Maggie, I think it's meant for you."

I shrugged. The way my life was going I figured the odds were good she was right, but I didn't tell her that.

"Did you meet the guy?"

"I'm meeting a guy for a dinner date. The one I told you about, the cop."

"So this is like the third date with him, right?"

I nodded. I'd given her an abbreviated version of the debacle of a date Aunt Loretta had invaded.

"So you must really like him."

And that was the million dollar question. Did I like Paul? On the one hand he seemed overly sure of his sexual attraction and had the nerve to order me a meal without even consulting me. On the other hand, he hadn't yet been scared off by my crazy family, and he'd been awfully kind to Aunt Leslie.

"He brought me flowers. I hate them."

"Flowers are a point in the winner column," Armani

mused. “And he took you to Angelo’s, that’s another thing in his favor.”

I nodded, but was thinking that God didn’t trust him.

“And he is hot enough to melt an iceberg.”

“I didn’t say that.”

“I guessed. I mean you did agree to go out with him during your first meeting.”

“I’ve freed my inner Chiquita, and I’m living dangerously,” I said dryly. At least the living dangerously part was true, though if her doomsday prediction was on the money, I might not be doing that for too much longer.

Chapter Thirty-Six

Stacy Kiernan, the social worker who'd spilled her guts to me, was laying in wait when I got to the hospital for my daily after-work visit with Katie. To the untrained eye it probably looked as though she was just joking around at the nurse's station, but I knew from the way her eyes darted in my direction the moment I walked through the doors that she was like a lioness after prey.

There was a time, not that long ago, when remarkably unremarkable Maggie Lee would have been alarmed by this development, but now I regularly interacted with hitmen and mobsters. . . . I ate hospital administrators for breakfast now.

"Maggie? Do you have a minute?"

"Sure." I followed her to the waiting area, amused that she chose the same seats we'd used last time. "How are you?"

"That's one of the things I wanted to talk to you about. I never really got the chance to thank you, but after our talk . . ." She glanced around to make sure no one was listening.

They weren't. Why would they?

"After our talk my life got so much better. It's done a complete turnaround." She smiled an ear-to-ear grin as though that would prove that she was deliriously happy.

Considering it had only been a few days, I thought she was probably exaggerating. "That's nice."

"No, you don't understand." She grabbed my hand. "Everything's changed. I inherited a house, I met a great, new guy, and I got a new job."

"Congratulations. I'm happy for you." I wasn't. I was wondering if somehow she'd managed to transfer her bad luck to me, like you'd see in a movie or something.

"And I owe it all to you, Maggie. That's why I'm sorry to bring this up."

She let go of my hand, sat back, and put on her reading glasses, her own personal Bat-signal that she meant business. "About your niece's bill . . ." She waited, one of those long expectant pauses that probably usually compelled whoever she was dealing with to blurt out a reply.

Just to fuck with her life-is-so-freakin-great head, I held my tongue. Not because I disliked her, but because I was sick to death of having everyone, Harry, Delveccio, Gary the Gun, call the shots.

She was finally forced to ask, "Have you come up with the money?"

"I'm waiting to find out if an investment I made will pay off."

"Will you know soon?"

"In the next couple of days."

She nodded approvingly. "Good. Good. I gave notice and leave in five days."

"Your new job isn't here?"

She shook her head. "No. I hate this job. I never wanted this," she waved her hands as though to encompass the whole hospital. "I want to help people. Like you helped me."

"Oh." Now I was feeling guilty for messing with her.

"I'm going to bury Katie's paperwork as best I can, but at most, you'll probably only have a week or so."

"You're going to do that for me?" I've got to admit I was surprised by her generosity. I'd only let the poor woman cry on my shoulder that one time, and here she was doing this incredibly generous thing for me. I felt guilty for my earlier thought about eating her.

"Oh course," she said, flashing that huge smile again. "That's what friends are for. It's against company policy for us to socialize, but I hope that once I've left, we can get to know each other better."

"I'd like that."

"Okay, like I said, I'll do what I can to keep her." With that, Stacy hurried over to another patient's family.

I made my way to Katie's room. "Hey there, Baby Girl."

No response.

I read *Where the Wild Things Are* to her for about the hundredth time, wondering if she heard me, wishing I knew whether or not she even knew I was there.

I fussed with her bedclothes, making sure she was

tucked in just like she liked, with the covers pulled up to her chin, but not tucked too tight. I tried to tuck Dino under her arm, but I couldn't find the stuffed toy. I looked under the bed, felt the sheets to make sure he hadn't gotten lost under them, and even searched under the visitor's chair. He was nowhere to be found, so instead I took her sagging hand and began singing "The Itsy Bitsy Spider."

I remembered how she'd been giggling over the song when the car accident had occurred. It came back to me in flashes. Her crooked smile. Her twinkling eyes.

The skid. The roll. The screeching and squealing of metal. The impact. The pain.

I closed my eyes, trying to tamp down the remembered terror that was making my heart race.

"Quite the touching scene."

Opening my eyes, I whirled to find Gary the Gun standing in the doorway.

"Fuck you!"

"If you want, but I'm not knocking any money off what you owe me." He grinned, amused by his own joke.

"Get out!" I raised my voice, hoping it would attract the attention of a nurse or orderly.

"But I just got here."

"You said I had seventy-two hours."

"Indeed I did. I just wanted to see if you were sticking to your regular schedule."

A chill skittered down my spine. This animal knew my schedule? "You'll get your money."

"As long as we understand one another."

I didn't reply; I just glared at him.

He didn't look particularly intimidated.

"Oh hello," Aunt Loretta called from the hallway. "Are you a friend of our Maggie?"

For once I was grateful for her interfering.

"Get out of my way," Gary growled, pushing past her and stalking away.

I sagged weakly against Katie's bed.

I couldn't take much more of this.

"What a rude little man," Aunt Loretta complained entering the room. "Is he a friend of yours?"

I shook my head.

Tilting her head, she examined me closely. "Are you feeling all right? You look . . . funny."

That was probably because I was feeling sick to my stomach after my exchange with Gary. "I'm just tired."

Aunt Loretta pressed her lips to my forehead and held them there for a long beat. This was her tried-and-true method of determining if one was running a temperature. "No fever," she declared.

"I told you, I'm just tired."

"That's because you're burning the candle at both ends, working, coming here, dating . . . how did your date go with that nice young man?"

So that was how she wanted to play it, like she hadn't joined us uninvited, told him my father's in the big house, and then fled the table in tears.

"It was nice." I played along, and then because she was apprehensively eyeing me as though waiting for me to rip into about her meddling, I let her off the hook. "We're going to have dinner again tonight."

Before she could finish opening her mouth to speak, I told her, "And no, I'm not telling you where we're going."

She had the good grace to look away.

"Did Aunt Leslie make it home okay this morning?"

"About that . . ." Aunt Loretta didn't often get cross with me . . . or with anyone for that matter. So when she did, it was something to behold. She crossed her arms over her barely covered chest, tapped her stilettoed foot impatiently, and gave me a look that would have made Aunt Susan proud. "She said you took her key away."

"I asked her to leave it."

"Why on earth would you do that?"

"I need my privacy."

"That's what you said when you moved out," Aunt Susan complained from the doorway.

Loretta and I both spun in her direction. Neither of us had been aware of her arrival.

"Yes, that's what adults do," I countered. "They grow up. They move out. They value privacy."

Strolling over to Katie's bedside, Susan said, "You make it sound as though you were forced to share a room with twelve other orphans."

Aunt Loretta chuckled at her sister's joke. I did not.

Growing up, I'd shared a room with Theresa. Even though she had been older, I'd been the first to move out. My aunts had never forgiven me for "breaking up the family," even though Marlene had actually been the first to jump ship, running away after her twin Darlene died.

The thought of Marlene squeezed my chest and caused my eyes to burn. Yet another loss I was never going to recover from. I'd spent so much time searching for her that first year after she ran away. Trying to find her, desperate to make things right. But every lead had resulted in a dead end. And when we didn't hear from her after a couple of years, I gave up any hope she was still alive, let alone ever going to come home.

"Leslie is family," Loretta reminded me, as though I hadn't been aware of that little fact. "It's not like she's a stranger or something."

"Aunt Leslie can't be coming over to my place and passing out in front of my front door. If Paul hadn't been there, I don't know how I would have gotten her inside."

"Who's Paul?" Susan asked.

"Paul was there?" Loretta asked simultaneously.

"Paul is not the point!" I snarled.

"Just as I told you, she's in an ill temper." Loretta said to Susan who nodded in agreement.

If I'd had any doubts about whether or not they'd planned to gang up on me, now I was certain, when at that instant, Aunt Leslie stumbled in, "Sorry I'm late."

"Only two visitors at a time," I called, as though it could somehow ward off whatever spell the three witches were about to cast. I know you think that I'm exaggerating, or maybe just plain crazy, but when the three of them put their heads together about something, or in this case someone, which unfortunately meant me, they're extraordinarily evil in their own "helpfully" meddlesome way. Okay, maybe not evil like Gary the Gun or Alfonso Cifelli, but they can make mere mortals, such as me, do things they normally wouldn't.

As head of the coven, it fell to Aunt Susan to mutter the ancient incantation, "We want you to move home."

"No."

They looked a bit surprised that their spell hadn't worked right off the bat, but, undaunted, the twins chanted the spell together. "We need you to move home."

Crossing my arms over my chest, I shook my head. "No way. And who are you," I asked, pointing at Aunt Loretta, "to ask me to move home, when you're practically selling the place out from under Aunt Susan?"

"But I'm not, Darling."

"You're not?" I looked to Susan for confirmation. She was nodding serenely.

"You dumped the rat?" I asked hopefully.

Loretta blinked her mascara-heavy eyes. "Templeton? Of course not."

"Of course not," I muttered dejectedly. That would have been too much to ask for.

"And I'd appreciate it if you wouldn't call him that."

Bringing the conversation back on track with icy efficiency, Aunt Susan said, "We want you to move home. For a while. Nothing permanent. Just until things settle down."

I shook my head. I was already going around killing people and talking to a lizard; moving in with these three would surely buy me an express ticket to Crazyville.

I looked at their hopeful faces. Loretta and Leslie were looking at me like kids hoping to receive permission to get a puppy, and Aunt Susan was regarding me with undisguised curiosity.

I wanted to shout, *Hell no!* Instead I said, "Thank you for the offer. I do appreciate it, but I just can't accept."

Loretta and Leslie looked crestfallen. You'd have thought I'd told them that *The National Enquirer* isn't a real newspaper or something. Usually I felt annoyance when it came to my aunts, but at that moment all I felt was guilt for letting them down. After all, they had done a lot for me over the course of my life, and now all of them were showing up with regularity for Katie. "I will however make an effort to visit . . . and more . . . and more regularly."

"Oh Maggie, that's wonderful!" Aunts Loretta and Leslie cried out simultaneously, enveloping me in what they called an "L-and-L hug" when I was a kid.

"Family dinners!" Leslie cried.

"Sunday breakfasts," Loretta declared.

While being smothered by the twins, it occurred to me that Aunt Susan hadn't said a word. Craning my neck to peer around my other aunts' arms, I looked for her.

When we made eye contact, she mouthed, "Thank you." Then she hurriedly left the room, leaving me in the embrace of my two more emotional aunts.

And in that moment I felt pretty damn good.

And then Templeton the Rat sauntered in, his face still bruised from the attack by Aunt Loretta's portrait.

He looked awfully damn smug.

"Look what I found," he called, breaking up our family hug. He held up Dino and waved the stuffed toy like it was a winning lottery ticket. "It was in the waiting area."

I eyed him suspiciously. I hadn't seen it while I was with Stacy Kiernan. How had it gotten there?

"Oh that's wonderful, Templeton." Aunt Loretta rewarded him for his find with a hug. "It's Katie's favorite. I'm sure that when she wakes up she'll be thrilled it's here."

"I wonder how it got out there," Aunt Leslie mused, voicing my own thought.

"Strange things happen in hospitals," Templeton said. "Why I once heard of a patient who just up and disappeared out of a hospital once. Paraplegic, poor fellow. One minute he was in his bed, the next he was gone. Some people said it was aliens who took him for experimentation."

I walked out of the room as he spun his story.

I wasn't buying his bullshit.

Not any of it.

Chapter Thirty-Seven

"It's just a little too convenient that he's the one who found it," I complained to God as I got dressed for my date with Paul.

The lizard was barely listening to me. Most of his attention was focused on whatever idiotic true-crime show he was watching on television. He was convinced that he would find the solution to the Gary the Gun problem in an episode.

"I mean Templeton walks in with the "found" toy, and all of a sudden he's the great rescuer or something? What's that about? Manipulative, that's what it is, if you ask me."

"No one's asked you," God drawled. "No one cares."

Just for that I turned off the TV.

"Hey, I was watching that."

"No one cares."

"I can't believe you're going on this date."

"Patrick says I should maintain as normal a schedule as possible."

"Normally you live like the proverbial old woman with too many cats," the lizard reminded me. "Theresa was always worried you were going to end up alone, a bitter, old spinster."

"Don't tempt me with the cat idea," I warned. "I bet you'd make a nice snack for one."

"You wouldn't dare."

Flopping on the bed, I looked him in the eye. "We have to talk."

"I thought we were already doing that."

"It's about your future."

"A cat-free future I hope."

"I'm going to take you to the hospital tomorrow."

I'll be damned if the lizard didn't jump up in the air and clap his hands.

Regaining his composure, he said haughtily, "Finally. I've been waiting forever to see Katie."

"And as I told you, about a hundred times, they don't allow pets there."

"And as I told *you*, you could always just tell them I'm a service animal."

"Dogs are service animals. Monkeys are service animals. Lizards are not service animals!"

"Have you ever tried talking to a dog?" God asked. "Their grammar is atrocious."

Determined to get through this conversation without losing my cool, I told him calmly, "I'm going to leave you in Katie's room."

"Does she have a TV?"

"She's in a coma! Why the hell would she need a TV?"

Despite my best intentions I found myself shouting at the reptile. I took a breath and counted to ten.

"Have you ever considered anger-management classes?"

"Have you ever considered dropping dead?" Flinging myself off the bed, I stalked into the kitchen. I glared at the stinking lilies propped in my pitcher and considered sticking them in God's enclosure since he hated the smell as much as me.

A cell phone rang, disrupting my evil plan. It was one of the throwaways Patrick had given me.

"Please tell me you have a plan," I said as way of greeting.

"You really need to work on your phone skills, Mags," he teased. "One usually says something like, *hello*. Followed by *what's new? or how are you?* You should give it a try sometime."

"Hello," I said grudgingly.

"Hi, Mags. How are you?"

"Not good. Not good at all. Gary was at the hospital again."

On the other end of the line, Patrick crunched on his Lifesaver. "What did he say?"

"He was making sure I was keeping to my schedule. It freaked me out that he knew I even had a schedule. Please tell me that you've come up with a plan."

"I have."

Silence.

"And . . . ?" I coaxed.

"I'm working out the details. I'll tell you about it tonight."

"I've got a date tonight."

Again with the silence.

"You're the one who told me to act as normal as possible. Wouldn't it look suspicious if I turned down a date with a cop?"

"So this is with Kowalski?"

"Uh huh." I got the distinct impression he didn't approve. I wonder what it meant that my aunts thought my going out with an officer of the law was the best thing ever, while Patrick and God seemed to think it was a terrible idea.

Not that Patrick said that. He didn't say anything.

"You still there?" I knew he was since it sounded as though he was chomping on an entire roll of mints.

"I'm here."

"So about the plan?"

"It's gotta be tonight."

"Okay, I'll cancel my date."

"Don't do that!" His tone was uncharacteristically sharp.

"I thought you didn't want me to go."

"I don't want you to cancel even more."

"So what the hell am I supposed to do?"

"Go on your date, go home, and whatever you do, don't let Kowalski inside."

"Why not? He's already been here."

"More information than I needed," Patrick muttered. "You can't let him in, because I'm going to be there. Waiting for you."

"Oh." I wasn't sure how I felt about this relative

stranger being alone in my home. After all, I'd just been preaching about the value of privacy a little while earlier.

As though he could read my thoughts, Patrick said softly, "I promise not to snoop . . . except maybe in your fridge if I get hungry."

"Fair enough. Don't eat the leftover Chinese food, I'm pretty sure it's covered in fungus."

"Good to know. Bye, Mags." He disconnected the call.

As he'd instructed, I opened the phone, pulled out the SIM card, and cut it into tiny pieces which I then flushed down the toilet.

"The redhead thinks this date is a bad idea too, doesn't he?" God called from the bedroom.

I'd forgotten that the little guy would have eavesdropped on my entire conversation. I don't know why I was worried about Patrick invading my privacy; the lizard had already obliterated it.

Ignoring the Paul question I strolled back into the bedroom. "He's come up with a plan to get rid of Gary the Gun. He'll be over later to tell me about it."

"Good, good. Now tell me again why you're taking me to Katie tomorrow."

I'd really been hoping he wouldn't ask that question. This was one discussion I didn't want to have, but he deserved the truth. "I'm worried about what could happen to you if . . . if I don't survive the hit on Gary. If I end up dead. . . ."

"You're not going to end up dead," God said dismissively, as though he thought that the possibility was itself an impossibility.

"Armani had another premonition. She said Doomsday is coming."

"Yeah? So what? Do you have any idea how many people predict that every single day? Haven't you ever seen them on the news carrying their signs?"

"He's a highly trained, highly motivated killer. I could die. And if I do, I want to make sure that you're not forgotten here. I need to make provisions for you to be cared for."

The lizard pressed up against the glass, as though to get a better look at me. "You're kidding me, right?" he sounded incredulous.

That stung. "I thought we'd become . . . friends." I swallowed the lump in my throat. "Is it really so hard to believe that I'd care what happens to you?"

"Don't be an idiot."

"Fine! Stay here. Rot here for all I care. They'll probably forget all about you, and you'll starve!" I stormed out.

"Come back here, you moron!" He shouted. There was a slight pause, in a tone that sounded pretty close to groveling he added, "Please."

I came back inside, switched on the TV for him, and walked out again.

"I'm sorry I hurt your feelings. Please come back and talk to me, Maggie." His reasonable tone had some sort of hypnotic effect. I did what he said. I turned the TV off again.

"Sit," he requested.

I did on the edge of the bed.

"You misunderstood me."

"You called me an idiot and a moron. You think there are other ways of interpreting those words?"

"I meant them as terms of endearment."

"Yeah, right."

"You can't leave me when you go to kill Gary."

"I told you, I'm going to make sure you're cared for. That's why I'm taking you to the hospital."

"No, you nincompoop. What I mean is, you have to take me with you when you go after Gary."

"Why?" I refrained from pointing out he'd done a half-assed job as a lookout when we went hunting Alfonso Cifelli, considering he'd missed Gary the Gun's presence

"Because friends don't let friends kill alone."

"I think that's the nicest thing you've said to me."

"Yeah, well don't get used to it. Now turn on the tube for me."

I switched on the television. "If I live through tomorrow, I'm going to get you some more crickets."

"Live crickets."

"Yes, live crickets."

A sudden banging on my front door startled us both. A glance at the bedside clock told me that either Paul was half an hour early for our date, or I had an unexpected visitor.

Would Gary the Gun knock? He did seem to enjoy scaring people, and, if he'd been following me, he would know where I lived. He hadn't hesitated to threaten me in the hospital. There was no reason to think he wouldn't hurt me here.

"Arm yourself!" God cried nervously.

Trembling like a dog during a thunderstorm, I picked up a hairbrush.

"That'll scare them for sure," he said.

I threw the brush back down. "Maybe I'll just throw your cage at him."

"At who?"

"Gary."

"How do you know it's Gary?"

I stared at him. "Who else would it be?"

"Why don't you ask?"

I hate when he makes perfect sense. "Who is it?" I yelled with false bravado.

"It's Lamont. I'm sorry to bother you like this, Maggie, but I need your help."

Sighing my relief, I ran to my front door to let Alice's baby-daddy in. "Hey, Lamont."

"I need your help."

"Come in, come in." I waved the big guy inside and pointed to my couch.

"Who's this one?" God called from the bedroom.

I ignored him. "You didn't eat the love muffins, did you?"

He shook his head.

"Good, because short of recommending a trip to the emergency room, there's not much I could do for you if that was your problem. So what can I do for you?"

"Forgive me for being rude but . . ." He trailed off as though unsure of how to continue.

"My aunts are driving you crazy?"

He shook his head.

That surprised me. I thought my aunts drove everyone crazy.

Then he nodded.

Which just served to confuse me. "Where's Alice?"

Lamont had the good grace to look uncomfortable. "Visiting your dad."

I rolled my eyes. Alice had always had a soft spot for my father.

"She told me what he did for her." Lamont cracked his knuckles. "It was a good thing he did."

I really didn't give a shit what the big guy thought of Archie Lee, but I was interested in something else he'd said. "She told you?"

He nodded.

I considered that for a long moment. I didn't think she'd ever told anyone that before. Hell, she didn't even talk about it with me. The only conclusion I could draw was that Lamont was special, really special.

The special man wrinkled his nose. "Forgive me, but what is that smell?"

I ignored God's chortling from the bedroom. "Lilies. My . . ." Oh crap, what the hell was Paul to me? "They were a gift from my date."

"Oh. I'm sorry. I didn't mean to—"

I cut him off with a raised hand. "I know. I know. It smells like something died in here."

Relieved, he nodded.

"But I'm guessing that you didn't come here to tell me that my home stinks."

"I want to ask Alice to marry me," he blurted out.

"Oh." I'd been so sure he'd been here about the witches. Now he was telling me he wanted to become a permanent fixture in my best friend's life. I wasn't sure how I felt about that. While I wanted Alice to be happy, I really wasn't thrilled with the prospect of having to share the most stable person in my life with someone else. Not right now when I was struggling to figure out which way was up.

"You think it's a bad idea?" The big man took my long silence to mean I didn't approve. He looked like he was about to crumple.

I shook my head, thinking fast. "No, of course not. It's just that . . . well geez, up until a week ago I didn't even know you existed, and now you're telling me you want to become part of the family. It's a lot to absorb."

"I understand."

"You really love her that much?"

"I can't imagine my life without her."

"You do know she's not perfect, right? I mean I know she's beautiful and smart and so sweet she puts diabetics into sugar shock, but she does have her faults. For one, she faints at the sight of blood, even her own. Two, if you're not careful she'll steal the marshmallow shapes out of your bowl of Lucky Charms."

"I don't eat Lucky Charms."

"Three," I said, warming to my task. "She's been obsessed with naming her kid Kaitlin, since we were like ten. What are you gonna do if it's a boy?"

Lamont chuckled. "You forgot to mention that she

grinds her teeth in her sleep, makes sure her foods don't touch when they're on her dinner plate, and she's tone deaf."

Impressed, I nodded. He seemed to know her pretty well. Could it be that after a string of losers, Alice had gone halfway around the world and found a winner?

"Where are you planning on living?" I asked.

I guess he heard the challenge in my tone, because he raised an eyebrow. "Wherever she wants. Though between you and me, I'm really hoping that she doesn't choose the B&B."

"Not Chicago?"

"Have you ever been to Chicago in the winter? It's cold."

"You've never spent an August in New Jersey," I countered. "It's humid. And muggy. And smoggy. And if you're not careful, the mosquitos will drain you dry."

"I'm a big guy to drain," he replied easily.

I couldn't argue with that.

"The reason I'm here, Maggie, is that I don't know how to propose to her."

"Ring. Question. From what I've heard, it seems like a fairly simple process."

Lamont rolled his eyes. "C'mon. The woman's had her unborn kid's name picked out for decades. Are you really going to try to tell me she doesn't have some dream proposal she's always imagined?"

"And you want me to tell you what that is?"

He nodded. "That's why I'm here."

He was, of course, absolutely right. Just about the time

Alice had picked out the name Kaitlin, she'd decided how she wanted to be proposed to. I was duly impressed that Lamont had figured that out and come to me.

"You must really want to make her happy."

"I do. You'll help me?"

"You're not going to like it."

He shrugged. "I don't have to like it. It's for her."

That, of course, was the response I was looking for.

"Don't say I didn't warn you. On one knee. In the middle of Couples Skate. At The Starlight Roller Rink."

I gotta give the guy credit. He blinked, but didn't bitch and moan about it. I'm pretty sure that meant the guy was officially smitten.

"Thank you, Maggie."

"My pleasure. You just make her happy. Just remember, if you hurt her, I'll have to kill you." Assuming I was still alive.

"She means it!" God shouted from the bedroom. "It's why she doesn't have a vase!"

I walked Lamont to my front door.

"You won't tell her, will you?" he asked.

"Of course not. It'll be our secret." I opened the door to let him out.

"Thanks, Maggie. You're just as Alice describes you."

"And how's that?"

"Gruff but good."

I made a mental note to tell my best friend that she should come up with a nicer way to describe me. *Gruff but good* sounded like a tire slogan. "Glad I could help."

"One more thing I wanted to ask."

Behind him, I saw Paul's car pull into the parking lot. "Sure, shoot."

"A ruby, right? Not a diamond ring."

I beamed. "You must be a hell of a listener, Lamont. My friend is a lucky girl to have ended up with a catch like you. Welcome to the family!" I moved to hug him and gasped when he lifted me off my feet in a giant bear-hug.

"See you soon, Maggie." He put me down and walked away waving and smiling.

As soon as he was gone, I waved at Paul's car. I held up a single finger indicating I'd be just a minute and dove back inside my apartment.

I snagged my purse and checked to make sure the lizard had enough water.

"Don't forget I think this is a bad idea," he grumbled.

"Duly noted."

Paul was leaning against his car when I got out to the parking lot. His T-shirt looked as though it might split across his pecs if he crossed his arms any harder. "Who was that?" he asked by way of greeting, making no effort to conceal his jealousy.

"Just a friend." I wasn't really into answering to the overly possessive type.

"Seemed awfully chummy for just a friend."

"He's just excited. He's going to ask my best friend to marry him and wanted some advice for the proposal."

"Oh." He walked around the car to open my door for me. "So you were telling him how to pick out the diamond and stuff like that?"

I pecked him on the cheek. "Stuff like that."

"Do you know a lot about that kind of stuff? Jewels? Gems?"

"I'm a girl, so I should know about that stuff. Is that what you're saying?" I held up both my bare hands. "In case you didn't notice, jewelry's not really my thing."

He laughed. "Is steak?"

"You bet!"

"Let's go to dinner."

Chapter Thirty-Eight

If a condemned man (or in this case, woman) is entitled to one last meal, Artie's Steakhouse is the place to get it. A local joint that features autographed headshots of celebrities who are now milking the last of what passes for their fame on a slew of celebrity "reality" shows, Artie's has a last-century vibe, but they serve the best beef in the county.

I must admit I was pretty darn excited when Paul announced where we were going. My attitude seemed to cheer him up, and we chatted amiably, mostly about Aunt Loretta and Aunt Leslie, all the way to the restaurant.

The mood in the car soured the moment we turned into the parking lot. It was empty.

Artie's is never empty. It's always packed. Even with a reservation, there's usually a wait.

"What the hell?" Paul threw his car into park, leapt out, and stalked over to the front door.

I could see there was a sign taped to it. I could see that Paul moved his lips while he read the sign. I could also see he was none-too-pleased about whatever the sign said.

I, however, was resigned to my fate. I should have known that a decent dinner was not in the cards for me. That's the way my luck was going.

"Health inspector shut them down." Paul slid back into the car. Suddenly the air in the enclosed space took on a negative charge.

"Some other time. Have you ever been to—"

"Goddammit!" He punched his dashboard.

I cringed.

"Dammit!"

"It's okay," I soothed, thinking that a guy who attacked his car because a restaurant was closed probably wasn't the one for me. Armani must have been wrong about him.

"It's not okay!" He drove his fist into the roof.

Swiveling in his seat, he glared at me, like it was my fault the health inspector had found something wrong with the place.

I leaned away from him. Suddenly the seatbelt that held me in my seat didn't feel so much like a safety device as a trap. Gulping, I reached for the release.

"I wanted this . . . this was supposed to be . . . this isn't the way . . ."

He was so angry he seemed incapable of completing a sentence. I had to calm him down before he totally went ballistic. I had to calm myself down before my heart beat right out of my chest.

"It's early. There are plenty of other places we can go." *Crowded places*, I thought. *Places where there are lots of people. Witnesses.*

"Like where?"

"Chinese?"

"I don't like rice."

"Mexican?"

"I don't like spicy."

"Italian?" He had to like Italian, otherwise we wouldn't have gone to Angelos.

"Had it for lunch."

I cast about for other options, desperate to find a place to go, if only so I could get out of the car. "How about . . . seafood?" I hate seafood.

He considered that one thoughtfully. "I guess so . . ."

"Oooh, I know," I said feigning excitement. "We could go to Crabby Sam's. Have you ever been there?"

He nodded. "You like that place?"

"*Love* it!" The lie came easily.

"Okay." He put the car into drive, rolled all of about ten feet, and put it back into park.

"What's wrong?"

"I shouldn't have lost my cool like that."

"It's okay."

Turning to face me, he said, "I was just so . . . frustrated."

I'm not proud of what I did next, I'm really not. You've got to understand that what I did came from a place of sheer desperation.

"I'm sorry to hear that. Are you okay?" Yes, I fell back on my Insuring the Future spiel!

"I had a terrible day at work," he confided. "My boss was on my ass and nothing went right . . ."

"Mmmm," I hoped that sounded like an empathetic murmur.

"And I was looking forward to tonight and then I saw you with that guy . . ."

"Lamont?"

"Is that his name? Lamont?"

I nodded.

"And I thought . . . I thought maybe the reason you and I haven't . . . haven't . . . is that you're hooking up with him."

"I told you, he's about to become my best friend's fiancé."

He nodded as though that made sense to him, but I got the distinct impression he was still puzzled as to why I hadn't slept with him.

I felt kind of bad knowing that it wasn't going to be happening at the end of this date either. Not with Patrick waiting back at my place.

"Maybe you should just take me home," I suggested.

"Cuz I lost my temper?" he asked sheepishly, hanging his head.

"Because I'm not sure you and I are going to work. Maybe we're not compatible."

"Oh, we're compatible." He leaned toward me, pressing his lips to mine, to prove his point.

I considered not kissing him, but I was all-too-aware we were in a deserted parking lot. It probably wasn't the best idea to rebuff his advances. Besides, he is one hell of a kisser.

So we kissed and groped and kissed some more.

"Want to go back to my place?" He finally asked.

I'll admit part of me did, but I couldn't get over the fact that both God and Patrick seemed to think this date with Paul was a bad idea.

Thankfully, I was saved from making a decision by the ringing of my cellphone. "Sorry. It could be the hospital." I squirmed out of his grasp, snatched up my purse, and fumbled for my phone. "Hello?"

"You have got to come to the B&B right now!" Alice shrieked.

"I'm kinda in the middle—"

"Now, Maggie!" she screamed.

Nearly-perfect Alice doesn't yell at people.

"What's wrong?"

"Templeton's going to die."

My heart dropped into my stomach. Gary the Gun. "Call the police."

"What are they going to do?"

"Stop him."

Alice of course thought I was referring to Templeton. "The police can't beat gravity."

"What?" I was thoroughly confused.

"Templeton's hanging from the weather vane!"

The bed and breakfast is three stories high and has a pitched roof, topped with an ancient, iron horse-and-buggy weather vane.

Paul, who could hear every word Alice shouted, was already peeling out of the parking lot.

"Tell him to hang on," I said weakly.

While I didn't have any use for Templeton the Rat. I sure as hell didn't want him to die.

Chapter Thirty-Nine

I WON'T BORE you with the details of Templeton's rescue, but I will say that Paul was pretty impressive when he swung into action. He got us to the B&B in record time, and he clambered up onto the roof without a moment's hesitation.

In the parking lot of Artie's, I'd been sure I was never going to go out with Paul again. My life was unstable enough as it was without adding a boyfriend with a hair-trigger temper to the mix. By the time Paul had performed his heroic deed complete with rippling muscles and assurances to my aunts that they shouldn't worry because he was a professional, Alice was whispering in my ear, "Where'd you find him?"

We ended up staying there for dinner. And by the time we were done with the meal, Paul had charmed my aunts, deflecting any attention they might have directed at me in the process, providing a much needed respite from their constant questioning. He'd even won over Aunt Susan by insisting she give him a room-by-room tour of the place.

During which I grilled Templeton on just how he'd managed to find Katie's dinosaur. Aunt Loretta didn't seem to realize it was an interrogation. She took it as an effort on my part to connect with the man she wanted to spend the rest of her life with and beamed and tittered through the entire questioning.

By the end of the evening, instead of thinking I'd be lucky if I never set eyes on Paul again, I was hoping that our next date would be sooner rather than later.

Assuming, of course, that I didn't end up dead or incarcerated before then.

"Thank you," I said, as he pulled into my parking lot to drop me off. I'd pretended to have a headache and had begged out of after dinner drinks. A request he'd accepted with an easy grace. "I know the evening didn't turn out the way you'd planned."

"You can say that again. I'm finding that being with you, Margaret Lee, is never boring." He slid the car into a parking space, threw it into park, and let the engine idle. "You don't like that Templeton guy do you?"

"I don't believe anything that comes out of the man's mouth."

"So you don't think he was trying to get a bag off the weather vane?"

"Hardly. Maybe he thinks that since it's an antique it's worth some money and he wanted to get a closer look at it."

"Could be. I'm sorry that I misunderstood about your relationship with Lamont earlier. He and Alice sure seem . . ."

"Smitten? In love? Head over heels?"

"All of that and more."

"How's your shin?" When Lamont had joined us at the dinner table saying he'd just gotten in from shopping, I'd had to kick Paul to signal he shouldn't mention the impending marriage proposal.

"I'll survive. Though you're going to have to make it up to me."

"I'd like that. But not tonight," I added in a rush before he got any ideas. I was all-too-aware that Patrick was waiting in my place. For all I knew he was watching us. "How about next time I make you dinner?" Yes, I know you're probably thinking that all I was capable of making was Lean Cuisine meals, but I knew my way around a stove. Sort of.

"I'd like that."

I reached for the door handle.

"What? No goodnight kiss?"

I hesitated. "Just a kiss."

"I promise."

True to his word, all Paul did was kiss me, making no move at all to even feel me up. I was sorta disappointed.

Once we broke apart, I leapt from the car, tossed an "I'll call you!" over my shoulder, and bolted for my apartment.

Once my front door was unlocked, I turned and waved good-bye to Paul. He flashed his headlights at me and then drove away. I slipped inside.

"I'm in the bedroom," Patrick called.

"You said you weren't going to snoop. So much for that promise!" I hissed.

Marching into the bedroom, I found Patrick sitting on the floor, his face inches from the television. I didn't bother to turn on the light. The flickering glow from the set gave us enough light.

"Find anything interesting?" I asked.

"I told you I wouldn't look around. I didn't."

"Then what the hell are you doing in here?"

"I thought you left the TV on for me."

"I left it on for him!" I pointed in the general vicinity of the lizard's terrarium.

"He didn't snoop," God informed me. "Go easy on the poor fellow."

Patrick slowly got to his feet. "Look, I'm sorry you had to cut your date short, but I'm not really in the mood to argue with you all night. So if you feel the need to unload on me, that's fine, but can we put a time limit on it, so that we can get to the plan?"

He delivered his request in such a reasonable tone, that I felt about as small as the lizard. "I'm sorry. I didn't mean . . . It's just that . . ."

"I didn't look through your stuff, Mags."

"I believe you." Normally I wouldn't have, but since the lizard was backing him up, I gave him the benefit of the doubt.

Patrick shook his head. "You always believe the worst of me. Half the time you think I'm out to kill you."

"If it makes you feel any better, I tend to think the worst of everyone. You're not special. Plus, you've had your chance to kill me a couple times now, so I'm starting to believe you won't."

"So that's why you've made sure to keep the bed between us this whole time? Because you're so sure I don't mean you any harm?"

He had me there, but I wasn't going to give him the satisfaction of confirming it. Instead I did my best to act casual as I sat down on the bed. "Why were you sitting on the floor?"

"It seemed presumptuous to lie on your bed, like an invasion of your privacy or something."

I patted the mattress, inviting him to sit down. He didn't budge. "You can use my bed anytime."

That hadn't come out right.

An awkward silence stretched between us. Finally I blurted out, "What are you doing here, Patrick?"

He seemed to consider the question a long time, as though he was trying to puzzle out that very question for himself. "The plan . . . remember?"

"I remember. I mean why are you helping me? Gary the Gun isn't your problem, he's mine."

"I feel responsible."

"Why? You did your job. You taught me how to kill Alfonso Cifelli. You gave me a plan. I was the one who screwed up."

"So I should just leave you to deal with it on your own?" A hint of anger tinged his words.

It intrigued me, but didn't cause me any concern, unlike when Paul had blown his top. "You have other responsibilities. Which reminds me . . . are you ever at home? Either home."

"Not unless it's absolutely necessary."

"And your wife . . . wives . . . are okay with that?"

"Thrilled," he replied dryly. "As long as I make regular deposits into the bank accounts, everything is just fine."

I glanced over at him. He'd stuck his hands in his pockets and was watching me closely, waiting for something.

"I'm not one of your responsibilities, Patrick." Turning my back to him, I pretended to examine God's enclosure.

"We need his help," God said. "Talking him out of giving it to us isn't the smartest idea."

Patrick was on the move. He sat down on the bed beside me, the mattress dipping beneath his weight. I didn't take my eyes off God.

"You don't have to do this. I got myself into this mess. I can get myself out of it." I'd done it my whole life; I didn't need a hero cop to come in and save the day.

He leaned his arm against mine, forging a physical connection while I was trying to tear apart our emotional bond. I wanted to lean away, but there was something so comforting about his touch. He wasn't asking anything of me, just giving.

"You don't have to do everything alone, but for some reason you seem to think you do. Why is that, Mags?"

I didn't have to answer him because Fate decided to intervene and do it for me.

My phone rang.

Not my cell phone. My house phone. The one I keep under the bed.

I must have tensed, because pulling away Patrick said, "If you need to get that, I can go wait in the other room."

As he moved to stand up, I grabbed his arm, anchoring him to the bed beside me. "I don't answer that phone."

"Ever?"

It rang again.

"Ever."

"Why not?"

It rang a third time.

Only certain people have my home number. People I don't want to talk to. People like bill collectors, the HR department of Insuring the Future, the administrators of the facility where my mother resides, and . . .

My answering machine picked up. I held onto Patrick's arm like it was a lifeline. My own recorded voice, proper, to the point of stilted, started speaking from beneath the bed. *"This is Margaret Lee. I am not available to take your call. Please leave a message."*

I held my breath as the machine beeped.

"Maggie May, it's Dad. Are you there?"

I didn't move. I didn't breathe. My father never called to just chat.

Patrick plucked my fingers from where I was attempting a death grip on his forearm.

"I've only got a minute. I'm using the cellphone of one of the guards. I just . . . I felt bad about how you left."

I shook my head. Typical. He was totally ignoring his part in our conversation. The part where he'd selfishly refused to help his own granddaughter.

"I think you misunderstood. I want to help Katie. I really do. I need you to believe that, Maggie May."

His arm free, Patrick wrapped it around my shoulders. I hadn't realized I was trembling until then.

"And I'm sorry I said what I did about you making your request being a strange coincidence. I know you couldn't hurt a fly."

God laughed at this.

"I've gotta get off, but I want you to know, Maggie May . . . I need you to know, I love Katie . . . and–"

The call ended suddenly. I didn't know whether he'd hung up or if we'd been disconnected. Not that it mattered.

"So . . ." Patrick said slowly.

I closed my eyes. I really didn't want to get into a heartfelt conversation about my incarcerated parental unit.

"I don't mean to pry, but . . . you keep your phone under the bed?"

His question was so unexpected, I burst out laughing.

He followed suit.

We sat there on my bed laughing our asses off. Of all the things he could have asked after hearing that message, I was so relieved that he asked about the phone that, at least for a few minutes, I forgot Doomsday was coming.

Chapter Forty

"HE SAID TO make sure to eat a decent breakfast," God reminded me. We were both sitting at my kitchen table. I was nursing the last of my coffee. He was pacing the length of his terrarium as though he'd been the one to consume a full pot of caffeine.

"Coffee . . . the breakfast of champion killers." I toasted him with my mug.

"Didn't your mother ever tell you that breakfast is the most important meal of the day?"

I thought about it for a second. "Nope." That job had fallen to Aunt Susan. "But she did tell me furlies live behind the couch."

"What the hell is a furlie?"

I shrugged. She'd imparted that particular bit motherly advice during one of her delusional stages. "I dunno. The way she talked about them I suspected they were some sort of rabid dust bunny."

"That reminds me," the little guy said a little too casually. "I wanted to ask you what your father did for Alice."

I jumped up under the guise of putting my mug in the sink, buying myself a moment to compose my answer. "He almost killed her father."

"And that was a good thing?"

I shrugged. "It was the right thing. Not the legal thing, but the right thing. My dad overheard Alice telling me that her father was . . . touching her, so he went over and beat the crap out of him. Her father left town right after that. He might be my dad, but Archie Lee is her hero."

"Sounds like you're a lot alike," God mused.

"Keep saying stuff like that, and I will let you starve," I warned.

"Speaking of food, you do know that that Patrick fellow is the professional. If he said to eat breakfast, maybe you should."

"I ate dinner. A real dinner. Meat. Vegetable. Starch. Real food from a stove instead of a microwave."

God didn't look convinced.

He did look tired, kind of pale, or at least less brown than usual. I was pretty sure he'd gotten even less sleep than me.

"I still have time to take you to the hospital, if you've changed your mind about coming along."

He flicked his tail, signaling his irritation. "I did not change my mind."

"Okay."

"It's just that I'm not so sure about this plan."

I nodded. I wasn't either, but Patrick had insisted it was our best chance. "Patrick said—"

"I know what Patrick said. I don't need you quoting him."

"You're the one who started in on me about Patrick saying I should eat breakfast."

"I notice you're picking and choosing which of his advice to follow."

"You do remember that he said we're going to have to be quiet, right?"

"Of course."

"That means you, too. Even though no one can understand you, they can still hear you chirping."

"I don't chirp. Birds chirp."

"Squeaking then."

"I certainly don't squeak. Mice squeak."

I drained the last of my coffee. It was way too early to have one of these conversations with the little guy. "What do you do?"

"I vocalize."

"Fine. No vocalizing!"

"I wasn't aware you're fluent in Sign Language." He said snootily.

"I wasn't aware you could keep that mouth of yours shut!"

Thankfully it was a Saturday, so I didn't have to miss work. Plus, I wasn't locked into a schedule. Patrick had said this would actually work in my favor in terms of creating an alibi.

Leaving God in the kitchen, I showered (because it's important to be fresh as a daisy when you're attending a murder) and went to pick out my killer's outfit. As Patrick had instructed, I selected jeans, a plain black T-shirt, a zip-up sweatshirt (yeah, I know, some marketing genius came up with the brilliant idea to call them "hoodies," but c'mon, we all know they're just sweatshirts.) and a pair of sneakers.

"Are we leaving soon?" the lizard called.

"I just have to get dressed."

This ended up being more complicated than I'd anticipated. Because I didn't have any underwear. At least not any clean underwear. (Aunt Susan had also been big on the "always wear clean underwear" drill.) I dimly remembered making a mental note to buy clean underwear; obviously I had forgotten.

"Crap."

"What's wrong?"

"Nothing."

"It doesn't sound like nothing."

"It doesn't matter."

"It sounds like it matters."

"I forgot to buy underwear."

The lizard was uncharacteristically silent. I didn't know whether he was too shocked to speak or was just laughing at me.

"It doesn't matter," I assured him.

"What are you going to do?"

"What do you care?"

"I think you should—"

"I don't care what you think I should do! I am a grown woman. I'm a capable adult. I think I can figure out how to solve my own fucking underwear dilemma!" I shouted.

"Patrick said not to attract attention. Neighbors notice when you shout."

"Will they notice when I strangle you?" I muttered.

I solved the underwear crisis . . . and no, I'm not telling you how, got dressed, and walked out to the kitchen.

My personal cell phone (as opposed to the burn phones Patrick gave me) buzzed. I didn't recognize the number. "Hello?"

"Hey, Chiquita."

"Hey," I tried to remember whether my work friend had ever called me on a weekend before. "Everything okay?"

"I had a terrible night's sleep."

"I'm sorry to hear that. Are you—"

"Cut the Insuring speech crap. I had a terrible night's sleep because I kept dreaming 'Doomsday is coming' and then a loud explosion."

The explosion she heard could very well be a gunshot. Of course I couldn't tell her that, so I asked, "Just one?"

"One explosion isn't enough?"

If she only heard one, that meant that only one shot would be fired. Mine. It had to be a good sign that Patrick's plan was going to work.

"I've got a really bad feeling about this," Armani whispered.

"You worry too much."

"Promise me you'll be careful today, Maggie."

"I'm going to the mall," I told her, feeling a twinge of guilt as I used her to shore up my alibi. "The worst thing that could happen is that someone might spray me with perfume."

"I hope you're right. See you Monday, Chiquita." She hung up.

"What was that about?" God asked.

"My psychic friend wanted to warn me that there's going to be an explosion."

The lizard swallowed hard.

"Last chance to change your mind. There's still time for me to run you over to the hospital."

God shook his head.

"Have it your way." I lifted the lid of his terrarium and extended my hand.

He eyed my palm suspiciously. "Don't forget. I have very sensitive skin and bruise easily."

"Did I hurt you last time?"

"No, but that time you hadn't recently threatened me with bodily harm."

"Stop being such a wuss."

Tail flicking, he climbed into my palm. I lifted him out of the terrarium and slid him into the pocket of my sweatshirt. "How is it in there?"

"Dark."

As per Patrick's instructions I drove to the mall, ran inside, bought a lip gloss, making sure to get a dated and time-stamped receipt, and then left the mall.

"I don't understand how you stand such temperature changes," the lizard complained.

"I don't know how you can stand to eat live bugs."

We continued this line of discussion for the entire eight blocks I had to walk, in order to meet Patrick at our prearranged rally point.

"He's here." I told God when I spotted the redhead sitting in a non-descript sedan. "Remember to keep quiet."

Leaning across the car, he opened the door for me.

"Is this a cop car?" I asked. It had a distinct aroma of stale coffee.

"No."

"Where'd you get it?"

He didn't answer. In fact he didn't say another word for the twenty-minute drive out to where Gary the Gun lived. I guess he was pretty nervous, too. That didn't make me feel any better.

I tried practicing Alice's stress-reduction breathing exercise. I didn't feel any different. I fiddled with the four-leaf-clover necklace Leslie had provided. I didn't feel any luckier.

Patrick didn't speak until he parked the car in an empty office building lot around the corner from Gary's place. "When this is over, there's something we have to talk about."

Noticing that his cheeks were slightly flushed and that he was having trouble making eye contact, my anxiety ratcheted up another ten notches.

"I know, I know, I owe you your cut."

"It's not that."

"What?" I joked, trying to break the tension. "Are you trying to break up with me, Mulligan?"

He shook his head.

"Then what?"

"Not now."

"Why not?"

"Now's not the time. It's personal."

"So why'd you mention it?"

He shrugged. "I don't know. I shouldn't have. It was a mistake."

I was thoroughly confused.

"We need to keep our heads in the game. Forget I said anything. You're absolutely sure you can make the climb."

"Positive."

Reaching into the sweatshirt he wore, he pulled out a gun and handed it to me.

"Another Magnum." I knew it wasn't the same as the one I'd used on Cifelli. While I'd been waiting for him in the park I'd noticed that the barrel of that particular weapon was scratched up. This one gleamed.

"I figured it was what you're comfortable with."

I nodded.

Which was weird. I shouldn't be comfortable with any kind of gun.

"What time does your watch say?"

"Eleven twenty-eight."

He glanced at his own watch. "Okay, so we go at noon. That should give us both plenty of time to get inside. You remember the plan, right?"

"I remember." Regardless, I was sure that God would remind me just as soon as we were out of Patrick's earshot.

"Okay." He reached for his door handle.

Trying to ignore the nervous churning of my gut, I followed his lead and felt for mine.

"Mags?"

I turned back toward him. My breath caught in my throat when I saw the intensity of his gaze.

"You asked me why I'm doing this."

"And you said you felt responsible . . . but if you've changed your mind . . . I can handle it from here."

"Rule Five."

"Did I learn Rule Four?"

"Rule Five is: Trust your partner."

I blinked. "We're partners?"

"For this job we are. I promise you Mags, I'm not going to let you down."

A balloon of panic swelled inside me. If he was counting on me . . . "I . . . I wish I could promise you the same."

"Just do your best."

"My best isn't usually enough," I confessed, ashamed.

"I'm not worried, Mags. I'll know you'll do great. The reason I'm doing this is that I like you. A lot. I've liked you since the moment I first laid eyes on you."

"People usually get past that once they get to know me," I joked weakly.

"People are usually fools."

With that he jumped out of the car and jogged away down the road.

I just sat in the sedan watching him disappear. Endangering my own life for the sake of saving Katie was one thing. Risking his life . . . I wasn't sure that was a gamble I was willing to make.

"You do know that in order for the plan to work you actually have to get out of the car," God reminded me.

I knew he couldn't stay silent forever . . . or even for an hour.

Grudgingly, I climbed out of the sedan. My legs were rubbery, but they carried me to the back of Gary the Gun's property. Just as in the photograph Patrick had shown me the night before, his home, an old colonial, was flanked by large trees. My job was to climb one of those trees, get into the house through the second floor balcony door that was open, and get down to the kitchen undetected.

Patrick had been convinced Gary would be in his kitchen. Apparently, besides being a first-rate hitman, the guy considered himself to be a gourmet cook.

"It looks awfully high," God said. "You do know I usually only climb about twelve inches at a time, right?"

"It's not that high." But it was. "What? Are you afraid you're going to get altitude sickness or something? It's a tree, not Everest. But if you want, you can wait in the car."

"Put me down. You can follow me up," he offered. "I'll scout out the best handholds."

"Okay." I carefully placed him on the ground, not wanting to bruise his sensitive skin. I had no doubt that if I did, I'd never hear the end of it. He scampered ahead of me. "Just remember," I warned on a whisper. "We *both* have to be quiet."

He scaled the tree, disappearing within seconds.

Leaning against the trunk, I took a moment to collect myself. I knew I had to do this. If I didn't, my family was in danger, I could go to jail, and I'd never collect the money I so desperately wanted for Katie. Now, on top of everything else, Patrick was counting on me.

I wasn't quite sure how he'd gotten the impression I'm count-on-able. I'd come from a genetic line of less-than-dependables. And yet his faith in me had seemed pretty unshakeable.

"Do my best," I muttered, finding my first handhold on the tree.

For a moment I imagined I was six again, making my first attempt to clamber up the tree behind my aunts' place.

"Just do your best, Maggie May," my dad urged, hovering below me with outstretched arms in case I should fall.

One of the reasons I love to climb so much is that I didn't learn on my own. I was taught. I wasn't alone.

I wasn't alone now either.

I heaved myself upward. Yup, I was climbing a tree so that I could take out a contract killer before he got me or those I loved.

If my best wasn't good enough, a whole lot of people could end up hurt or dead.

Chapter Forty-One

I WAS HUFFING and puffing like a beached whale by the time I reached the level of the balcony.

God raised a finger to his lips, a mocking reminder to be quiet. I was trying, but the climb had been more difficult than I'd anticipated. Plus, I'd shredded the skin on my left palm. It stung like a bitch.

Gingerly, I swung myself from the tree to the balcony, taking care not to bump into the glass door that was propped halfway open. Gripping the railing, I took a minute to catch my breath.

I glanced at my watch. 11:45. I had fifteen minutes to get down to the kitchen. That meant I had at least ten minutes to kill.

The lizard tapped on my sneaker. I crouched down as low as I could.

"I'll go make sure he's in the kitchen," he whispered.

"Be careful," I whispered back. He scampered inside, and I settled in for my wait. Taking out the shiny gun Patrick had provided, I examined it carefully, making sure it was loaded and the safety was on. I could practically hear him coaching me. *Breathe in, focus along the sight, and as you exhale, you're going to squeeze the trigger.*

That lesson in the barn seemed like it had taken place a lifetime ago. I'd been a different person.

It's personal, Patrick had said. I'd been so caught up in my worries, I hadn't given much thought to what it was he wanted to discuss, but now, with nothing to do but wait and think, I found myself wondering what he'd meant.

Assuming we both lived through the day, I had sort of thought this would be the last I'd see of him. That's how I'd want it if I was him. I'd been nothing but trouble from the moment he'd met me. Still, his saying he wanted to have a discussion of a personal nature seemed to indicate he thought we had some kind of future.

It caught me off guard when I realized how much that possibility pleased me.

God scuttled up to me.

I bent down to listen to his whispered report.

"I've got good news and bad news."

I rolled my eyes. Of course there had to be bad news.

"The good news is that just like Patrick said, he's in the kitchen, watching the Food Network . . . blasting it really."

I waited for the bad news.

"But . . . he's handling knives."

I nodded. I had figured that if we did indeed catch him in the kitchen, there was a good chance he'd have cutting implements within reach.

"And . . ."

My stomach flipped nervously. There was more?

"He's wearing a chef's hat."

I couldn't see how headwear was a problem.

"And nothing else. I didn't want you to get distracted by his . . . um. . . . uh . . ."

I'd never seen the little guy at a loss for words. "Nudity?"

He shook his head. "Tumescence."

"Huh?"

"Apparently cooking is a turn on for him. Literally."

It took me a beat to figure out what the hell he was talking about. "Oh. O. . . . h."

"I didn't want your attention to get diverted by his—"

"I got it." Of all the weird conversations I'd had lately, I was pretty sure this one took the cake.

"I just want you to be prepared."

"Forewarned is forearmed."

"Exactly."

"Ready?"

I nodded. It was a lie. About the only thing I was ready to do was throw up.

God led the way.

I followed, skirting around the balcony door and entering Gary the Gun's house. Even from up here I could hear the television blaring downstairs.

Running ahead of me, the lizard disappeared around a corner. I surmised, from the tangled sheets on the bed, that this was Gary's bedroom. I aimed the Magnum at the pillow, pretending his smirking face was on it. I pretended to pull the trigger.

I could do this. I could kill the son-of-a-bitch threatening everyone I loved. A sense of calm filled me, settling my nerves and stomach. I followed after the reptile, ready to do my job.

Gary the Gun's home was not what I'd expected. Not that I'd given much thought to what the devil's lair might look like, but I certainly hadn't expected it to look so . . . normal. Then again the only other killer's home I'd been in was Patrick's sparse apartment.

Glowing Thomas Kinkade prints lined the walls. Yes, the Prince of Darkness was apparently a fan of the Painter of Light. I was surprised they were prints. You'd figure with the kind of money he was probably pulling in he could afford an original or two. He seemed particularly fond of Main Street scenes. Personally Kinkade's idyllic view of the world, with its shimmering highlights and deep pastels, makes me want to retch.

I noticed that the furnishings looked like they'd been pulled piece-for-piece from a Pottery Barn showroom. Apparently Mr. Tough Guy was also Mr. Gullible Suburbanite.

The noise from the TV grew louder as I approached the stairs. God peeked through the railing slats, and waved me forward, indicating that the coast was clear. Glancing at my watch, I saw that it was 11:56. I disengaged the safety of the gun and moved toward the stairs.

Suddenly the lizard streaked toward me. "Doomsday is coming!" He shouted.

I made a shushing gesture. All I needed was for Gary

to hear the lizard vocalizing and leave the kitchen to check out the noise.

"Doomsday is coming," God whispered.

"So I've been told," I whispered back. "You're the one who told me—"

"Doomsday is here." He covered his eyes as though the sight were too much to behold.

Just so you know, Doomsday arrives with a low rumble, sort of like thunder rolling in the distance.

It was behind me. I almost dropped the gun. The insistent rumble grew louder.

I turned slowly.

I gotta admit that Doomsday wasn't exactly what I expected, but it sure as hell scared the crap out of me.

Seventy pounds of growling bared teeth and coiled muscle glared at me. The Doberman pinscher looked as though it was about to attack.

"Nice doggie," I whispered.

"Give it a donut! Give it a donut!" God urged in a panicked whisper. He had insisted that I put the three stale crullers in my pocket before we'd gotten out of the car at the mall. I'd told him that if I hadn't eaten them when I bought them, I wasn't going to eat them today. He'd argued that they might come in handy. I hadn't seen how the practically-fossilized paper weights could be of any use, but I'd compromised and taken one with me.

Slowly, so as not to startle the animal waiting to tear me limb-from-limb, I pulled the baked good from my pocket. "Nice doggie. Would you like this?"

It stopped growling and sat down.

I handed it over, making sure not to lose any fingers in the process. The mutt wolfed it down and then looked at me expectantly.

"I'm sorry. I don't have any more."

It growled.

"If I'd known you were going to be here, and you'd be hungry, I would have brought more." As I spoke, I brought the gun up and leveled it at the dog's head.

No doubt the gun shot would alert Gary to my presence, but if the animal made a move for my jugular I wouldn't have a choice. The prospect of shooting this dog made me queasier than the idea of shooting its owner. "Please don't make me shoot you," I begged.

In response it snarled at me.

"What?" It sounded as though the mutt had said something.

"Doing here what?" Despite the guttural growl, I heard a high-pitched, breathy woman's voice. If this dog had a soul, she was a blonde along the lines of Anna Nicole Smith.

"What am I doing here? Is that what you're asking?"

"I told you their grammar is terrible," God grumbled.

She growled at him.

"If you don't have anything nice to say, don't say anything at all," I said. I smiled at the dog, trying to ignore the fact that I was scared to death of her. "I'm Maggie and this is Godzilla. What's your name?"

"Doomsday," she replied.

Armani really needed to work on these predictions of hers.

"We're not here to hurt you, Doomsday."

"Leave the guy hurts before."

I looked to God for a translation. "She said, Leave before the guy hurts you."

I nodded. "Thank you. I appreciate that advice, Doomsday, I really do, but I can't leave."

She cocked her head to the side and looked at me quizzically. "Hurt Doomsday are you?"

"She wants to know if you're going to hurt her."

Realizing I still had the gun pointed at her head, I lowered it to my side. "No, sweetheart. I'm not going to hurt you."

Lying down on the floor, she crawled over to me on her belly and licked my sneaker.

"Oh look, you've made a new friend," God drawled with all his annoying superiority.

Ignoring him, I bent down and stroked the top of the dog's head. Her coat was softer than I expected, silky almost.

"Mean guy. Take home me?"

"She wants to know if you'll take her home. Apparently Gary is mean to the creature."

"Who could be mean to such a sweet girl?"

She rolled over, inviting me to rub her belly.

"I'm not sure my apartment complex even allows dogs, otherwise I'd—"

"Hey Dog Whisperer, you're going to be late," God reminded me.

I glanced at my watch. Twelve o'clock on the dot. "Oh crap. Doomsday, I need you to stay here. Stay."

There was a crash in the kitchen.

Patrick must have already been there, and I was late.

Without waiting for the gecko to tell me if the path was clear, I ran down the stairs, through a sitting room, and straight into the kitchen, failing to register that the TV had been muted, which meant there was no noise to cover my approach.

Then I tripped.

I went sprawling, losing my gun as I landed on my hands and knees. As I fell, I realized that what I'd stumbled over was Patrick—more specifically, his body laid out across the doorway.

This did not bode well for our plan.

Neither did the fact that I'd lost my gun. I scanned the kitchen floor for it. The damn thing had skittered halfway across the room. As I crawled toward it, my ribcage was thunked.

Okay, I wasn't really thunked, I was kicked, but the sound that was made as Gary the Gun's foot connected with my side made a definite thunking sound. And it definitely hurt. A lot.

I lay on my opposite side trying to catch my breath, but I couldn't because it hurt to breathe. Out of the corner of my eye I saw Gary scoop up my gun.

This plan was definitely not working out.

Chapter Forty-Two

"YOU SHOULD HAVE just paid up," he said, walking toward me, the weapon dangling casually from his fingers.

As God had told me, he was naked except for a chef's hat which was perched on his head at a rakish angle. And as God had warned, Gary was . . . tumescent. I averted my eyes.

Struggling into a sitting position, I stole a quick look at Patrick's still form. I couldn't tell whether he was breathing. "Why'd you tell Delveccio you killed his son-in-law?"

"Because that job should have been mine!"

"I wasn't trying to horn in on your territory. He offered me the job. I didn't ask for it." As I spoke, I slowly got to my feet. I surveyed the area. I was nearest the pantry. The knives were on the counter on the opposite side of the room. There was no way to reach them. He'd shoot me first.

"And now that idiot," he waved the Magnum toward Patrick, "he decided what? That he was going to play hero and help out the pathetic girl? Talk some sense into me? Get me to give up those pictures of you? Was that the plan? For the two of you losers to try to make a deal with me?"

He didn't know we were there to kill him. That had to work in my favor. I just wasn't sure how.

"Well I've got news for you, I don't deal."

"Okay, I can see we made a mistake." I inched toward Patrick. If I could just figure out if he was still alive . . .

Gary waved the gun at me. I inched back in the opposite direction.

"You're not going to deal, I get that now. But here's the thing. If you don't let us go, how are you going to get the money?"

"Delveccio will pay up."

"The blackmail money, the extra hundred-twenty grand I'm supposed to give you."

"You've got it?"

"I'm getting it. It's not like I brought it with me."

"Okay, just to show you what a nice guy I am, I'm gonna let you go."

I breathed a sigh of relief.

"But your partner, he ain't getting so lucky. This ginger's been a thorn in my side for way too long." He kicked Patrick's side for emphasis.

Groaning, Patrick instinctively tried to roll away.

I took this as a good sign.

At least he wasn't dead.

Yet.

"How do you expect me to get the money without

his help?" I asked, unwilling to leave my murder mentor behind. I finally understood the *honor among thieves* crap Delveccio and my dad talked about. "We both walk out of here, or you don't get a dime."

"Or you both end up dead." To illustrate his point, Gary advanced on me, the gun leveled at my face.

I backed away, until my butt connected with the butcher block island in the center of the room. Gary kept coming, jamming the barrel of the gun under my chin. The metal was cold. His breath was garlicky.

I leaned backward, trying to get away from both. I put my hands behind me, trying to balance on the cutting surface, and felt something cool and slimy. It felt suspiciously like flesh.

At that moment I was pretty sure skipping breakfast had been a good idea, otherwise I'd have started spewing like a Las Vegas fountain.

"You interrupted my cooking time," Gary told me. "It's my chance to relax, my one pleasure."

"What about all those crappy paintings you've got?"

Grabbing my chin with his free hand, he pulled my face toward his. "They're art!"

"Those are prints."

"Art!"

"They're not even serigraphs."

"I collect art and I cook. I am a Renaissance man!"

"No, you're a short, ugly dude with really bad breath." Yes, I actually was stupid enough to say that out loud.

Just for that he kissed me. It was about as repulsive as licking the brush I use to scrub my toilet bowl.

I'd like to say that I remembered Patrick's self-defense lesson about going for the Eyes, Nose, Throat, and Groin. I didn't. I froze. Terror and revulsion acted as paralytic agents, rendering me helpless against Gary's assault. Trying to reach my tonsils with his tongue, the evidence of his . . . tumescence rubbing against me, Gary apparently decided that my paralyzed state was his chance to get lucky.

"Don't just stand there!" God shrieked. "Do something."

It took me a second to realize that he was perched between Doomsday's ears and they were watching us from the doorway.

"Hit him!" God coached.

"Teeth the guy! Teeth the guy!" Doomsday urged.

The Doberman's barking caught Gary's attention and he half-turned his head to yell at the dog. "Shut up, you worthless mutt!"

I took the opportunity to knee the bastard in the balls.

Surprised, and bent over with pain, he released me.

Unfortunately he didn't let go of the Magnum. Waving it in my general direction, he squeezed off a round.

For the record, in case you couldn't guess, being the person shot at is infinitely worse than being the one doing the shooting.

I dove behind the butcher block island for cover.

"Use the torch!" God yelled. He'd crossed the room and was standing on the counter by the stove pointing to a small butane torch. The kind that is used for melting sugar on top of crème brulee. Apparently the Renaissance Man had a bit of a sweet tooth.

"What the hell is that?"

Apparently Gary had taken note of the little lizard gesticulating wildly on his countertop. He took a shot at God too.

The lizard took a header off the counter, joining me behind the relative protection of the island. "I told you this plan was a bad idea!"

"It wasn't my plan," I muttered.

"I don't care whose plan it was. You're dead. Do you hear me, you're both dead." As though to illustrate his point, Gary stalked over toward Patrick, brandishing the gun.

With no other weapons in sight, I made a mad grab for the torch.

He laughed when he saw me snatch it up. "That thing isn't going to help you. You'd need a flamethrower to take me down."

I threw it at him. It bounced off his gun arm. Encouraged, I grabbed the next thing my hand hit and chucked that at him too. The jar of mint jelly caught him squarely in the gut. (Aunt Susan was right, my job as a newspaper delivery girl had taught me something!) The glass crashed to the floor and shattered, sending minty green goop everywhere.

The next thing I found was a large can that had to weigh about eight pounds. That wasn't good for throwing, so I left it. Instead I went for a roll of aluminum foil.

When I raised my arm to throw it, Gary roared, "Enough!"

He aimed the gun at me and took a step forward.

Right onto the broken glass.

"Dammit!" He looked down at his now bleeding foot.

I charged like a bull at a waving cape, intent on taking him down.

Somehow I managed to tackle the naked man. We rolled around amid the glass and jelly, each intent on dominating the other.

"Hit him!" God yelled.

"Teeth the guy!" Doomsday urged.

Superior strength and a lifetime of experience were on Gary's side. Within moments, he had gained the upper-hand.

"Help! Help!" I cried desperately.

And help arrived.

Patrick dragged him off of me. The two men fell backward to the floor. I made a grab for the gun while Patrick struggled to subdue the smaller man who was thrashing about like an animal caught in a net.

Gary squeezed the trigger and a bullet cut through my hair, missing my ear by inches and momentarily deafening me.

Briefly deprived of one of my senses, my others became more acute. I could suddenly smell garlic, mint, and . . . gas.

Chapter Forty-Three

"GAS! I SMELL gas!" I panted, struggling to keep the barrel of the gun pointing away from my head. Now I knew what Armani's predicted explosion was. It wasn't a gunshot, it was a gas explosion!

"I smell it too!" God shouted.

"Teeth the guy!" Doomsday urged.

And I finally understood what she meant. I bit Gary's wrist as hard as I could. It was a disturbing sensation to sink my teeth into this soft skin, feeling his malleable tendons shifting beneath the onslaught.

Howling, he released his hold on the gun. Grabbing it, I crawled a few paces away from the two grappling men, just in time to see Gary ram his elbow backward into Patrick's head, causing his skull to bounce off the tile floor. The hollow thud it made caused me to cry out.

Patrick went limp.

"Don't move," I warned Gary.

Ignoring me, he got to his feet, his chest puffed with his perceived victory.

Unlike with Cifelli, I had no hesitation about ending this man's life. I squeezed the trigger.

And nothing happened.

Not a damn thing.

I squeezed it again. Still nothing. The damn thing had jammed.

Realizing I was helpless, Gary made his move.

He was almost on top of me when 70 pounds of growling Doberman got between us.

"Run!" Doomsday told me.

I scrambled away. God was beckoning for me to join him behind the butcher block island.

I heard Gary scream, "You stupid mutt!"

Then there was a sickening thunk and the dog let out a pained whine that lanced my heart.

I looked back to see Doomsday cowering on the floor, Gary looming over her.

"Bad dog!" He screamed, looking like more of a rabid animal than she. He kicked her again. Her pained yelp bounced off the kitchen walls.

I had to do something. Desperately I scanned the kitchen for a weapon.

Gary reached into the pantry and pulled out a big long gun. I'm not expert, but I was pretty sure it was a shotgun. The man kept a shotgun in his kitchen cabinet.

"Meet the guy," Doomsday whimpered, her big brown eyes pleading with me. "Meet the guy."

I turned to God for a translation, but all he could do was shrug.

Gary kicked her a third time.

"Meet the guy," she begged in an agonized moan.

As her owner aimed the weapon at the poor dog's head, God made his move.

"Leave her alone, you coward!" He roared . . . vocalized . . . chirped as he charged straight at the naked man's toes.

"Meet the guy."

And suddenly I understood what she meant, what Armani's premonition had meant, and how it was a matter of life or death. Damn those pesky homonyms!

With God providing a distraction (Gary was trying to stomp him to death) I grabbed the hunk of flesh on the butcher block. The leg of lamb, with the bone still in, weighed a good eight pounds.

Swinging it like a baseball bat, I connected with Gary's shoulder. Stumbling, he tried to bring the shotgun up at me.

Doomsday "teethed the guy" clamping onto his ankle and dragging him down to the ground. The shotgun went off.

Gary tried to fire the remaining round at me. I swung the meat at his arm. The shot went wide, but there was a deafening boom.

For a third time I swung as hard as I could at his ugly face and was rewarded with the sickening sound of his neck snapping.

He fell to the floor, his head flopped at an unnatural angle to his body. His eyes were open, but as empty as a doll's.

"Dead is dead," I muttered.

"Fire! Fire!" God shouted, pointing at the opposite side of the room.

I turned. Sure enough the kitchen was going up in flames. From the location of the fire, I guessed that Gary's last wild shot had hit the heavy can on the counter, and that must have been filled with something flammable.

"Oh crap."

"That's an understatement." God muttered.

Kneeling beside Doomsday, I stroked her soft head.

"Are you okay?"

She licked my hand.

"Can you get up, Sweetheart?"

"Take now home you?"

"She wants to know if we'll take her home."

I nodded.

She got to her feet.

I swallowed the painful lump that rose in my throat. If I'd been able to cry, I'm sure I would have shed a tear or two when I saw that she was going to make it.

"You have to get out of here," I told her as the little lizard scrambled up her leg and perched himself between her ears. "Go with God."

Turning away from them, I ran over to where Patrick lay. "Patrick? Patrick, we have to get out of here."

His eyes fluttered open, the blue-green as empty as a tranquil sea.

The kitchen was getting hotter. The flames crackled.

"We've got to get out of here."

His eyes drifted back closed. He wasn't going to get out of here under his power. It was going to be up to me.

I crouched down, slid my hands under his arms, and pulled.

Can I just say that I now understand the meaning of the phrase *dead weight*? I could barely slide him across the kitchen tiles. He weighed a ton. The fire was getting closer, the ceiling above was starting to crumble.

It was hard to breathe.

"Help me let."

I was startled to find that the animals hadn't left the kitchen. They were standing beside me.

"She wants you to let her help you," God told me. "I think that's a good plan. Otherwise we're all going to roast."

"How?"

"Pull him I."

"She says she'll pull him. She'll take one arm you take the other. C'mon hurry up. Give her one of his arms."

"Try not to hurt him," I said, giving one of Patrick's arms to the Doberman.

She grabbed onto his sweatshirt sleeve and started tugging as she walked backward. I pulled on his other arm. Together we dragged him out of the kitchen.

"This way to the door," God directed, leading the way.

A noise that sounded like popping corn on steroids reached our ears.

"Bullets!" God and I said simultaneously.

"Who knows what else he has in there." God sounded panicked. "The place could go up any second. Hurry! Hurry!"

I happened to agree with him that we were on the

verge of being blown to smithereens, so I redoubled my efforts. The dog and I dragged poor Patrick through the rooms of the house, bouncing him over doorsills, getting him caught up on corners, and smashing him into furniture along the way.

I wasn't sure if we were saving or killing him.

Finally we reached the door and hauled him outside.

"Go get the car!" God ordered.

"He's too close to the house."

"Move myself I can." Doomsday assured me.

"Someone's going to call the fire department and then the police will be here," God reminded me.

He was right.

I took off running.

"Come back!" God yelled.

I stopped in my tracks. "You just told me to go!"

"You forgot the keys, you ninny!"

He was right. I jogged back.

"This pocket! This pocket!" God jumped up and down on Patrick's right hip.

I pulled out the keys and stumbled away again.

It felt like an eternity had passed as I ran to the car and drove it to Gary's place.

By the time I got back to the house, black smoke was filling the air. As she'd promised, Doomsday had somehow managed to get the redheaded man to the curb.

I had no idea how to get him into the car.

"Patrick, wake up!" I begged, slapping his face like they do on TV all the time. It didn't work.

"Hit no!" Doomsday nudged me out of the way and began slathering him with big, wet doggie kisses.

They did the trick.

Patrick stirred.

"Wake up, Patrick. Come on, I need you to open your eyes."

He blinked, struggling to focus.

"Help me get you into the car."

"Wha— Wha—"

I thought I heard the wail of sirens in the distance.

"We have to get out of here now." I half-lifted, half-dragged him into the backseat of the car. Doomsday hopped into the front.

"Not the driver's seat!" I told her.

Obediently she moved over to the passenger's side. "Wind."

"She wants you to open the window," God supplied from the backseat, where he'd curled up on Patrick's chest.

I opened the window for the dog. She stuck her head out. I drove away.

"Mags?"

"Yes, Patrick?"

"Did you bring your lizard to a hit?"

"Yes, Patrick."

"Oh."

Behind us, Gary the Gun's house blew up.

Chapter Forty-Four

PATRICK INSISTED HE didn't need to see a doctor. I told him he'd been knocked unconscious twice. God helpfully mentioned he might have brain damage. I told him to shut up.

Patrick thought I was telling him to shut up. I couldn't exactly tell him I was talking to the vocalizing lizard, so the topic of conversation got dropped.

We went our separate ways at the mall. Patrick drove off to return the mysterious sedan. I left the Doberman and the gecko in my car—yes, all the windows were cracked, and no, it wasn't too hot for them—and went to complete my alibi. If anyone asked, I'd say I spent the day at the mall. I had my lip gloss receipt to prove when I'd gotten there, and now I went in to buy live crickets for you-know-who.

The same creepy clerk helped me, but this time he eyed me as though I had crawled out from under one of the rocks in the critters' cages. In addition to the crickets, I realized Doomsday needed some stuff, so I added a bag of dog food and a box of biscuits to my order. Then, since she struck me as a girly-girl kind of girl, I got her a pink studded collar and a pink-nylon leash. I also couldn't resist getting her one of those squeaky toys that looks like a squirrel's tale.

It wasn't until I'd gotten back in my car and caught my reflection in my rearview mirror that I understood why the clerk had regarded me so strangely. Half my face was covered with dried mint jelly.

I drove home, fed the animals, took a shower, and left them to argue about what to watch on TV, but not before I heard another phone message from my father. In this one he asked me to come to visit him as soon as possible.

On my ride over to the hospital, I listened to reports about a local home that had blown up. Fire officials were blaming the tragic explosion on a gas leak.

It was sort of a letdown to find that Tony/Anthony Delveccio wasn't at the hospital. Then again, what self-respecting mobster . . . alleged mobster, would spend his nights sucking down chocolate pudding in a hospital cafeteria?

I'd waited this long to get paid. It wouldn't kill me to wait a little longer.

I hoped.

Aunt Susan was asleep in the visitor's chair beside Katie's bed.

I tiptoed into the room, bent over, and whispered in my niece's ear, "Everything's going to be okay, Baby Girl."

Aunt Susan stirred. Not wanting to startle her, I didn't move. She woke slowly, stretched, and then realized I was there. "Oh, hello. I didn't know you were coming by today."

"I come by every day."

She nodded. "Of course. Have you made a decision about tomorrow?"

"Tomorrow?"

"Your mother's birthday. Will you be going to visit her?"

I hesitated.

"I knew it!" She didn't bother to hide her disappointment.

"What time are you going?"

"Noon. We're bringing her a birthday lunch, just like we do every year. Which you'd know if you ever joined us."

I hadn't joined them for years. I told everyone I hated the place, but the truth was it scared the shit out of me. The fragmented minds and incoherent ramblings of the residents frightened me, not because I thought I was in physical danger, but because I knew, I *knew* how someone could go from normal to nuts in the blink of an eye. I didn't feel love for my mother when I saw her there. I didn't even feel pity. All I felt was a sense of foreboding that I was next.

"Theresa always brought the cake." Aunt Susan looked at me expectantly.

"Well I'm not saint-fucking-Theresa."

"Margaret! Language!" She looked over at Katie as though I was rotting the child's soul with my word choice.

"I'm sorry." I wasn't certain whether I was apologizing to the kid or the adult. "It's just been a day."

"We all have our days, Margaret."

Not like the one I've had, I thought. "Can I ask you something, Aunt Susan?"

She nodded.

"Why'd you make me work that paper route? Theresa never had to do one."

"And you think that's because I liked her more than I liked you?"

The thought had occurred to me.

She shook her head sadly. "I bet that it never occurred to you that you were always the most responsible of the four and that maybe, just maybe, I thought you deserved some recognition for that over-developed sense of responsibility you had."

"No, gotta say I never considered that way of thinking about it."

"You were a great paper girl. You delivered them dry and on time, every single day. You received all sorts of commendations and you received darn good tip money."

"I did?"

"You don't remember that?"

I shook my head.

"You've always had a selective memory. Remembering all the bad stuff. Sometimes I think you don't recall a moment of happiness."

She might be right.

"Do you have dinner plans?" I asked.

She shrugged. "Loretta and Templeton are out on a date night. Alice and that nice young man of hers . . ."

"Lamont."

"They're going roller skating. And Leslie . . ."

I could fill in that blank.

"She's gone to a Narcotics Anonymous meeting."

You could have knocked me over with a feather.

Aunt Susan nodded. "I'm trying not to get too excited, but yes, apparently she's recognizing she has a problem."

"Wow." It was all I could think to say.

"I guess we have you to thank for it."

"Me?"

"You hurt her feelings when you asked for her key to your place."

"That wasn't my intention. I just wanted—"

She raised a hand to silence me. "I know what you wanted. You were embarrassed that your boyfriend saw her like that."

"I . . . no . . . actually Paul was cool with it. His mom's a drunk."

"Lovely."

"I just meant he's had experience with . . . difficult family members."

"Whatever. Apparently, according to the new lingo she's spouting, you asking for your key back was her "bottom." That's when she realized she needed help."

"Wow."

"Wow indeed."

"So can I buy you dinner? This place serves a mean chocolate pudding."

"I know," she confided. "I'd like to have dinner with you, Margaret."

"Great, because I'd really like to know why you signed me up for softball."

"What's with all the questions about your childhood activities?"

"I'm making a list of my skill sets."

Chapter Forty-Five

I CALLED THE number I had for Patrick, but got a recording saying it was no longer in service. Maybe he'd changed his mind about that personal talk he'd wanted to have.

I didn't get much sleep. Doomsday seems to spend a great deal of her sleeping time chasing something through her dreams. Since I'd made the mistake of letting her sleep on my bed with me, that meant she spent a great deal of time kicking me.

It would have been easy to blame my insomnia on the dog, but the truth was I was worried.

I was worried that Patrick had brain damage.

I was worried Delveccio wouldn't pay up.

I was worried because at some point during my dinner with Aunt Susan, I'd had the unsettling realization that I'd left the Magnum, covered with my fingerprints, in Gary the Gun's kitchen.

I was worried that my father had called twice in two days. Usually he only called twice a year, Christmas and my birthday, though that may have been my fault because I had never answered a single one of his calls.

I was worried that if I went to see my mother, that I'd find I'm more like her than I want to admit.

I was worried because Alice had called and asked me to be her maid of honor (apparently the Couples-Skate-one-knee thing had worked for Lamont) and I really didn't want to get stuck footing the bill for an ugly-ass bridesmaid dress.

I was worried Katie would never wake up.

Somehow all that worry had me in my car and driving out to the prison to see my Dad.

He looked a little better than the last time I'd seen him. His bruises had faded to varying shades of green and yellow.

"Thanks for coming, Maggie May."

"It's not often I get a royal summons to come visit you in your royal kingdom."

If my smart-ass comment bothered him, he didn't let it show. "What happened to your face?"

"I got a dog."

It was the response I'd given to Aunt Susan when she'd asked the same question over our second round of pudding. Apparently having a gun shoved under one's chin leaves a bruise.

My aunt had believed the implausible explanation. My father did not.

"What have you gotten yourself into, Maggie?"

I sure as hell wasn't going to confide in him, so I countered with a question of my own. "Why did you want me to come here?

"I wanted to explain about why I couldn't give you what you asked for."

"For Katie. Let's be clear here. I wasn't asking for myself. I asked for Katie."

"Do you remember when I pawned your bike?"

"Uh huh." Dragging up ancient history wasn't the best way to endear himself to me.

"Do you know why I took it?"

"You wanted to bet on a horse."

He nodded. "Do you know why I wanted to bet that horse?"

"Because you thought it was going to lose?"

He ignored my sarcasm.

"It was running at twelve-to-one odds. It was going to have a hell of a payout."

"But I'm guessing it didn't. Otherwise I would have gotten my bike back, right?"

He nodded.

"And what does this have to do with why you asked me to come out here."

"Do you know why I robbed that bank?"

"Because you wanted to bet on racehorse?"

"For the same reason I pawned your bicycle."

I was starting to think a visit with mom at the crazy-house might be less insane than this conversation.

"Why am I here?"

"Because I need you to understand."

I sat on the edge of my chair, thrumming with anger I could barely contain. "Understand what? That you're a compulsive risk-taker, whether it's placing a bet, running a scam, or robbing a bank? I understand that. I've understood it for a long time. You do what feels best for you at any given moment. Screw what's best for anyone else!"

A single tear trickled down his face. "I did it because I loved her."

"Mom? You're going to blame this on Mom? She's been locked up in the loony bin for a long time. You don't love her. You just love to play with her."

"Maggie May, please."

"Do not Maggie May me like you have any right to pretend that we share any kind of relationship! You blew your very last chance for that when you refused to help Katie!"

"I don't have them," he murmured.

"What?"

"I don't have the jewels."

That let the air out of my sails. I sank back on my seat. "What do you mean you don't have them?"

"I gave them to someone to keep."

"Who?"

He shook his head. I knew he'd never tell me.

"And what? This person ripped you off? This whole no-honor-among-thieves thing again?"

"I don't know."

"You don't know. That's just great, Dad. You kill an innocent woman, end up in here, and on top of all that you lost your big score? Explain to me again why the D.A. called you a 'professional' criminal."

"I didn't kill her," he said quietly.

And I believed him. I knew in my core that the man who'd spent the majority of my life scamming and hustling and conning was telling the truth. Because it made sense. My dad had been many things, but mostly he'd been a crook. Just a crook. He'd never used a gun in any of his earlier crimes. He wasn't a killer.

I was the only killer in the family. My stomach roiled traitorously as the knowledge sucker-punched me in the solar plexus. I barely heard his next words as my head buzzed and the room spun treacherously.

"I just wanted you to know that if I'd had the jewels, I would have helped Katie. I'd do anything to help my family. Anything."

I believed him about that, too.

I got up to leave. I had to get out of there. Get away from his admissions that should have made me feel better, but were making me feel worse. All this time I'd thought the worst of him, and he hadn't deserved it. I'd judged him for doing something I'd deemed unforgivable, something he'd never done, but I had.

"Tell me you believe me, Maggie May." His plea was desperate.

"I'll let you know if her condition changes," I muttered. I walked out.

I was still trying to recover my equilibrium when I spotted a familiar face in the visitor's parking lot of the prison. For a second I thought it was a new symptom of my insanity . . . seeing people who weren't there.

I blinked three times trying to clear the mirage from my line of vision. It didn't work. He was still standing there, deep in conversation with one of the prison guards. I considered getting in my car and driving away, but then he turned and spotted me.

He exchanged a few more words with the guard, nodded in my direction, and then headed straight for me.

I tucked my chin into my chest with the hopes of hiding my bruise.

"Hi Maggie! What brings you here?"

"Hi Paul. I was visiting my father."

"Did you have a nice time?"

I glanced back toward the building. "Not particularly. What are you doing here?"

"Parole board hearing . . . for a guy I put away a couple of years ago."

"On a Sunday?"

He shrugged. "Federal judge, kind of on the quirky side."

Just as sure as I'd known my father was telling me the truth, I knew that Paul was lying.

"Hey," he said, in a none-too-subtle attempt to change the direction of the conversation. "When am I going to get that dinner you promised me?"

"Soon. I've got some family stuff over the next week." Plus, I was exhausted. "Can we do it next week?"

"I'd like that." He glanced at his watch. "I gotta go. Don't want a bad guy getting loose on my account."

With a quick kiss to my cheek, he hurried toward the prison building.

I had no doubt he'd lied to me, but before I could puzzle it out, my cell phone buzzed.

"Hello?"

"Hey, Mags."

"You're still alive!" I felt as though a great weight had lifted from my shoulders.

"We've talked about this. You're supposed to say *how are you?* or something like that."

"How are you, Patrick?"

"I'm still alive!" he crowed, clearly mocking my reaction to hearing his voice.

"I was worried about you."

"I told you not to."

"I did anyway."

"Can you come by my place, say around one?"

"Yes," I replied automatically, forgetting that that was smack dab in the middle of when my mother's birthday luncheon was called for.

"Great, see you then. Bye."

"Bye."

Apparently it was time for our conversation regarding a personal matter. I wished to hell I had a clue what it was about.

Chapter Forty-Six

Since I had some time to kill before my meeting with Patrick, I swung by the apartment, walked Doomsday (well more accurately she walked me), and picked up God. He'd been haranguing me mercilessly about taking him to visit Katie.

"Remember," I told him as I walked into the hospital. "No vocalizing."

"I'll be as quiet as a statue," he pledged from the dark confines of my sweatshirt—excuse me, "hoodie"—pocket.

I was making a beeline for Katie's room when my name was called.

Grudgingly I turned to see Stacy sitting in her usual seat in the waiting area. I started to wonder whether the chair had a plaque with a name on it or something.

"Come here for a second, Maggie." She waved me over.

I walked over and sat beside her. "Everything okay?" It wasn't until I sat down that I realized that the other person in the waiting area, his face hidden behind a newspaper, was Delveccio. I recognized him because of his pinky ring.

"Everything's great!" Stacy chirped. "Your investment banker wired the funds over to cover your niece's bill."

"He did?" I slid a sidelong glance in the alleged mobster's direction. He was still obscured by the paper.

"So you're all set. I did the paperwork myself. Katie's staying here."

"Thank you." I meant the expression of gratitude to be directed at Tony/Anthony.

"No problem. Just doing my job," Stacy said. "Speaking of which, I've got other things to wrap up. Today's my last day." She handed me a card with her contact information written on the back. "Let's keep in touch."

She jumped to her feet and hurried away.

I felt God stir restlessly in my pocket, but thankfully he stayed quiet.

"Damndest thing," Delveccio said, pointing to an article. "This guy's house blew up with him in it."

"I heard about that."

Folding up the newspaper, he looked me in the eye. "You did good."

"Thank you for taking care of Katie's bill."

"A deal's a deal. You should be rewarded for a job well done. Knowing my grandson's safe, that's a load off my mind. Gotta say, I really didn't think you were gonna be able to pull the second job off. Gary was a pro."

"I had help."

"Yeah, he told me that."

"He's the one that deserves the credit for . . . eliminating that particular problem." I didn't want Delveccio starting to think that Patrick wasn't up to the job. The man had two families to support.

"He said you were the one who did it."

"It was a team effort."

The mobster nodded. "Told me he's thinking of taking you on as a partner on a permanent basis. You interested in that?"

I glanced in the direction of Katie's room. The bills for her care wouldn't stop piling up any time soon. "Maybe. If the circumstances are right."

"You want a deal like the redhead's got? You get to pick and choose who you hit?"

I nodded.

"I think we could work that out. I'll be in touch. You go visit that little girl now."

Obediently I got up and walked down the hall to Katie's room. I glanced back in Delveccio's direction, but he was already gone.

Closing the door behind me in the hopes a nurse wouldn't notice I'd brought a reptile into the sterile environment, I walked up to Katie's bedside.

"Hey there, Baby Girl. I brought you a visitor."

"Why do you insist on calling her that?" God snapped. "She's three, no longer an infant."

Taking him out of my pocket, I placed him on my niece's chest. He just stood there staring at her still face.

"When she was born Theresa and Dirk couldn't agree on a name for her. It took them three days. During that time she was called Baby Girl Albers." I smoothed Katie's hair off her forehead. "Godzilla came to see you."

The lizard crawled up until he was level with Katie's ear. He lay on her pillow whispering to her. I couldn't hear what he said. After a few minutes, he said, "I'm done."

I extended my hand and climbed onto it. Against the white background of the sheets, I realized he was looking the worse for wear. Bruises covered most of his body, evidence of the ordeal we'd been through the day before.

"You okay, buddy?"

"I'm just tired," he told me. "Usually all I do is stay in a ten-gallon container. I exerted myself more than usual yesterday."

"I never thanked you."

"You bought me crickets. That's thanks enough. I really don't need you subjecting me to some heartfelt declaration of gratitude."

"Thank you." I pressed a light kiss to the top of his head.

"Gross."

I carefully placed him into my pocket.

"We're going to have to do something about the lighting in here!"

Chuckling, I slipped my finger into Katie's small hand. "Everything's going to be okay, Katie."

She squeezed my finger.

My heart stopped.

I couldn't have felt what I'd just felt. She couldn't have been responding to my voice. It must have been some sort of involuntary muscle spasm, right?

I looked at her once again limp hand and began to sing, my voice cracking with emotion. "The itsy bitsy spider went up the water spout. Down came the rain and washed the spider out. Out came the sun and dried up all the rain, and the itsy bitsy spider went up the . . . went . . . up . . . the. . . ." I could barely get the words out. Part of our game had always been that she'd squeeze my hand when I reached the word 'again' to indicate I should repeat the song. "Went up the spout . . . again."

She squeezed my finger.

And for the first time since the accident, I cried.

Chapter Forty-Seven

I WAS OVER an hour late for my meeting with Patrick.

It had taken all of my willpower to leave Katie's bedside to ask a nurse to get a doctor. The next couple of hours had been filled with a battery of tests and consultations. In the end, I got a genuine smile from the doctor who informed me that Katie's prognosis was improving.

"She needs her rest," a kindly nurse had told me as she'd ushered me out of Katie's room. "It looks like you do, too. Go home."

I'd gone home long enough to return God to his terrarium and give Doomsday a potty break. I would have tried to contact Patrick, but he'd blocked the number he'd called from earlier.

So I showed up to his door an hour late.

"I was getting worried." In pure Patrick fashion, he wasn't angry or annoyed, just concerned, but I was in defensive mode and ready for a fight.

"You should give me a number I can actually reach you at."

"You're right. I'm sorry about that." He motioned for me to enter his man cave. There were no weapons in sight.

"You can be maddeningly reasonable."

He stared at me, his gaze cataloging everything from my bloodshot eyes to the bruise beneath my chin. Reaching out, he used three fingers to gently tilt my head back so that he could examine my injury.

"He hurt you."

"He hurt you worse." Remembering the sickening thunk Patrick's skull had made as it bounced off the tiled floor had my eyes filling with tears. The floodgates had opened when Katie latched onto me, and I'd been on the verge of sobbing uncontrollably ever since.

"Shhh." Patrick led us to the couch. Sitting beside me, he wrapped both arms around me and rested his chin on top of my head. "It's okay. You're safe. Everything's fine."

I closed my eyes, allowing him to weave a cocoon of shelter around us with his murmured words. It felt warm and safe and right.

"Delveccio paid Katie's bill."

"Good."

"I couldn't have . . . I'd never have been able to . . . The reason I was late . . . Katie responded to me today. I was singing to her and she grabbed my finger."

Hugging me more tightly, he exclaimed, "That's great news, Mags!"

I nodded.

"So why the tears?"

"You almost died yesterday."

"But you saved me. I told you that your best would be good enough."

"You should know . . . I screwed up."

"How?"

"I left my gun in his kitchen. Do you think they'll find it? Do you think they'll be able to trace it back to me?"

He chuckled. "No, Mags. You're perfectly safe."

"How can you be so sure?"

"Even if they did survive the heat of that fire—and I'm guessing nothing did, considering how hot I heard it burned due to all the explosive material Gary had stashed there (that is, after all, why I'd blown out the pilot light, in the hopes of destroying the evidence)—your prints aren't in the system. With the exception of the speeding ticket you got a few years back, you've got no record whatsoever. I checked you out before I met with you the first time."

"Oh."

"You sound disappointed that you've got one less thing to worry about."

"I'm not." I was actually relieved, but that reaction was immediately replaced by another worry. "It's just that I don't know what this personal thing you wanted to discuss is about."

I felt him tense.

My sense of safety evaporated.

Releasing me he got up, crossed the apartment, and leaned against his kitchen counter. I didn't like the look of this.

"Can I ask you something first?"

"Sure."

"Why'd you take the dog?"

"She needed a place to stay . . . besides, I owed her."

"You owed her?"

I nodded. "She saved me. She helped to save you."

"How do you figure that?"

"She helped me to drag you out of the house."

"She helped . . ." he trailed off, deciding not to voice his disbelief. "Do you remember when we were at the cemetery the second time?"

I nodded and hung my head. Yet another of my mistakes. I'd been convinced he was going to kill me and had attacked him.

"I tried to tell you there."

"Tell me what?"

"But you weren't listening. You were so wrapped up in that stuff that's always going on in your head."

"Tell me what?"

He rubbed his chin nervously.

Now I was really getting worried. Whatever he was about to reveal was causing Mr.Unflappable consternation. It couldn't be good.

"It took me a while to put the pieces together," he said slowly.

"Pieces of what?"

"I need you to promise to not freak out."

"You taught me to use a gun, you helped me to plan two murders, you partnered with me to pull off one of them, and in all that time you never asked me to promise not to freak out, but now you're asking? *That* is freaking me out!"

"Your sister Marlene is alive."

It felt like all the air had been sucked right out of the room and I was oxygen-deprived.

"You said you'd buried two sisters and the third was probably dead too, but she isn't. At least she wasn't six months ago."

After the emotional roller-coaster ride I'd been on today from the low of my visit with my father to the high of Katie's response, this news was just too much. I swayed woozily.

Patrick rushed toward me, catching me as I pitched forward. I would have fallen face-first onto the floor, but he knelt in front of me, his hands on my shoulders holding me up.

"I'm sorry, Mags. I couldn't think of another way to tell you."

He had to be wrong. I'd given up on the hope that Marlene was still alive years earlier. It was easier to believe that horrible reality than it was to think that she just wasn't getting in touch, because that would mean she'd never forgiven me.

"I busted her six months ago. I didn't know then who she was. I didn't figure it out until I saw that old picture of her in your place. And even then I wasn't sure. I had to do more research."

"She's alive?"

He nodded. "If you want to try, I might be able to help you find her."

My niece might wake up, and my baby sister was alive. I'd never been so happy in my life.

I tried to smile. I tried to thank Patrick, but the feelings were just too much for me.

Falling into Patrick's arms, I burst into tears. Not the trickling droplets that had dripped down my face in Katie's room, but great, big, heaving, body-wracking sobs. I'd never been so fucking happy in my life.

Epilogue

So NOW YOU know how I got into this line of work.

And no, I know you're wondering, but I didn't visit my mom on her birthday. I was afraid that in my highly emotional state they might lock me up, too.

I couldn't take that risk. I had too much to do:

- a niece who needed curing
- an aunt who needed help staying clean
- talking animals to care for
- a new career to nurture
- bridesmaid duties

And, oh yeah, even though I didn't know it at the time, I found out not long after that that I needed to kill someone at a wedding. . . .

About the Author

A lifelong resident of New Jersey (something she hopes you won't hold against her), JB Lynn doesn't care if the cup is half full or empty; all she cares about is whether it's regular or decaf! She writes with a parrot on her shoulder, two dogs at her feet, and a patient husband in the next room. To learn more about JB and her books, please visit www.jblynn.com.